PRAISE FOR PETER BRANDVOLD AND HIS NOVELS:

"Make room on your shelf of favorites; Peter Brandvold will be staking out a claim there." —Frank Roderus

"Lots of action . . . If you thought they didn't write 'em like this anymore, this is the book for you." —Bill Crider

"Brandvold creates a fast-paced, action-packed novel." —James Reasoner

"Action-packed . . . for fans of traditional Westerns." —*Booklist*

"Takes off like a shot." —Douglas Hirt

"A writer to watch." —Jory Sherman

"Brandvold writes a lot like L'Amour." —*The Fargo Forum*

"One of the best writers of traditional action Westerns in the business right now. He's very prolific." —*Bookgasm*

"Brandvold's rousing adventure . . . feels more cinematic with every passing chapter." —*Cowboys & Indians*

WESTERN

APR 0 5 2012

.45-CALIBER CROSS FIRE

PETER BRANDVOLD

BERKLEY BOOKS, NEW YORK

THE BERKLEY PUBLISHING GROUP
Published by the Penguin Group
Penguin Group (USA) Inc.
375 Hudson Street, New York, New York 10014, USA
Penguin Group (Canada), 90 Eglinton Avenue East, Suite 700, Toronto, Ontario M4P 2Y3, Canada
(a division of Pearson Penguin Canada Inc.)
Penguin Books Ltd., 80 Strand, London WC2R 0RL, England
Penguin Group Ireland, 25 St. Stephen's Green, Dublin 2, Ireland (a division of Penguin Books Ltd.)
Penguin Group (Australia), 250 Camberwell Road, Camberwell, Victoria 3124, Australia
(a division of Pearson Australia Group Pty. Ltd.)
Penguin Books India Pvt. Ltd., 11 Community Centre, Panchsheel Park, New Delhi—110 017, India
Penguin Group (NZ), 67 Apollo Drive, Rosedale, Auckland 0632, New Zealand
(a division of Pearson New Zealand Ltd.)
Penguin Books (South Africa) (Pty.) Ltd., 24 Sturdee Avenue, Rosebank, Johannesburg 2196,
South Africa

Penguin Books Ltd., Registered Offices: 80 Strand, London WC2R 0RL, England

This is a work of fiction. Names, characters, places, and incidents either are the product of the author's imagination or are used fictitiously, and any resemblance to actual persons, living or dead, business establishments, events, or locales is entirely coincidental. The publisher does not have any control over and does not assume any responsibility for author or third-party websites or their content.

.45-CALIBER CROSS FIRE

A Berkley Book / published by arrangement with the author

PRINTING HISTORY
Berkley edition / April 2012

Copyright © 2012 by Peter Brandvold.
Cover illustration by Bruce Emmett.

ISBN: 978-0-425-24693-1

BERKLEY®
Berkley Books are published by The Berkley Publishing Group,
a division of Penguin Group (USA) Inc.,
375 Hudson Street, New York, New York 10014.
BERKLEY® is a registered trademark of Penguin Group (USA) Inc.
The "B" design is a trademark of Penguin Group (USA) Inc.

PRINTED IN THE UNITED STATES OF AMERICA

10 9 8 7 6 5 4 3 2 1

ALWAYS LEARNING   **PEARSON**

In Memory of Buck

1997–2010

1

CUNO MASSEY SET his feet a little more than shoulder-width apart, the right one slightly forward of the left, and pivoted sharply as the Yaqui brave lunged at his bare belly with the antler-handled, razor-edged bowie knife.

The knife's talon-like point missed Cuno's hard midsection by a little more than a hairsbreadth. The Indian gave a shocked yowl as the momentum of his thrust left him open for a split second. Cuno took advantage of that opening, using his left hand to chop at the Indian's knife wrist and lunging forward with his own bowie, the curved point angled up.

Cuno heard himself grunt with the violent thrust and thought the knife's savage tip would disappear in the brave's bronze belly. But at the last eighth of a second, the fleet-footed brave pivoted back and sideways enough that the tip of Cuno's knife merely etched a thin, red line between two of the Indian's clearly defined ribs. The brave's eyes brightened with a fleeting look of fear that changed instantly to glee as he lunged forward with his own knife extended and drew a similar line across Cuno's lower left side.

The warrior grinned and stepped back, constantly shuffling his feet, his long black hair held back from his face by a braided deerskin band. His round, flat features were tight with menace, black eyes dancing and glittering. Cuno could hear Camilla groaning anxiously as she watched the fight. She sat by the freight wagon that the Yaqui had been pulling across the desert and which they'd likely confiscated from a train heading north toward Nogales, before they'd spied Cuno and Camilla and decided to have some fun.

Five other braves sat in a circle around the two fighters, whooping and hollering and passing a bottle they'd likely found on the wagon. A sixth held Camilla on his lap near the wagon, squeezing one of her breasts through her calico blouse while pressing a bowie knife against her throat. She did not move but grunted and cursed against the Yaqui's assault, her dark, worried eyes on Cuno.

The Indians had attacked his and Camilla's camp at the first wash of dawn, riding in with the fury of a hundred demons, and took the pair by surprise while they'd still slumbered in their blanket rolls. He and Camilla hadn't taken turns keeping watch like they normally did because they'd been exhausted from outrunning a Rurale troop and had badly needed the sleep. Besides, they hadn't seen any Yaqui or Apache signs in the past three days, since they'd crossed over the border into Sonora from Arizona.

Cuno had managed to grab his Winchester and kill three of the braves before another, galloping through the camp on his war-painted mustang, had smashed the butt of his Spencer carbine against the back of Cuno's head. The braining had laid Cuno out for several seconds. When he'd regained his senses, he was being dragged to his feet by two braves while another pulled the freight wagon into the camp and yet another held his rifle on Camilla, who was bent forward at the waist, screaming at the bronco braves in a mix of her own native Spanish and broken Yaqui.

They found the pretty, sharp-tongued senorita dressed in men's trail garb quite amusing and told Cuno that, despite his killing three of their party, they'd set both him and Camilla free if he could defeat the best fighter amongst them in a fair fight with bowie knives. Cuno wasn't fooled. They merely wanted to enjoy themselves further here before killing him and then most likely raping and killing Camilla. Which was why, now, as the brave facing him lunged toward him once more, Cuno had his next moves clearly etched in his mind.

He chopped down hard with his left hand, knocking the brave's knife down and to one side so hard that he heard the Yaqui's wrist crack. Grunting, Cuno bounded off his heels, lunging forward with his right foot while dragging the left one for balance, and drove his own bowie smoothly into the brave's belly, just beneath his breastbone. He dropped his wrist and, gritting his teeth, angled the knife point up and under the breastbone. He knew immediately that he'd punctured the warrior's heart as hot blood washed over his hand.

Quickly, before the other braves had even realized what had happened, he jerked the knife out.

The brave staggered forward as his shoulders sagged, the light in his dark eyes fading and a befuddled expression washing across his face. A gob of blood oozed over his bottom lip. One of the other braves gave a shout that broke off abruptly when Cuno grabbed the dying brave's wrist, jerking him forward and throwing him into a stocky brave lounging on the ground, a little apart from the others, and just now bringing his Spencer carbine up.

The dying brave's foot kicked the carbine out of the other Indian's hand, and releasing the dead brave to sprawl over the living one, Cuno dived onto the rifle as the others shouted and squealed and scrambled to raise their own carbines. Cuno came up fast, the Spencer in his hands. He'd seen the other brave cock the weapon, so he drew his right index finger over the trigger, taking hasty aim on the brave nearest Camilla. His eyes wide with exasperation, the Indian held the bowie down by his side, as though he'd decided to reach for his own rifle and try for Cuno rather than kill the supple senorita in his arms.

It was the reaction Cuno had been betting on.

The carbine roared in Cuno's hands, and the brave who

still had one arm wrapped around Camilla's neck jerked backward as the .56-caliber hunk of lead slug punched a hole through the middle of his chest, opening a veritable cavern. As the brave yowled and looked skyward, instantly dead, the bowie dropped from his right hand into the red desert caliche.

Only about six seconds had elapsed since Cuno had thrown the dying brave atop the one raising the Spencer he now held in his own hands, and the others, drunk and reeling in confusion from all that had happened so quickly, were just now stumbling to their feet and raising their own rifles. Cuno rolled twice to his left as two braves triggered their carbines, kicking up dust behind and around him while another slug spanged off a rock to his right.

Cocking the Spencer, Cuno rose to a half-sitting position, drew the hammer back with his right thumb, aimed quickly, and fired. He fired two more times, shooting and levering the Spencer's trigger-guard cocking mechanism. He was familiar with the weapon. He'd owned a similar one when he'd first headed out on the trail to find the men who'd killed his father and stepmother four years ago in what now seemed another lifetime, in Valoria, Nebraska Territory.

But firing the old, creaky, .56-rimfire seven-shot repeater was still an awkward maneuver. His position made it all the trickier and so did the fact that the drunk braves were now on their feet and scrambling around, screaming wildly as they returned fire with their own carbines, blowing up dust and gravel around Cuno. Thick puffs of blue powder smoke rose as the Yaqui stumbled around, startled and frightened, drunk and enraged.

Cuno managed to deliver two killing shots, spinning both braves around and down, screaming, one accidently shooting the other one in the thigh before dropping his carbine. When Cuno had emptied the weapon's seven-shot tube, the other three attackers had twisted around and fallen in the brush lining the notch between low, rocky hills, two of the three moaning and thrashing, still alive.

"Here!"

Cuno glanced to his right. Camilla stood about ten feet away, holding up his ivory-gripped .45, which the brave who'd been molesting her had wedged behind the waistband of his deerskin breeches, keeping it for a trophy. She tossed it to Cuno, who flipped open the loading gate and spun the cylinder, making sure each chamber showed brass. Clicking the gate home, he cocked the perfectly weighted piece as one of the braves gave a squeal and began half running and half crawling up the rocky hill to the north.

One of the other two warriors was on his hands and knees, trying to bring up a Spencer he'd found in the brush.

Cuno walked purposely over to the brave fumbling with the carbine in his bloody hands and dispatched the warrior with a single round through his right temple. He cocked the pistol once more and strode up the slope rising to the rocky hill beyond, which the other brave was scrambling up heavily, streaking the rocks and twisted buckbrush clumps with blood, his breaths rising heavy and ragged.

Cuno wasn't one to back-shoot a man, but he'd make an exception for this brave who'd intended to kill Cuno and rape his girl. He and Camilla had been lying low, minding their own business out here as they slowly drifted deeper into Mexico on their desperate search for a new life. Camilla and her brother's gang, all of whom were now dead, had busted Cuno out of a federal pen in Colorado, and they'd been chased to the border by a stubborn old lawman and a younger sheriff—the very man who'd wrongfully arrested Cuno in the first place and nearly condemned him to a lifelong stint in the federal pen run by a sadistic, diabolical warden.

Cuno raised the Colt Peacemaker .45—a gift from the old pistoleer Charlie Dodge, who'd taught him how to shoot it back when he'd first started dusting the vengeance trail—straight out from his right shoulder, planted a bead on the back of the fleeing Yaqui's head, and squeezed the trigger.

The pistol barked.

The Yaqui made no sound. His head bounced off the red-painted rock in front of him with a cracking thud. He fell onto his side, tumbled back down the rocks he'd just climbed, and lay still, curled up as though he meant only to nap.

Most of his forehead was gone, leaving a gaping, bloody wound.

Cuno lowered the smoking pistol and was about to turn back toward the camp when he heard something. Frowning, he glanced back at Camilla standing where he'd left her and holding her hand up to shield the rising sun from her eyes, her long, dark brown hair blowing about her shoulders in the breeze that was picking up. She'd found her own pistol, a Schofield .44, a heavy piece that normally sagged low on her thigh but which she now held low by her side.

Cuno held up a hand. "Stay there!"

He bounded up the rocky hill, leaping the dead Yaqui and skipping from rock to rock, sweat dribbling down his back and chest and burning in the slight cut the Indian had opened in his side. He gained the top of the hill and stared into a broad, rocky bowl in the northeast, where gray morning shadows stretched out from the greasewood shrubs, barrel cactus, and tall saguaros pocked by nesting cactus wrens.

The sound he'd heard, indistinguishable before, rose again—a savage war whoop.

This time it was accompanied by the drum of galloping hooves. Cuno shaded his eyes with his hands, squinting across the bowl, his stomach tightening. A dozen or so riders were galloping around the shoulder of a distant hill and snaking into the bowl, heading toward Cuno.

They were small, dark riders in red calico shirts, red headbands, and they were riding short, sinewy mustangs.

Cuno raked out a curse and ran back down the rocky hill, again leaping the dead brave and landing flat-footed in the canyon where the other Indians lay strewn and bleeding, flies already beginning to buzz around them as the Mexican sun climbed higher and the heat intensified. He ran over to Camilla, who watched him gravely, and placed his hands on her shoulders.

"You all right?"

Her eye was swelling, and her lower lip was cracked, her blouse torn. She nodded, frowning impatiently. "What did you see?"

"More Injuns. Headed this way."

Cuno—a former freighter with the bulky physique to prove it—grabbed his shirt from where he'd dropped it on the ground before he and the knife-fighting brave had squared off and drew it over his stout, broad shoulders. Camilla grabbed her saddle, which she'd been sleeping against when the Yaqui had stormed into their camp.

"How many?" she asked.

"Around a dozen, I'd say," Cuno said fatefully, looking around for his Winchester repeater, which he'd dropped when the first brave galloping into the camp had brained him.

He found it hidden in a clump of Spanish bayonet. Setting the octagonal-barreled '73 on his shoulder, he grabbed his own saddle and canteen and glanced at Camilla, who was quickly shoving small food pouches into her saddlebags.

"Leave it," he told her. "They'll be on us hard in five minutes!"

He started running south, toward the low, grassy notch where he and Camilla had picketed their horses the previous night, by quiet starlight in sharp contrast to the dawn's sudden fury.

"I bet you wish I'd left you in that Colorado prison," Camilla yelled as she broke into a run behind him, hefting her saddle and saddlebags onto her shoulders.

"You jokin'?" Cuno shot her a taut smile as he dashed between two large boulders and into the notch where their horses stood, snorting and kicking and pulling at their picket line, indignant at the recent commotion. "And miss all the fun we've had since?"

2

CUNO AND CAMILLA pushed their horses hard off and on for most of an hour before Cuno, reining up suddenly, said, "Hold on."

He studied their dusty back trail meandering across the flat desert on which only cacti and wiry tufts of brush grew. Camilla checked her own mount down and turned to Cuno. "If we keep pushing, we will make my uncle's rancho just after nightfall."

Cuno shook his head, slowly shuttling his gaze from left to right across their back trail, spying no movement except the occasional jackrabbit or dun coyote slinking around the brown foliage growing up out of the tan sand and gravel. Everything was a shade of brown out here except the black rocks and the lime-green branches of the creosote or the occasional mesquite growing along a wash. "That's what they want us to do."

"They might not be following. We've seen no sign of them."

"They're following, all right." Movement straight back about a mile caught Cuno's eye, but he eased the tension in his back when he saw a hawk rise up above a hillcrest and trace a lazy circle as it scouted a fox or a rabbit den. "And they're wanting us to blow out our horses. Be easy to run us down, then, when we're on foot out here . . ." He glanced at the brassy sky in which not a single cloud shone. "Under that sun."

Out the corner of his eye he saw the hawk rise suddenly, bank, and wing off toward the south, as though something had startled it.

Cuno looked around quickly. Spying a low ridge about fifty yards north, he said, "Come on!" He touched his dull spurs to the ribs of his skewbald paint mustang, Renegade, and galloped off the trail and up the side of the hill. Camilla galloped behind him.

Cuno put Renegade up and over the crest of the hill and into a dry wash lined with mesquites and willows on the other side. He grabbed his father's old spyglass from his saddlebags and ran back up the side of the hill, doffing his hat about ten feet from the top. Hunkering between two boulders at the hill's crest, near an old rattlesnake skin, he extended the brass telescope and cupped his gloved hands over the lens to keep the sunlight from flashing off the glass.

He brought the ridge over which the hawk had been hunting into sharp focus just as two Indians rode up and over it through a slight notch in the crest and halted their mustangs beside a one-armed saguaro. Both Indians looked around carefully, holding carbines butt-down on their bare thighs.

Another rider rode up behind them and then gigged his horse to one side while yet another rode up behind the first two and continued on between them. Cuno adjusted the spyglass's focus, clarifying the female rider straddling a cream, gold-tinged mustang—almost a palomino. She stopped her horse and looked around, holding her regal chin in the air.

Cuno's heart skipped a beat as he stared at the Yaqui queen through his spyglass. It was hard to tell from this distance, but the clean, even lines of her face framed by the stygian hair hanging straight down to her shoulders and secured with a dark pink calico headband told him she was a heartbreaking beauty. She wore a dark brown deerskin vest over a black blouse with white polka dots, but her legs were bare beneath a short, slitted deerskin skirt. Long and cherry tan, they angled down the cream's sides, knees bent forward and drawn taut against the pony's ribs. On her feet were the traditional Yaqui moccasins, though, while the Yaqui men rarely decorated their footgear, hers appeared trimmed with red beads.

She wore a big knife in a beaded sheath on her waist. A rifle of some kind hung down her back by a leather lanyard—Cuno could see the barrel poking up from behind her right shoulder. She dipped her chin as she batted her heels against the cream's sides and started forward, turning her head back and moving her mouth, as though speaking to the others. As she gigged the cream into a trot down the hill, likely following Cuno and Camilla's trail, the others fell into a ragged line behind her.

Cuno collapsed the spyglass, doffed his tan hat, and scrambled down the slope to where Camilla stood, holding her hat while her chestnut bay drew water from it, liquid beads dribbling through the felt crown and onto the ground around her boots. She was looking anxiously at Cuno.

"We got shadows, all right."

"Shit."

Cuno grabbed Renegade's reins and swung up into the saddle, the image of the straight-backed Yaqui queen blazed behind his retinas. It wasn't lust he was feeling but a knife edge of apprehension. Sharper than before. Yaqui women were known to be even more savage than the men. And the young and pretty ones could be the most savage of all.

Camilla stepped off a rock onto her bay's back and neck-reined the mount around until she sat off Cuno's right stirrup. "What is it?"

"Nothin'. Let's ride." He gigged Renegade up the wash that was paved in fist-sized gravel. "Maybe we can lose them in these rocks and avoid being slow-roasted over a low fire."

"That's a pretty thought, amigo." Camilla booted her

bay behind Cuno. "Who'd you see back there—the entire Yaqui nation?"

"No, just one girl who reminds me a little of you."

He chuckled to ease the tension.

"Was she pretty?" Camilla asked later that night, when they'd made camp in a narrow canyon about six miles beyond where Cuno had seen the queen. At least, if she wasn't a bona fide Yaqui queen, she should have been.

The nights were cold now in October, and because Cuno believed they had finally lost the Yaqui, since they'd seen no telltale dust plume behind them for hours, they built a low fire from branches of the nearly smokeless catclaw shrub.

Cuno had been with enough young women in his young life to know the importance of treading cautiously in these waters. "Ah, you know—she was Yaqui."

Camilla bit off some jerky from the chunk in her fist and frowned at him from across the fire. "That doesn't exactly answer my question."

"She was a long ways away, a couple hundred yards. And you know how a spyglass picks up a glare."

"So she was pretty."

Cuno sipped from his smoking coffee cup and shrugged as he slid his diffident gaze toward the sandstone bank flanking Camilla. "Well, she didn't look ugly from that distance. I'm just glad to not be lookin' at her close up, 'bout now. Got a feelin' it wouldn't be a healthy experience, no matter how pretty the girl is."

Camilla chewed her jerky slowly, staring into the fire, the orange flames dancing in her round, brown eyes. Her round face was pretty with its small nose and broad mouth. She had a small, white scar on her lower right cheek, and he could see it best by firelight.

God knows they'd shared enough campfires in their short time together. They'd met in Colorado, when Cuno had guided her and several Anglo ranch children to safety from marauding Utes and before he'd been arrested by Sheriff Dusty Mason for killing four rogue territorial marshals who'd been intending on attacking Cuno's party, ostensibly because they thought Cuno had been trading rifles to the Indians, though what they'd really wanted were the girls.

It was remote country up in Colorado and Wyoming, where lawmen were often impossible to distinguish from the worst of the curly wolves.

Cuno enjoyed seeing Camilla's face on the other side of the fire from him, though he often wished they could settle down for a while and get to know each other better. For as long as they'd been together, during the long over-mountain run from the Utes until Cuno had surrendered to Sheriff Mason in exchange for the safety of Camilla and the Lassiter children, and then after Camilla and her brother Mateo de Cava had busted him out of the federal pen, they'd been on the run from either red men or white.

Sometimes he wondered what they'd have to say to each other if they weren't both about two steps from bloody death.

"You did well back there," she said now, biting off another hunk of jerky and chewing it slowly as she stared into the fire. "With the Yaqui, I mean. I didn't know you could fight so well with a knife as well as a pistol and a rifle."

"Like I told you before," he said a little defensively, setting another slender catclaw branch on the crackling flames, "my pa taught me all about fighting. Fists and knives, mainly." He paused. "Pa was an old drover, and while he didn't talk about it all that much, I think he rode the long coulees for a while. That's Anglo talk for outlawin'. I reckon Ma burned that out of him, set him on the straight and narrow."

Cuno gave a wistful smile, remembering the old man whom he hauled freight with until Lloyd Massey had been killed by Rolf Anderson and Sammy Spoon, after Anderson had raped and killed Cuno's stepmother, Corsica Landreau.

Cuno glanced over the flames at Camilla. She was still chewing slowly, pensively, while staring into the flames. She'd extended her legs straight out in front of her, cowhide boots crossed. Sometimes it was damn hard to know what

what was going on behind those brown eyes, and the thought that she continued to sit in judgment of him burned him.

"Don't tell me you're still tryin' to figure me out, Miss Camilla."

She lifted her gaze to his, wrinkling the skin above the bridge of her small, tan nose.

He said, "You shoulda done that before you and your brother busted me out of that pen."

"I know who you are, amigo." She smiled thinly. "I found out who you were when you left that stolen money behind with Mason. You could have kept the money. You could have killed Mason . . ."

"Like your brother would have done," he reminded her, letting her know where she came from.

"*Si*, like Mateo would have done." She nodded, still regarding him with that faintly puzzled expression. "But you didn't. You left the money on the other side of the border, and you left the man alive who saw you jailed for no reason." She smiled.

"Did I pass the test, then?"

"What test?"

"You know—the one that tells you whether I'm worth hangin' around with . . ."

Cuno couldn't keep the irritation from building. He wasn't sure what had caused it—his having left a load of money behind that could have made their lives so much easier, or that it had been her, the sister of notorious outlaw Mateo de Cava, who had convinced him to leave it. If not for Camilla, he would have kept that loot, which made him wonder who in hell he was now.

Certainly not the man his father had raised him to be.

Life had become so much harder and more confusing than he'd ever expected it could.

The frown lines cut deeper into her forehead, and her face reddened beneath her natural tan. "You really think I rode all the way to Colorado to test you? What—you think I need a man so bad that I—!"

Cuno had scrambled around the fire on his hands and knees, and now he wrapped an arm around her shoulders and clamped his other hand over her mouth. "Easy! You're gonna bring every Yaqui in Sonora down on top of us!"

She looked at him over his hand, which he cautiously removed from her mouth. Scowling, she whispered through gritted teeth, "Feel free to leave whenever you want, gringo. I only busted you out of prison because I felt I owed you that much. The payment has been made. Neither of us owes the other anything. We're both free to ride in whichever direction we want."

She grabbed her Winchester carbine and her low-crowned Stetson. "I'll take the first watch and wake you in a couple of hours." She donned the hat, the horsehair thong dangling beneath her dimpled chin, and rose to her feet. "If you're still here."

She racked a cartridge into the Winchester's breech and stomped away from the firelight, the Schofield sagging low on her hip, her spurs chinging softly as she climbed into the rocks sheltering their camp.

Brooding, feeling guilty for getting angry at her when without her he'd still be in the federal lockup, Cuno poured himself another cup of coffee.

What the hell was wrong with him these days, anyway?

He sat back against his saddle with a sigh.

3

CUNO HAD THE last watch of the night, and when he came down from his perch in the rocks around dawn, he built up the fire, set coffee to boil, and found himself kneeling beside the crackling flames, watching Camilla sleep.

She lay curled on her side, resting her face on her hands. Her features were dark tan—almost Indian dark—and smooth, nearly round, though her prominent chin gave her face more of an oval shape. Her chocolate-brown eyelashes rested gently as feathers against her cheeks.

It was about six o'clock, time to get moving, though where Cuno himself was headed, he wasn't sure. His intention during most of his and Camilla's trek south from the federal pen had been to follow Camilla to a wild horse ranch, where an old *mesteno*, Tio Larosa, who had raised Camilla and her bronco brother until Mateo had run off with banditos when he was only fifteen years old, and whom Camilla considered her uncle, trapped and broke wild mustangs to sell to the Mexican Army as remounts.

Now, as they approached the Larosa ranch—only about a half a day away, in fact—Cuno felt himself having second thoughts. He'd let little grass grow under his feet in these four years since his father and stepmother's deaths. Although he'd been married for a short time and had tried to farm and run his own freighting business, he wasn't sure he was ready to tie himself to one woman.

Or if Camilla even wanted him tied to her . . .

The uncertainty rankled him.

He stared down at Camilla, who shifted a little beneath her blankets and wrinkled her nose. On their trip down from Colorado they'd discussed settling down together and possibly working on Uncle Tio's ranch. But did Cuno love her enough to build a home with her, possibly even marry her? Could he love her the way he'd once loved his late wife, July, who, while carrying their baby inside her, had been killed by bounty hunters chasing Cuno?

Just the thought of her was still a knifepoint in his belly. It was a strong fist clutching his heart. Could he give Camilla the love she deserved for the devotion she'd shown him while he was still in love with his bride left behind in a grave in Nebraska?

His doubt made him feel tender toward the girl sleeping before him, and he bent over her now and touched his lips to her cheek. She jerked with a start, opening her eyes and staring up at him.

"Easy," he whispered. "Just me."

She continued to gaze up at him, three small, vertical lines etched into the bridge of her nose. "You're not coming to Uncle Tio's, are you?"

He brushed a speck of fire ash from her cheek with his thumb. "I've run a freight wagon with a team of mules, but I've never broke horses before. I'm afraid I'd just get in the way at Uncle Tio's."

She lifted her arms from beneath her blankets and set her wrists on his shoulders. "You could learn."

"I reckon I could."

"If you wanted to."

Cuno nodded. "I'm sorry. I should have known my mind

well enough before to tell you what you could expect from me."

"Shh." She lifted her face and pressed her lips gently to his, working her mouth slightly, nibbling his lips gently with her fine, small teeth. "We had a good run, as Mateo used to say. But it was a run. What do we really know about each other, anyway? Maybe it's for the best this way."

"You're not mad?"

"No, I am not mad. I am sad." She hardened her eyes and her tone. "Not because I was looking for a husband when we busted you out of that prison, but because, if I had been, I could have done a lot worse than you." She quirked an ironic smile. "And you could have done worse than me."

He sat back on his butt, drawing one knee up and resting his arm on it and looking speculatively off at the rocks turning pale now as the dawn thickened. "You'll do better. You lost your brother saving my hide. You'll do much better."

"Mateo was never long for this world. I loved him for the blood we shared, but the last good thing he did was help me bust you out of the prison." She reached up and gave Cuno's long, sandy-blond hair a little tug. "Hey, what was her name, anyway?"

Cuno glanced at her. There was no jealousy in her clear, brown eyes. Only genuine curiosity.

"July."

"That's a funny name."

"She was a funny girl. And she was carrying our baby."

"I am sorry." Camilla wrapped her hands around his upper arm, pressed her cheek against it. "You should have told me."

Cuno sighed as he grabbed a leather swatch and lifted the boiling coffeepot off the coals. "Let's have some mud and hit the trail. I'll see you off to Uncle Tio's, then fog the trail for the gulf, maybe. I've never seen that much water."

She threw her blankets aside and rose quickly, showing her tough side though he knew she felt as badly as he did about their imminent separation. They'd shared a long, hard couple of months, as well as each other's blanket rolls, and they'd both be leaving a lot behind them when they forked trails.

But Cuno didn't see how there could be any other way. He was still searching for something, and he had to find it alone first before he'd be any good to a woman.

They ate a quick meal of biscuits and beans cooked in the bacon they'd bought in the last village they'd ridden through. When they'd scrubbed their dishes out with sand and dumped the remaining coffee on the fire, they rigged their horses, mounted up, and rode on out of the hollow.

Just after sunup, they crossed a broad, sandy flat that stretched away from them in all directions and held their horses to trots, so they wouldn't lift dust that might be seen by the Yaqui, if there were any still behind them. Cuno had tramped a broad circle around his and Camilla's camp the night before, and he'd spied no sign of anyone out there but a hunting bobcat whose large, clawed prints had been freshly stamped in the mud around a run-out spring.

On the other side of the flat, they slipped into a shallow arroyo that meandered along the base of the low, rocky hills on whose slopes grew only sparse clumps of brown brush and cacti. Near the arroyo, however, mesquites, paloverde, and greasewood offered cover. Just after noon, they followed the floor of the arroyo to the crest of a hill and checked their horses down.

Camilla looked at Cuno but said nothing for several seconds. Then she turned her head to stare out across a vast expanse of rocky desert hemmed in on all sides by steep bluffs and mesas. "You see that notch to the south there?" she said, pointing. "Between those two highest ridges?"

"I see it."

"A trail there leads to the mountain range in which Uncle Tio built his ranch. You can't see it from here, but there's another trail that will take you through a notch in those western mountains. If you keep following it, you will ride through several *pueblitos* before you finally, after three or four days maybe, reach the Sea of Cortez."

She leaned over and kissed him, then glanced at the faint horse trail that followed the ridge they were on almost due south. "We separate here, amigo. Tio's ranch is deep in the mountains and too far out of your way."

"Hell, I'll ride with you to Uncle Tio's. Those Yaqui could still be followin' us."

She pursed her lips. Her eyes grew bright, and she shook her head sharply. "No. It's best like this."

Cuno wrapped his arms around her and kissed her, fighting the knot in his throat. She returned the kiss, passionately, then pulled away from him, jerked her horse around, and spurred the bay on along the ridge crest.

"Hyah!"

She did not look back before she disappeared around a towering knob of rock, leaving only her sifting dust and dwindling hoof thuds.

Cuno stared at the rock. The dust settled. His belly felt like a well being slowly drained of water through a fissure. Suddenly, he became aware of Renegade canting an incredulous glance back over the stirrup at him. The horse's expression demanded to know why he'd let such a good woman get away.

"Ah, hell," he said, booting the horse westward down the hill, following a meandering Indian trail. "Might as well disappoint her now as later." He rode too tensely in the saddle, and his back started aching in addition to his belly. Annoyance tugged at him. "What the hell would you know about it, anyway?"

Renegade merely twitched an ear and continued walking.

No longer worried about the Yaqui, Cuno booted the skewbald paint into a lope across the sage- and cedar-stippled bench toward a series of tall sierras foreshortening against the western horizon. Strips of ragged-edged pancake clouds gave the ranges a mysterious, brooding look. He glanced around him as he slowed Renegade to a walk and saw little life but a jackrabbit sitting in the shade of a rock shelving out from a gravelly slope, munching something in its paws. A few hawks hunted the nearer ridges.

A while later, a flock of blue quail raced onto the trail before him, their odd, gaudy plumage jouncing as they disappeared into the thorny brush on the trail's other side. A young coyote dashed after them, and then there was a loud peeping as the flock dispersed.

Then, for a long time, except for the breeze and the thuds of Renegade's shod hooves, there was only silence.

Cuno looked around at the vast Mexican sky bowling over the near and distant ranges. His chest felt as hollow as an old gourd, and he half wished he'd ridden on with Camilla. So many people had passed through his life; first his mother, and then his father's second wife, Corsica, whom Cuno had grown to love like an older sister.

Then his father.

And then, a year later, just when they'd been building a life together, a family, July had followed them all over the Divide. There was no one left. No family that Cuno knew of.

He was as alone as the first and last man. If he should fall prey to Yaqui or a stalking wildcat, no one would know or care. His body would rot slowly in the dry desert air, the bones strewn far and wide by predators. Soon, they'd end up white as porcelain, bleached by the sun, and strewn along the bottom of a dry arroyo to be moved later by the floods of the next summer monsoon.

A January chill rippled through him. Staring at the ridges leaning away from the vast, brown-and-lime-green desert that swallowed him like an ocean swallows a single fishing boat, he felt as though the air were being sucked out of his lungs. He gripped his braided leather bridle reins and shook his head against the dark, turgid thoughts.

"Be nice to reach the ocean," he said, taking comfort in the sound of his own voice.

Where would he go after that?

It would take many years for the law to forget about him and his escape from the federal pen during which many guards were killed and Warden Castle was seriously wounded. Tortured, even, by Mateo de Cava, who blew the tip of the man's nose off. Then, fleeing south, Mateo's gang had shot up a town and nearly an entire contingent of bounty hunters as well as Sheriff Dusty Mason, who had been riding with the old deputy U.S. marshal Spurr Morgan.

Cuno and Camilla were accessories to those crimes if for no other reason than they had been riding with the desperadoes. Cuno and Camilla had left behind the loot the gang had stolen from a stagecoach, but they'd still taken part in stealing it. Most likely, bounty hunters and lawmen north of the border would be gunning for Cuno for many years to come.

Maybe forever.

When the sun had set, Cuno made camp in a dark hollow. He took a shot of tequila from the half-empty bottle in his saddlebags that he and Camilla had shared several nights before, celebrating their border crossing and a new life in Mexico.

The tequila tasted sour, and it made his head ache. He tossed the bottle into the brush, kicked dirt on the fire, and lay back against his saddle. For a long time, he listened to the coyotes.

He rose early the next morning but rode slowly west, sparing his horse, not in any hurry. In the midafternoon, he crossed a low pass and cast a look behind him to see five Yaqui galloping toward him from the rocks and brush on either side of the trail, just below the pass.

His heart jumping, he looked around. There were two more groups of the small, dark riders galloping toward him from straight out on either side of the trail, on fleet-footed mustangs. Closing on him quickly, the Yaqui started to whoop and holler like banshees.

4

SPURR MORGAN OPENED his eyes and stared for a time at the stamped tin ceiling, frowning, blinking, rolling his dry tongue around in his mouth, trying to remember where in hell he was. He could hear a rooster crowing and the slow clomps of a horse or a mule, and the clattering of rickety wheels. Someone yelled in the street beyond the dusty, cracked window to his right—*"¿Clara, usted tiene tacos alla?"*

Clara, do you have any tacos over there?

Spurr blinked, ran his wrist across his broad nose that was tanned to the color of ancient whang leather by over sixty years of the frontier sun. He was in Mexico. What the hell was a deputy United States marshal—especially an old one with a creaky heart—doing in Mexico? And where in Mexico was he?

Someone sighed to his left.

He turned his head and saw a long, tan body lying beside him, black, sleep-mussed hair hanging down her back and across her shoulders. The bed's single sheet was pulled down to her waist. Her round hip curved up beneath it, drawn so taut against her buttocks that he could see the crack between them. Her upper arm lay against her side, her forearm curving down out of sight against her belly. Spurr rolled onto his side and stared at her tan arm that showed three small, white scars on the outside of it, just above her elbow.

Cigarette burns.

He'd seen those burns last night, as he'd been toiling beneath the *puta*'s spread legs and she was pretending that he was giving her the ride of her life when he'd long ago stopped giving any woman much of a ride at all—though for some reason he had never stopped enjoying it himself—and it all came back to him.

He was in Mexico. He'd crossed the border illegally but for good reason—a pack of outlaws who'd been calling themselves cavalry soldiers had sacked Fort Bryce near the Mexican line and stolen the fort's entire cache of weaponry it had been storing in advance of its planned distribution to the other forts around Arizona Territory in the hopes of finally quelling the Apaches. Spurr's good friend, Colonel Abel Hammerlich, had been gut-shot by his own second-in-command and left to die in the house Abel had shared with his only daughter before the daughter had been kidnapped by the conspirators.

Spurr, who'd been on the trail of the Mateo de Cava Gang after they'd sprung a firebrand named Cuno Massey from a federal pen in Colorado, had been in the area when he'd heard the news of the fort's sacking by a good third of its own soldiers. When Massey and his girl had drifted over the border into Mexico, Spurr had picked up the trail of slave traders he'd once thought to be heading for the Indian Nations but who'd turned and headed into New Mexico Territory, where he and Sheriff Dusty Mason had run them down. Spurr had ridden from Las Cruces to Fort Bryce— what was left of it after the massive fire that had all but demolished it, leaving most of its honest soldiers either dead or dying—where he'd picked up the thieving killers' wagon trail.

No U.S. lawman was allowed to cross over into Mexico without special written permission by his own government

and that of Mexico, but Spurr had made a career of not following rules—at least not following the rules he hadn't
himself made up.

Spurr was a rawhide-tough, craggy-faced old lawman—
he rode for Chief Marshal Henry Brackett out of Denver—
and his best years were far behind him, but he was a
sentimental cuss, and seeing those cigarette burns on the
puta's arm the night before had twisted his heart and broken his concentration. Now he leaned toward the girl and
pressed his lips to the burns, as if trying to heal them.

The girl gasped and jerked with a start. She drew her
hand away and rolled onto her back, sitting halfway up and
curling her legs beneath her, as though she were about to
leap out of bed and flee.

"It's all right, darlin'!" Spurr said, holding his hands up,
palm out. "It's just old Spurr and I was only givin' you a
good-mornin' peck."

The girl's bare breasts rose and fell heavily as she studied
Spurr, then gradually her muscles relaxed, and she reached
up to sweep her hair out of her eyes. "I apologize, senor," she
said in broken English. "Sometimes . . . I am jumpy."

"Me, too. I should have known better." She had other
scars on her—some that looked like knife scars. It wasn't
easy being a whore in Mexico. "Pardon?"

Slowly, he stretched his hands out and drew her leg
down before him. He lowered his head and pressed his lips
to her knee.

She looked down at him, her breathing slowing, and she
smiled. She stuck a finger in the corner of her mouth, and
wagged her other upraised knee coquettishly. "Spurr," she
said as though just now remembering his name and remembering his drunken devilishness from the night before. He
and the girl, whose name he couldn't remember if she'd
ever told him, had danced at a little cantina down by the
creek that angled through the *pueblito*, whose name he also
couldn't remember—if he'd ever known it.

It had been a slow night, and the owner had bought Spurr
several drinks in addition to the cups of bacanora Spurr had

bought for himself and the girl. When Spurr had tired from the dancing, he and the girl had staggered up the stone steps from the cantina and taken a tumble in the lumpy corn-shuck bed they were in now, and which must have a goodly supply of bedbugs, because Spurr could feel the pinprick-like stings.

She spread her legs for him now and ran her hands along the insides of her thighs. "You want to go again, senor?"

She wasn't exactly pretty, but she wasn't missing too many teeth, and her breasts were nice and full. If Spurr had been about fifteen years younger and not quite as hung-over—the dirty window was firing javelins through his eyes and deep into his skull—he might have taken her up on the offer. If he remembered correctly, she wasn't cheap, but he could afford her even on his lawman's pay.

Spurr chuckled. "Girl, you flatter this old mossy horn." He kissed her knee again, ran both his knobby, brown hands appreciatively, affectionately, down her leg, then rolled over and dropped his feet to the floor. "Next time I'm in town, darlin'. Next time I'm in town."

He leaned forward with his elbows on his knees and ran his hands through his red-brown hair liberally stitched with gray that, badly in need of a trim, hung down past his neck. It was still a thick head of hair, if age-silvered and greasy. At least he still had that.

"How about breakfast, senor?" the girl said, scuttling up behind him and wrapping her arms around his neck, press-ing her breasts against his back. "Tortillas and chorizo? *Café?*"

Spurr saw a half-empty bottle standing on the floor be-side his bare feet. He reached down for it. "I reckon this'll do me." He tipped back the bottle, took a long swig. The liquor burned his tonsils and seared several layers of skin as it plunged down his throat and into his belly, which jerked upon impact. He swallowed several times to keep the liquor down, then eyed the clear bottle appreciatively. It reflected his lilac-blue gaze. "Mescal," he rasped. "Best tanglefoot invented by man."

"Senor?"

The girl leaned down to peer into his face.

"I was just complimenting your people down here on a job well done." He swallowed again, cleared his throat. "A job well done . . ." Spurr patted the girl's hand on his chest, then rose from the bed and walked over to the window, holding the bottle by its neck.

He cleared the film of dust and flyspecks from the glass and looked down at the narrow street meandering between adobe shacks and stock pens. The sun was well up, and blue smoke drifted over chimneys. A man in a frayed straw sombrero was pulling a cart loaded with mesquite branches, and several shopkeepers were sweeping their wooden boardwalks.

Spurr looked west along the street and then east, hoping for a glimpse of one of the men he'd been tracking. Likely, they were still asleep. He'd followed them into the *pueblito* last night, but he'd been too beat from the long trek across the desert to try to throw down on them alone. A man of Spurr's experience knew himself well enough to know when to hold back and replenish his energies, which, he thought now with a chuckle and a backward glance at the naked girl curled on his bed, he'd done last night.

The men he'd been tracking had split up from the rest of the group south of the border, probably knowing it would be harder for three or four sets of wagons hauling stolen ammunition to be tracked than the entire group together. They were probably expecting a contingent of soldiers from Fort Huachuca to fog their trail—or bounty hunters—but if a posse had been sent out, Spurr had seen no sign of them. Likely, the soldier in charge was awaiting permission from both his own superiors as well as from the Mexicans, and that could take weeks or even months.

Spurr knew he couldn't take down all the murdering thieves himself. He just wanted to find out where they were headed and maybe, if possible, rescue his friend's daughter. No telling what kind of horrors the girl was enduring at the hands of the killers.

Spurr took another pull from the bottle and when he could speak again, enjoying the mescal's incredible mind-clearing and painkilling properties, he shambled back to the bed. The girl was sitting in the middle of it Indian-style, no sheet covering her, closely inspecting her right big toe.

"Senorita, ole Spurr has a question for you."

She looked up from her foot.

"Did you happen to see two big freight wagons pull into the *pueblito* yesterday afternoon, about two hours before I showed up? They would have been driven by three gringos, with two other gringos on horseback."

She pursed her lips and nodded. "*Si*. They were a . . . curiosity," she said after flailing for the right word.

"Wasn't a young lady with 'em, was there?" Spurr ran a hand across his shoulder. "A *rubia?*"

"I saw no *rubia.*"

Spurr scowled. He'd figured it was a long shot that he'd followed the outlaw contingent hauling Hammerlich's daughter, but, being only one tracker, he'd had to choose one set of tracks.

"Can you tell me where they lit? Where they may have spent the night?"

"*Si, si.* They are over at Senora Corazon's place, across the street from St. Xavier's." The girl crossed her naked breasts quickly and glanced imploringly at the hammered tin ceiling.

"*Muchas gracias*, senorita." Spurr held up the bottle. "A morning libation?"

The girl shook her head. "My uncle never lets me drink before noon. It makes me sleepy and causes me to dance funny." She jerked her head back and laughed adorably despite the one tooth missing from her smile.

"A wise man, your uncle." Spurr tossed back another shot, lowered his chin against the burn as he swallowed, then shook his head, stood, and pressed his fist to his chest. "A wise, wise man, but I'll be damned if that don't invigorate a tired old ticker."

Spurr set the bottle on the small wooden table, which

was the room's only furnishing besides the bed and a small wooden crucifix hanging from a nail over the door. With a grunt, he bent over and began grabbing up his clothes from where he'd tossed them on the floor in his drunken, lusty haste the night before. He dressed in his threadbare balbriggans, patched buckskin pants, hickory shirt, beaded elk-hide vest, recently darned socks, and the high-topped fur moccasins he preferred to stockmen's boots. The moccasins were more comfortable for both riding and walking, and lawmen sometimes had to walk or even run, though Spurr had never been good at the former and, due to his ailing ticker, was now even less effective at the latter.

He drew his suspenders up over his shoulders that had once been broad and square but now, with the ravaging of the years, were pulled slightly forward and down to both sides of his chest, which was rather spindly but had once attracted the fond glances of comely females. The old lawman donned his battered tan slouch hat with the hawk feather sticking out of its band, then stooped once more to retrieve his shell belt with his walnut-handled Starr .44 positioned for the cross draw in its left-side holster and a sheathed bowie knife on the left hip.

"You dropped something."

Spurr followed the girl's gaze to his badge lying on the floor where'd he'd dropped his shirt. He'd removed the copper sun-and-moon from the garment when he'd crossed the border and stuck it in his pocket. It must fallen out in last night's high jinks with the *puta*.

Spurr picked up the badge then shoved it into a pouch of one of his saddlebags hanging over the back of the chair by the table. He looked at the girl. She regarded him gravely, her long hair hanging straight down around her face.

"They are bad men, those men you ask about."

"*Si*, senorita." Spurr slid his Starr from its holster, flicked open the loading gate, and spun the cylinder. Only five chambers showed brass; it was his habit to keep the one beneath the hammer empty so he didn't shoot himself in the leg.

"They are five. You are only one old . . ." She cut herself off and flushed, looking ashamed.

Spurr chuckled as he plucked a .44 cartridge from his shell belt and thumbed it into the empty chamber. "You got that right, senorita. I'm only one old man." He spun the cylinder, clicked the loading gate shut, and slid the weapon into its holster angled high over his left hip. "But sometimes us old men'll surprise you."

He gave her a wink as he draped the saddlebags over his left shoulder, then grabbed his old '66 model Winchester repeater from where it leaned against the wall by the door and brushed dust from the brass receiver. Fishing around in his pants pockets, he found a few coins and tossed them onto the bed near the girl's bare legs.

"That cover it?"

"Si, si. Gracias." She lifted her eyes to his and forced a smile. "You surprised me last night, Senor Spurr. The way a wildcat surprises a rabbit!" She cupped her breasts in her hands, mashing them against her chest, curling her legs, and giggling.

"Oh, I doubt that," Spurr said with an appreciative grin. "But I'm much obliged to you for sayin' so."

He pinched his hat brim to the girl and opened the door.

"Go with *Jesus*, Spurr," she said, her face grave again.

"Oh, I doubt he'd have me. But I do intend to send a few fellas to El Diablo."

Spurr blew her a kiss as he hefted the saddlebags on his shoulder, went out, and closed the door behind him. In the quiet room, the young *puta* crossed herself and lifted her imploring eyes to the crucifix.

5

HITCHING HIS CARTRIDGE belt and his pants higher on his lean hips, Spurr walked down the stone steps and into the dirt-floored cantina stitched with sunlight blasting through the dirty front window.

Three men were passed out in various positions about the cramped place, two on the floor. The previous night's tobacco smoke and tequila smelled heavy and stale. There was no sign of the proprietor, the *puta*'s uncle, but Spurr could hear someone moving around behind a curtain flanking the bar consisting of pine logs stretched across beer kegs.

He didn't cross to the front of the room but turned at the bottom of the stairs and went outside through a plank-board door. This north side of the high, narrow, adobe building was shaded, but when he started walking west the brassy Mexican sun found him and set his head to pounding so that he wished he'd brought the mescal. It was late in the year, so despite the sun it was chilly, and the cold slithered beneath Spurr's collar and down his back and made him shiver . . . and pine once more for the bottle.

He continued along behind the buildings and trash piles and privies and stock pens, until he saw the whitewashed church ahead. St. Xavier's was an ancient, crumbling ruin, with a cracked wall about six feet high around it. In several places the wall was open, having given way to the erosions of time, with ancient straw protruding from the old adobe and whitewash. In other places, the wall was pocked with bullet craters and large, faded bloodstains—mementos of the political upheavals and sundry violence that was part and parcel of daily life in Mexico.

About twenty feet from the wall, Spurr stopped and pressed his shoulder to the back of the livery barn in which he'd stabled his big roan stallion, Cochise, and where, the previous night, he'd thought he might also find the mules and wagons he'd been following. But the outlaws had been careful. Cochise and a burro were the only tenants. The traitorous killers must have swung the wagons through town and, maybe not liking the setup, parked them out in the desert somewhere. Maybe they feared that in town someone might get a look at what they were hauling and spread the word, eventually making its way to the army, the Federales, or the Rurales. Most of the rural Mexican police force were every bit as corrupt as the banditos and border toughs they fought against.

Spurr edged a look out from behind the barn. Across the *pueblito*'s narrow, dusty main street, a nondescript little building sat hunkered beneath a giant cottonwood opposite St. Xavier's. Its pink adobe was cracked in many places, its flat roof shingled with cholla branches. There was a wooden front gallery propped on stones, and several chairs and even a velour love seat outfitted it.

A water olla hung from the rafters, and a gourd dipper drooped from a nail in a gallery post. At the moment, a liver-colored cat sat on the porch rail, hunkered into itself, head bowed toward its front feet, awaiting the warmth of the rising sun.

Unlike most of the other buildings, no smoke lifted from the brothel's stone chimney. The windows were dark. No sounds emanated.

Spurr hoped he hadn't waited too long and let the killers

get away. But most desperadoes, especially ones that had been trailing hard across a vast, lonely desert, chose to sleep deep and hard once they reached a town—especially after a night of carousing. And maybe enjoy one more poke and a leisurely breakfast before heading out the next day into the Mexican wastelands.

Spurr shuttled his glance toward the wall surrounding the church. He saw a gap straight out before him, in the shape of an inverted V, and set his saddlebags down against the livery barn. Holding his rifle up before him in both hands, he pushed out from behind the barn and took three steps.

A click sounded from the other side of the street. Spurr turned his head to see the brothel's front door open and a figure emerge from the heavy shadows behind it, but Spurr continued walking, putting the ruined wall of the church between him and the whorehouse.

He hadn't been able to tell if the man had seen him. He stopped just inside the wall, gritting his teeth and cocking his ears. Had he blown his opportunity to take the demons unawares?

As if in reply, a voice rose from across the street. "Hey! You there! I *seen* you!"

Spurr glanced in the direction of the main street through a small, ragged hole in the church wall and saw the man—a rangy blond in dirty cream balbriggans and boots and wearing a pistol and cartridge belt around his waist—tuck his pecker back into his underwear bottoms as he stepped off the gallery. Apparently, he'd been coming out to piss in the street when he'd seen Spurr.

The old lawman cursed under his breath as the brigand passed out of his view as he crossed the street, heading for the churchyard. Spurr looked around quickly. The church bulked up before him, about fifty yards away. Around it were rock-mounded graves, some sporting wooden or stone markers, some marked by nothing but the sage and catclaw growing up around them.

About twenty feet to Spurr's right, a tall stone marker fronted a grave that was not a rock mound but merely a barren, grave-shaped depression in the earth. He could hear the outlaw's boots crunching gravel now as the man approached the wall. Spurr bolted over to the tall marker whose ancient inscription had been worn out by time—all he could make out was a faint image of *Jesus* holding his hands out in blessing.

Spurr grunted as he bent his arthritic knees, hearing them pop, and sat down in front of the marker. He cursed again in pain as he rested his stiff back against the marker and ground his bony ass into the gravelly ground, then rested his rifle across his thighs. Quickly, he tipped the brim of his hat down over his eyes and lowered his chin to his chest. He breathed slowly, feigning sleep.

"Hey!" The outlaw's slightly high-pitched voice echoed around the boneyard, off the sun-blasted adobe walls of the church. "You, there! I seen you. Don't think I didn't!"

Spurr poked up his hat brim up and opened one eye. The unshaven blond brigand stood in the V notch in the adobe wall, aiming a cocked Schofield revolver at Spurr. "Leave me be, damn you. Let a man sleep!"

He closed the eye and crossed his arms on his chest as though in frustration.

He could hear the man's boots crunch gravel. His spurs chinged softly as he approached the old lawman. The crunching and chinging grew louder.

The crunching and chinging stopped.

Spurr smelled rancid tequila sweat. The man kicked his right, moccasin-clad foot.

"What the hell you doin', sneakin' around out here, old-timer?"

Spurr opened his eyes again and stared up at the mean-faced, unshaven blond whose nose was burned as bright as a Mexican sunset. "I done got kicked out of the last bed I was in. Somethin' about my kickin' and snorin'. If a man can't get peace in a graveyard, where can he?"

The blond brigand stared down at him speculatively. He narrowed his right eye, then his left eye. Then deep scowl lines cut across his forehead, and recognition dawned in his gaze. "Hey, I know you. Why . . . you're . . . Spurr Mor—!"

Spurr slapped the gun out of his face with a sideways thrust of his right arm. At the same time, he gave an agonized groan, kicked his right moccasin up, and drove it squarely into the man's crotch. The pistol barked, the slug spanging off a gravestone somewhere behind Spurr. The outlaw folded like a jackknife, crossing his hands over his crotch and glaring at Spurr with bright blue eyes. Spurr whipped his rifle up and slammed the barrel across the outlaw's right temple.

The brigand screamed and half twisted around, dropping first to one knee, then to the other knee, and removing one of his hands from his crotch to cover his temple. He shook his head wildly as though to clear it. Slowly, both hands dropped, and he sagged over onto his side in the red dirt and gravel and lay still.

Spurr grunted as he heaved himself to his feet, leapt the unconscious killer, and ran in his arthritic, shambling, bull-legged gait to the churchyard's front wall and hunkered down beside a gap. Carefully, he edged a look through the gap and across the street at the brothel.

Nothing had changed. No smoke lifted from the chimney, no sounds emanated from behind the gallery. Even the cat lounged as before, its head maybe hanging a little lower toward its paws. Obviously even morning gunfire wasn't all that uncommon around here.

Spurr ran back to the unconscious outlaw on whose cut temple a pale blue lump was sprouting. Spurr grabbed a set of handcuffs out of a pocket of his elkhide vest and cuffed the brigand's hands behind his head. The man groaned, blinked his eyes. Spurr rammed the butt of his Winchester against the blond's other temple, laying him out again, cold.

It was not a move that Chief Marshal Henry Brackett would condone, if the sage old lawman ever learned of it. But Spurr was a not a by-the-book lawman. He couldn't count on all his fingers and toes all the by-the-book badge toters he'd known who were now pushing up stones and buckbrush.

He racked a cartridge into the Winchester's breech and ran around behind the church, leaping graves and trash piles of mostly wine and tequila bottles, and stepped through a gap in the far western wall. Limping a little on his game left leg—he'd just discovered it was game when he'd pushed himself up so quickly to lay out the blond brigand—he ran across the main street and stole around to the rear of the brothel, where there was more trash and a stinky privy pit that had only been partially filled in, beside a two-holer without doors.

A voice rose from the two-holer. "Del?"

Spurr froze about ten feet from the privy. He stared at the privy, thinking fast. "What?"

"Was that you that triggered that shot? Don't you know me an' the boys was wantin' to sleep in?"

Spurr stole forward on cat feet, until he gained the near front corner of the two-holer. "Sorry."

The voice of the man in the latrine was slow and gravelly—the voice of a badly hungover Texan. "Just cause you can't sleep past five thirty from your daddy wakin' you to milk cows when you was just a shaver don't mean you got a right to go firin' that pistol of yourn so early in the god-damn mornin'!"

Spurr looked through the door at the man sitting the hole—a stocky man with thin, curly brown hair and a week's growth of beard on his fleshy, red-eyed face. The man's eyes had just started to widen when Spurr slammed his Winchester's butt solidly against the man's forehead with a loud, crunching smack and then a wooden thud as his head smashed against the back wall.

Knowing the man's wick was out if he wasn't dead, Spurr whipped around, aiming his rifle at the brothel's back door that stood about two feet open. A well-worn path led from the door to the privy. There were no windows back here, and Spurr took advantage of that by taking his time, listening closely, as he tramped to the back door then listened for another few seconds before hooking the Winchester's barrel around the door and slowly swinging it wide.

He ground his teeth against the squawk of the dry hinges, then quickly stepped inside and pressed his back against the wall right of the door. He was in a hall, and there was a man standing in front of him, about eight feet away.

As Spurr's eyes adjusted, he made out a bearded face with two surprised eyes under the brim of a tan cavalry hat. A Colt Army pistol in the man's hand was tracking Spurr's move to the wall. Light from behind Spurr flashed off the Colt's bluing, and Spurr squeezed his Winchester's trigger.

The roar in the close confines made the entire building jump. The man in front of Spurr yelped and triggered his Colt out the open door as he flew straight back down the hall, which Spurr could now see opened onto the main part of the brothel, which wasn't much except a small bar and several large cots covered in animal skins. Two of the skin piles were now moving, and a man leapt off a cot against the brothel's right side, hit the floor on his ass, showed his wild eyes to Spurr, then reached under the cot for a sawed-off, double-barreled shotgun.

"Goddamn you, Little Dog," he shouted, lifting the shotgun. "You said we had nothin' to worry about here!"

"Hold it!" Spurr took long strides forward as he pressed his Winchester's brass buttplate hard against his right shoulder and levered a fresh round into the chamber.

"Hold this, you son of a bitch!"

The man on the floor raised the shotgun higher, and Spurr drilled him through the middle of his forehead. Another man emerged from a pile of skins on the room's left side, under which a girl was cowering and screaming, and grabbed one of several pistols off the bar planks and ran toward the brothel's front window.

"Stop, you devil!" Spurr shouted, ejecting the spent cartridge from the Winchester and racking another round, drawing a bead on the middle of the running man's back. He was big and naked and nearly as hairy as an ape. As big as he was, he managed to twist around and fire an errant shot toward Spurr before he bounded off his bare heels and dove toward the window.

Spurr squeezed the rifle's trigger. The Winchester's roar was nearly drowned by the screech of shattering glass as the big, hairy man dove on through to disappear onto the gallery while glass rained behind him.

Another girl began screaming and yet another began shouting Spanish epithets above and behind Spurr, who wheeled suddenly, levering the Winchester and aiming at a small loft area to which a wooden stairs rose, over the main room. The girl shouting at him was plump and naked and gesturing wildly while calling Spurr every name he'd ever been called in his long career, and a few he hadn't. No other men appeared to be with her.

Spurr tipped his hat brim to the angry *puta* then swung around and walked on out the front door and onto the gallery. The big, hairy, long-haired man was writhing in a bloody sea of broken glass, reaching down with one hand to grab his crotch.

"Well, if it ain't ole Alvin Little Dog," Spurr said, aiming his Winchester at the bloody half-breed's head. "Last time I seen you, you was bein' shipped off to Deer Lodge in the good ole Montana Territory."

Little Dog looked up at Spurr. His face was broad, pock-marked, knife-scarred, and unlike the rest of him, hairless. "Spurr," he grunted, holding his hand high inside his right thigh, where apparently Spurr's bullet had pinked him as he dove out the window. In a pain-pinched, quavering voice, he said, "What brings you to Mexico, you old son of a bitch?"

"You."

Little Dog squeezed his eyes closed and gritted his teeth. "Well . . . you got me. Figured . . . it might be you . . . who'd get me. Just figured it that way." He was cut up bad. A deep gash in his neck was spurting blood. Sweat popped out on his red-tan cheeks and forehead, and his entire body shook. "Go ahead—finish me!"

"Where you boys headed with them wagons, Alvin?"

Dying as painfully as he was, Little Dog only grinned and shook his head. "No, sir, brother. Won't give you that, you ugly old bastard."

He whooped triumphantly, jeeringly.

Movement on the other side of the street caught Spurr's eye. The blond outlaw was staring through a hole in the church wall, looking dazed, both temples bloody. Spurr wouldn't get the information he wanted from Little Dog. At least not before the Cree half-breed expired from blood loss. The lawman would get it out of this contingent of the gang's sole surviving member.

"All right, Alvin." Spurr raised the Winchester to his shoulder. "Go ahead and shake hands with Ole Scratch if you're in such a dangblasted hurry."

Alvin Little Dog laughed then whooped again, louder.

Spurr's Winchester bellowed.

Alvin Little Dog stopped whooping.

6

EVEN THE NEAREST Yaqui was still a hundred yards away from him, but as Cuno crouched low over the sleek neck of his galloping skewbald paint, the Indians' war whoops and devilish yowls seemed to be coming from inside his own head. He'd heard before that no matter what a man had ever been through on the frontier—and Cuno had been through a lot himself, including Indian battles—nothing ever prepared him for an attack by blood-hungry Yaqui raiders.

Their reputation for slow, excruciating torture was known far and wide.

Renegade's hooves thudded. Cuno could hear the horse's breaths raking in and out of his straining lungs. He glanced to his right and saw the Indians angling toward him across the desert, trying to cut off his westward route. Another pack of three was kicking up dust on his right, a little farther away than those on his left but not by much. He cast a quick glance behind. Five were behind him now, riding in a ragged line abreast of each other, hunkered low over their war ponies' necks, long black hair streaming out behind them. All five were reaching back to slap their mustangs' rears, coaxing more speed.

The war whoops sounded like the warbling of a demented demon freshly loosed from hell, causing the hair on the back of Cuno's neck to stick straight up in the air.

He stared ahead of him. He still had another five miles to the first line of hills where, if he could reach it, he might have a chance of losing his pursuers or at least have a fair chance of holding them off from higher ground. But Renegade would never make it that far at this pace. As game a horse as Renegade was, he was no match for the Yaqui's smaller, fleeter war ponies.

A low butte crested with a sandstone knob stood on the right side of his trail, about a hundred yards away. It was his only hope, though he had no illusions. Death was near, and it seemed just as cold and lonely as he'd imagined it would.

He slid his ivory-gripped .45 from the holster thonged low on his right thigh and squeezed off a shot at the Indians racing toward him on his right flank. It was a long shot for a short gun but he'd hoped it would slow them some. It did not. They kept coming, crouched low, whooping and hollering and wildly slapping their ponies' behinds.

Cuno triggered two more shots as he reined Renegade off the trail's right side and pointed him toward the butte. The move made the Indians on that side of the trail and to his right about sixty or seventy yards and closing fast, whoop all the louder and crazier.

"Yeah?" Cuno said. He holstered his Colt, slid the Winchester '73 out of its boot under his right thigh, and levered a shell into the chamber. "How 'bout one of these?"

Holding both the reins and the rifle, giving Renegade his head because the horse was smart enough to know where Cuno was heading to try to get some advantage against the Indians, he twisted back in his saddle, aimed quickly, and fired. His slug flew well wide of the lead rider he'd been aiming at, and blew up dust behind the man and in the center of the fast-approaching pack.

He aimed again, fired, and one of the Indians snapped his head back and to one side before bringing it forward and swiping a hand against his ear, which Cuno had apparently nicked.

Cuno grinned. It wasn't much, but it did appear to slow the riders in that group just a bit and temper their howling.

Now he and Renegade were within fifty yards of the base of the knob-crested butte. The Indians were behind and to his right, angling toward him, their ponies dashing, fleet and graceful as tigers, through the low clumps of cacti. Now the butte's rock-strewn base was before Renegade, and the horse drew up and turned sideways, his white-lathered sides heaving, foam licking back from his expanding and contrasting nostrils.

Cuno leapt out of the saddle and, holding the horse's reins, jumped onto a flat-topped boulder, and fired six quick rounds at the nearest group of Indians, knocking two out of their saddles and causing a third to check his mustang down so suddenly that the horse nearly turned a somersault, dirt blowing up in front of him.

The other two groups of Indians were closing fast.

Cuno jumped off the boulder and, jerking on Renegade's reins, quickly climbed the side of the butte, his boots slipping and sliding in the loose red rock that sloped down like a stout woman's apron from the base of the knob about a hundred feet above. The Indians were triggering their carbines now, and bullets plunked into the rocks and gravel around Cuno and Renegade. The horse whinnied and fought the reins, but Cuno held fast. He paused once to trigger two shots at the oncoming riders, then jerked Renegade on up to the knob, around it, and into the cool, blue shade behind it.

He was dizzy from the fast climb, his chest throbbing. Quickly, he tied Renegade to a stout, dried root angling out of a crack at the base of the towering knob then ran back to the side of it, thumbing fresh cartridges into the Winchester's breech. He edged a look around the tower of scaled, eroded sandstone.

The Indians were leaping out of their saddles about twenty yards below the butte's base and running through the sage and creosote, holding their carbines across their chests. None were howling now, but in the clear desert air, Cuno could hear their breathing and the snap of branches and the crunch of gravel beneath their moccasins. They sounded like hunting coyotes padding around a camp at night.

Some came running up the slope toward Cuno. Others angled around to both sides, nearly surrounding him. He had little hope, but he'd cull the pack a little, make them pay dearly for his life.

He dropped to a knee and started hammering away with the Winchester, empty cartridge casings flying over his right shoulder. In five shots he only managed to drill two of the Yaqui and merely slow the others running up the bluff toward him, weaving and dodging and howling as they triggered their carbines. As the Indians' slugs hammered the rocks around him, Cuno continued firing, pivoting on his hips, until he'd emptied the Winchester and maybe wounded only two more Yaqui.

Meanwhile, Renegade was screaming and bucking and trying to get loose, and Cuno was wishing he hadn't tied the horse but let him run. He was too good a horse for these savages to get their hands on.

The others were still coming, most from behind. As he whipped around to shoot down the backside of the bluff, he saw one warrior drop behind a boulder while another flipped his arm up and forward. The steel blade of the feathered hatchet winked as the grisly weapon turned end over end. It made a whooshing sound as it cut the air, and Cuno ducked and threw his Winchester up a quarter second before the blade would have embedded itself in his forehead, likely splitting his skull in two.

At nearly the same time, he glimpsed out the corner of his eye one of the other braves drop his own carbine and lunge toward him with a knife, screaming so loudly and bizarrely that Cuno thought his own back teeth would crack. Automatically, Cuno pivoted again and tried to ram the stock of his repeater into the brave's belly. He missed, only glancing the stock off the brave's side but avoiding the sharp point of the horn-handled knife in the brave's slashing right hand.

Hearing more shots rising from behind, and knowing he was a goner but unable to quit fighting until he was dead, Cuno dropped the Winchester and reached for his .45. Before he could palm the hogleg, however, the brave bulled him over onto his back, and he triggered the weapon wild. He looked up to see the brave suspended over him and his right hand wrapped around the brave's right wrist, the knife in that hand angled down toward Cuno's chest.

The brave's brick-red face was a mask of animal fury, his chocolate eyes white-ringed, his chapped lips stretched back to reveal his crooked, yellow teeth. Spittle frothed his mouth. The wolf claw necklace and an elkhide medicine pouch that smelled of gunpowder and lavender brushed Cuno's chest.

The brave writhed and fought against Cuno's outstretched right arm and clawed at Cuno's face with his left hand. Meanwhile, the shooting continued and Cuno vaguely wondered why he wasn't dead or mortally wounded yet when he also became aware of agonized cries instead of war whoops, and bodies falling around him.

Keeping his concentration on the brave with the knife, he drove his right knee into the brave's groin. The Indian gave a shriek and dropped the knife. At the same time, Cuno arched his back and twisted his hips and sent the brave tumbling downslope before quickly scrambling to his feet. Before the Indian could make another move, Cuno was on him, smashing his right fist into the brave's face—hammering the brave's jaw and cheek and nose.

The brave was too dazed by the pummeling to do much more than try to bow his head and shield his face with his arms. Propelled by a killing fury, Cuno kept at him, slipping a left inside the brave's arms and connecting solidly with the brave's chin. The brave twisted around and fell and was scrambling, beaten and bloody, back to his feet when his head snapped suddenly sideways.

A rifle thundered—cutting through the silence that Cuno had just now become aware of. A quarter-sized hole shone in the brave's right cheek. Blood oozed from another, larger hole on the other side of his face.

His head sagged, and then he fell upslope, rolled downslope several yards, and came to rest against another dead brave who lay on his back, arms and legs akimbo, several gaping, bloody holes in his naked chest.

Cuno blinked, his head spinning, his chest rising and falling sharply as he looked around. More braves lay dead on the downslope. Beyond them, five men in blue cavalry uniforms sat atop five sweat-lathered horses. One of the men was just now lowering his smoking Henry repeater from his shoulder and ejecting the spent cartridge.

Another, a tall, red-haired man with sergeant's chevrons on his sleeves, riding a copper-bottom mare, slipped down from his saddle, slid his Winchester into his saddle boot, and ran up the slope toward Cuno. He veered toward one of the dead braves, gave an Indian-like whoop, and shucked the bowie knife sheathed on his left hip.

The others on horseback watched as the tall, redheaded sergeant jerked the dead brave's head up by his hair and quickly and deftly lifted the scalp. He raised the bloody trophy high above his head, and gave another Indian-like howl.

Cuno watched him blankly, his mind still spinning too fast to comprehend what had just happened. And that he was still alive. Who were these soldiers and where had they come from? He'd thought he was alone out here and about to be dead and forgotten.

At the moment, the soldiers who'd saved him seemed to have forgotten him. They were all gazing up the slope at the tall redhead still holding the bloody scalp aloft and giving a little shuffling dance.

"Now, why in the hell did you go and do that, Lusk?" asked a man with lieutenant's bars on the shoulders of his blue cavalry tunic. He was potbellied and blond, with a brushy dragoon-style mustache, and two silver front teeth.

"Trophy to show my girl!" bellowed Lusk, leaning down to clean his knife blade on the Indian's calico shirt.

Cuno felt naked without his pistol. He looked around, spotted it lying in the rocks, and walked over to it.

At the same time, a rifle thundered, and a bullet kicked up gravel about six inches right of his ivory-gripped .45.

Cuno jerked with a start and spun around. The lieutenant was holding a smoking Winchester on him.

"Not so fast, amigo," he said in a drawling Texas accent as he ejected the spent cartridge and seated a fresh one. "First—who in the hell are you, and what are you doin' down here on the wrong side of the border?"

Cuno glanced at the soldiers staring back at him, squinting against the sun. To a man, they were hard-faced and flat-eyed. But Cuno had the tart vinegar following a close fight burning through his veins.

"I was about to ask you the same question, amigo."

7

THE LIEUTENANT AND the other soldiers stared flatly at Cuno. The young ex-freighter, dusty and disheveled and bleeding from his lips, held their gazes.

Finally, one of the soldiers, a corporal, chuckled and spat a wad of chew onto a flat rock near his bay's right foreleg and glanced sideways at the lieutenant. "He's got some grit, Sapp. Best let him be."

"Might be able to use him," said the corporal sitting beside the lieutenant. "He done kilt his share o' them Injuns. Might come in handy, the farther we head into Yaqui country."

"He killed his share o' them Injuns," said the lieutenant, Sapp, "but he'd be dead if it weren't for us." He sat up a little straighter in his saddle, and his silver front teeth flashed beneath his yellow, dragoon mustache as he said commandingly, "I asked who you were, mister, and I expect an answer, or I'll shoot you in both legs and leave you to die with them heathens."

Cuno relented. Whoever these men were—and something told him they were not soldiers despite the uniforms—they had kept him from becoming buzzard bait. Flatly, standing near his .45 on the slope across which several dead Yaqui lay sprawled, he said, "Name's Massey. Cuno Massey."

He saw no reason to use an alias. While the United States government no doubt had a warrant out for his arrest, they wouldn't have sent soldiers across the border for him. And if these men were soldiers, he was from Mars. "What I'm doing down here is no one's business but mine. I'm obliged to you for helping me out with these Injuns, and I'll try to repay you anyway I can. But that's as far as I go."

The lieutenant, Sapp, stared at him, canting his head a little to one side. The brim of his tan kepi shaded his eyes. The men's horses blew or shook their heads, twitched their ears, eager to be away from the blood smells. The redhead with the dripping scalp shuttled his expectant glance between the two parties. High above the butte's sandstone knob, a hawk screeched, likely waiting for the killers to abandon the carrion.

Finally, Sapp's eyes softened as they flicked up and down Cuno's muscular frame, and he said, reining his own horse away from the butte, "Bring your hoss, young feller. We got a camp yonder with grub and water."

He booted his coyote dun into a gallop to the northwest. The other mounted men glanced again up the slope at Cuno, then turned their own mounts away from the butte and spurred them after Sapp. Cuno stood staring after them, his ears still ringing from his head's impact with a rock earlier, in his fight with the axe-wielding Yaqui. The redhead stared at him as though taking Cuno's measure.

"You alone?"

Cuno nodded.

The redhead tucked the end of the Yaqui's long black scalp behind his cartridge belt. "This ain't no country to be alone in, partner." He walked up the slope, dragging his boot heels, his blue eyes friendly in an otherwise broad face with a broad, freckled, belligerent nose. As he extended a gloved hand toward Cuno, he said, "I'm Lusk."

Cuno stared at the man skeptically, then shook his hand. "Cuno Massey."

"So I heard." Lusk turned away and began striding down the slope, loosing shale behind him, the dust rising burnt-orange in the fading afternoon light. "And I heard another thing."

"What's that?" Cuno had started tramping up the slope to where Renegade stood tied to the root in the shade of the tall knob, the paint's eyes still white-ringed with anxiety and wanting to hightail it out of there.

"I've heard the name Massey before."

As Cuno grabbed his paint's reins, he glanced down the butte as Lusk stepped into his saddle. Cuno regarded the sergeant curiously as he led Renegade down the slope, the horse snorting his disdain for the dead Indians, his shod hooves ringing off stones.

At the bottom of the bluff, Cuno swung up into his saddle. Lusk sat his horse with the U.S. brand on its left wither, leaning forward on his saddle horn, giving a knowing, faintly jeering smile.

"Ever been to Valoria in the Nebraska Territory?" Cuno asked him as though they were having a normal conversation, not wanting to give anything away.

"Nope, never been to Valoria. Hell, I was through Nebraska maybe only one time."

"Well, I reckon there's plenty of Masseys around. Common enough name."

Lusk kept giving him that cat-that-ate-the-canary look as he booted his army remount in the direction the others had headed, Cuno cautiously spurring Renegade behind him. After they'd ridden a hundred yards, heading for a notch in a dark line of hills in the northwest, Lusk looked at him again as he rode off Cuno's right stirrup.

"Federal pen had 'em a prison break a few months back," he said. "I know, see, 'cause I ran the telegraph office back at Fort Bryce, and I took down the federal telegram ordering all cavalry patrols to be on the watch for escaped federal prisoners heading for the Mexican line. Especially for the young blond rascal that killed him some territorial marshals up Wyoming way. Had just enough of an usual name to stick in my memory."

Cuno eyed the man for a time. "Since you know so much

about me, how 'bout you tell me what blue-bellies are doing this far south of the border?"

"Oh, I can't do that," Lusk said. "No, sir—you see, that's a military secret." He chuckled, bit the end off a tobacco braid, and started working it around in his mouth. He returned the braid to his shirt pocket and glanced once more at Cuno, that satisfied, knowing grin still stretching his mouth. "But there's no need to worry, young Massey. I for one don't doubt them marshals deserved what they got, and your secret's safe with me." He winked. "As long as our secret's safe with you."

Cuno wasn't sure he shouldn't have thanked the soldiers, if they were indeed soldiers, and ridden out. But with the Yaqui on a rampage—and they'd likely be even more ornery when they discovered their fallen comrades on the butte—he might be better off spending the night around these men's fire, then lighting out first thing in the morning and continuing on to the gulf.

He cast a cautious glance behind him and was about to turn his head forward when something caught his eye on a low hill to the south.

"Hold up," he told Lusk, pulling back on Renegade's reins.

"What is it?"

"A rider." Cuno jerked his chin to where he'd spied the single rider sitting atop the hill, little more than a blue-yellow smudge against the southern horizon. But there was some white in the smudge, as well, as Cuno felt apprehension tingle along his spine as he reached back into his saddlebags for his spyglass.

He telescoped the lens and brought the sage-stippled hill into focus. The smudge clarified into a slender, tan figure mounted on a cream horse. He couldn't see much of her, but he could see enough to see that she was a woman—the same Yaqui queen he'd seen before trailing him and Camilla. Her bare legs and arms shone like liquid gold in the west-angling sun. Her face, angled toward Cuno, as though she were staring back at him, was a tan oval between the wings of her long black hair.

Cuno glanced back at Lusk, who was directing a pair of army-issue field glasses toward the hill. The redheaded sergeant lifted his upper lip above his tobacco-brown teeth. "There she is. The little Yaqui she-devil her ownself."

"You've seen her before?"

"*Ojos del Fuego*, the Mescins call her. Fire Eyes. Don't know her real name, and I don't know who started calling her Fire Eyes—or what hombre could have gotten close enough to see her eyes and live—but that's what they call her around here, even up in Arizona. She's the one leadin' the Yaqui in these parts on their miserable war parties. She's got several separate bands around Sonora and western Chihuahua, and she leads 'em all. Been devilin' us since we crossed the border. We was out lookin' for her when we ran into you." Lusk ground his teeth. "Slippery bitch."

Cuno was staring again through his spyglass at the comely queen sitting her cream war pony like some vision out of an old Mexican legend. She sat so still, glowing golden, that she might have been a statue. Suddenly she lifted her carbine high above her head and held it there—a mocking, threatening salute of some kind.

Then she lowered the rifle, reined the cream around, and disappeared down the other side of the hill. Gone, as though she'd only been a figment of Cuno's imagination.

"What the hell you suppose that meant?" Lusk said, lowering his field glasses.

Cuno reduced his spyglass and slipped it into its saddle-bag pouch. "I have a feelin' she wasn't welcoming us to Mexico."

Lusk chuckled. He booted his horse ahead, and Cuno reined the paint around, continuing to cast cautious glances behind him as he followed his guide for a mile or so across the desert, crossing a couple of shallow dry washes before dropping into a narrow canyon with fifty-foot limestone walls streaked with sandstone and granite and pocked with bleached, white dinosaur bones.

Lusk stopped at a bend in the meandering canyon floor, raised an arm, and shouted his own name.

Cuno saw the Gatling gun maw protruding from between two rocks in the right side of the canyon wall. A head covered in a straw sombrero rose from behind the Gatling gun, showing a bearded face with a cigarette dangling between its thick lips, and the gunner said, "Who's your friend, Lusk?"

"Jesus Christ."

"No shit?"

"Would I shit you, Carson?"

Carson told Lusk to do something physically impossible to himself, and Lusk chuckled as he glanced at Cuno, and the two continued riding along the gravelly canyon bottom, rounding the bend past the Gatling gun and entering a broad area where green started to show, even a few ironwood and paloverde trees lining a thin stream that flowed out of the rocks on the canyon's left side.

Seven or so wagons were parked near the stream. On the stream's other side, horses and mules were picketed in a long line, some now drinking water while men moved amongst them with feed bags and curry combs. Other men sat around fires on the canyon side of the stream, some sitting on rocks, playing cards, or sleeping in the shade of the paloverdes.

From a quick count as he and Lusk approached the group, Cuno figured there were around twenty men here—some in uniform, some half in uniform, some in trail-worn civilian clothes. Those who'd helped him out with the Yaqui, including Sapp, were just now unsaddling their sweaty, dusty mounts. Sapp was talking to a tall, middle-aged man riding a steeldust army mount, and they both turned to Cuno and Lusk with interest. Cuno and Lusk drew their horses up to the tall man while Sapp set his saddle on his shoulder and led his horse to the stream.

The tall man was smoking a long black cheroot. He sat regarding Cuno from beneath bushy eyebrows. His eyes were steel blue, his face broad and hard, the cheeks tapering severely to strong jaws. He wore a dark brown mustache flecked with gray. Muttonchop whiskers of the same color angled down to meet his lip corners with stiletto-sharp points.

He was dressed like a gambler or a southern gentleman in a black plantation hat, black clawhammer coat, string tie, and whipcord trousers tucked down into high-topped, stove-pipe boots. Two pearl-gripped .45s jutted from cross-draw holsters on both hips, and a bulge beneath the coat bespoke a shoulder gun.

"Who's your new friend?" he asked Lusk in the reso-nate, slightly gravelly voice of a longtime smoker, keeping the blue eyes, sharp and probing as knife blades, on Cuno.

"Major Bennett Beers, meet Mr. Cuno Massey," Lusk said, shuttling his gaze between the two.

If Beers recognized the name, he didn't let on. He didn't extend his hand but only drew deeply on his cigar and said while letting the smoke trickle out his nostrils, "What brings you to Mexico?"

Cuno wasn't accustomed to such bald questions, and this one annoyed him. He saw no reason to lie, however. Whether these men were really soldiers or not, their being in Mexico was most certainly illegal. He had no idea if it was as illegal as Cuno's business here—running from mur-der and other sundry hanging offenses—but those covered wagons and the hard looks of Beers and Sapp and Lusk and the others, he'd have bet silver dollars to navy beans it was. If not, they were obviously more concerned with their own business than trifling with one of the many wanted Anglos in Mexico.

Cuno said, "Had a run of bad luck, decided to see if I could turn it down here."

Beers glanced at Lusk. "What do you think?"

"I think he had run of bad luck north of the border, Major."

Beers turned back to Cuno. "You want a job, Massey?"

Cuno glanced at the wagons and the other men milling around them, most looking toward Cuno while smoking or playing cards or breaking out bottles. The wagons were California rack-bed freighters—good, rough-country im-plements for hauling moderate-sized loads up and down steep mountains or rocky trails. They all appeared to have double-thick iron-shod wheels, reinforced undercarriages, drag shoes, and rough lock chains. Whatever they had on board was probably heavy, and since it was being hauled this far into Mexico, it must also be valuable.

"We lost four men over the past couple of days to the Yaqui. I need scouts and drivers. If you've skinned a mule team before, I could use you in a wagon. Two dollars a day plus grub, whiskey, and group security. Down here, in case you hadn't noticed, security is a mighty precious commodity."

Before Cuno could reply, someone said, "I'd take him up on it, Massey. Not too many lone wolves survive this deep in Mexico. Not even handsome young men still cutting their milk teeth."

A woman's voice.

Cuno shuttled his gaze beyond Beers to see the voice's origin—a blonde about his own age sitting in one of the driver's seats. She was dressed like a man and she was lounging back in the driver's seat like a man, smoking a cigar similar to Beers's, and she was holding a bottle of whiskey by its neck. She was even drunk like a man, eyes a little bleary, slurring her words.

But the body inside her rough trail clothes was all female. And the brown eyes gazing admiringly across Beers at the parties' new teamster was as female as the rest of her. To a dangerous degree, Cuno instinctively noted.

Beers glanced over his shoulder at her and then turned back to Cuno. "Don't mind her. That's just Flora. And when I say don't mind her, it's for your own good. Flora may look as pretty and innocent as Christmas morning, but she's as mean as a whole nest of slithering Mojave green rattlesnakes. She's been known to cut a man's throat for passin' a single harmless glance across her tits."

Beers grinned broadly at Cuno, making his eyes narrow devilishly. "And she's all mine."

8

SPURR DROPPED TO a knee in the middle of the trail and traced the furrow of a wagon wheel with the index finger of his right hand.

The furrow, which appeared here at the intersection of the trail he'd followed out of the *pueblito* and another trail swinging in from the east, was about two days old. If there'd been little wind through here, that was. If wind had obscured the furrows, it might be newer, but he didn't think there'd been wind—you could tell by the amount of dust and broken branches on trees and shrubs, and the amount of leaves and mesquite beans on the ground—and certainly no rain.

So the furrow could have been made by one of the wagons he was following, time-wise. But this track was narrower than those he'd seen before, leading away from Fort Bryce and taking the shortest route over the border into Mexico. So . . . while it could belong to one of the wagons belonging to the killers masquerading as soldiers who'd sacked Fort Bryce, it likely was not. Which meant, after a day of scouring the terrain south of the *pueblito* he'd never learned the name of, he still hadn't cut the caravans' sign.

After he'd taken the blond gang member, Del Hammond, into custody, he'd found the two wagons belonging to Hammond's party, and hid all three wagons loaded with rifles and ammunition as well as dynamite, in a narrow box canyon and closed off the mouth of the canyon with rocks and brush. Of course, anyone familiar with the area would likely find them, if they happened upon the canyon, but it was a chance that Spurr had had to take. He hoped that after he'd rescued Abel Hammerlich's daughter he'd be able to somehow get the wagons back to the border, or summon the U.S. Cavalry to cither destroy them and their contents or take them into custody.

He'd spanked the mules back in the direction of the *pueblito*, where he hoped they'd be well cared for.

Spurr cursed as he straightened and looked back at the coyote dun he was trailing behind his big roan, Cochise. The blond brigand he'd brained in the boneyard, Del Hammond, lay belly down across the coyote dun's back, to which Spurr had lashed the killer's saddle. He'd taken Hammond with him as a guide of sorts, because he hadn't been sure what else to do with the man. The *pueblito* had boasted no hoosegow, and he couldn't very well just turn the killer loose, though trailing him along as he followed the other killers would likely slow him up.

And so far the man had been a tight-lipped trail guide . . .

Spurr walked over to the coyote dun, down the left side of which Hammond's head hung, one cheek pressed taught to the horse's belly, just beneath his own blue-striped saddle blanket. Hammond wore no hat, because one wouldn't stay on his head in such a position. So Spurr had stuffed the man's hat into his saddlebags, and with a strip of cheap twine he'd tied a burlap swatch over the man's head, to keep the sun from burning him raw. It made Hammond, whom Spurr had had run-ins with back in the Indian Nations, where Hammond and his brothers had sold whiskey to the Choctaw, look a little like an mannish old lady heading outside to hang wash on her line.

Spurr had tied Hammond's hands to his ankles beneath

the horse's belly. Now, as Spurr's shadow fell across the killer's head, Hammond blinked his eyes.

"How you feelin', Del?" Spurr said. "You enjoyin' the ride, are ye?"

Hammond licked his lips and squinted one eye up at the old lawman. "You're an ugly old bastard."

Spurr knelt beside the man, the better for the outlaw to see him. The lawman pressed his index finger against Hammond's cheek, through the burlap swatch. "If you were a little better trail company and told me exactly where your pards is headin' and who they intend to sell them guns and ammo to, I'd allow you to ride right-side up, like a normal man, stead of some smelly, old cadaver being hauled to town for bounty."

"I don't like you, Spurr."

"Don't like myself sometimes."

"I gotta piss."

"Piss down your leg. Er . . ." Spurr grinned. "I reckon in your position it'd come down your sleeve, wouldn't it?"

"You old bastard—you don't understand!" Hammond slammed his head against his horse's side, gritting his teeth and causing his face to swell up between the flaps of his ridiculous scarf. "I don't know where they're headed. Bennett didn't tell us—only that once we got there, we'd be rich enough to spend the rest of our lives in Mexico without ever havin' to work again!"

"Who is this Bennett Beers, anyway? That his real name?"

Hammond let his head sag against his horse. His shoulders rose and fell as he breathed, a picture of frustration. "I can't tell you that. Christ, you know what would happen to me if I so much as whispered a word about him?" His voice was shrill with exasperation, genuinely frightened.

"Who're they sellin' the rifles and ammo to?"

Hammond said nothing, just hardened his jaws and stared at the old lawman's boots.

"The girl still alive?"

"I can't tell you nothin', damnit!"

"All right." Spurr sighed, rose, and walked back over to where Cochise stood, glancing back dubiously at the man hanging belly down over his horse. He wasn't sure if Hammond knew the gang's destination or not, but he had a feeling he did, and that it would just take time for the blond outlaw to tell him what he wanted to know.

"Ain't that a sorry sight, Cochise?" Spurr said, stepping into his saddle. "That ain't the way a man's s'posed to ride his horse, now, is it?" He glanced back at Hammond. "Just wait till tomorrow. Gonna be mighty sore after two days ridin' with all the blood in his head and feet and his belly grinding against his backbone."

Spurr chuckled, clucked the big roan into motion, pulling the dun along behind by its reins, and heading off down the trail at a fast, jouncing trot. Chief Marshal Henry Brackett wouldn't approve. But the chief marshal wasn't alone down here in Mexico. Spurr was.

Hammond's voice quavered beneath his horse's clomping hooves. *"Spurr . . . you . . . son of a bitch!"*

They continued south across the Sonoran Desert, Spurr watching for sign of at least one of the three groups of wagons that had split up at the border. Finding one trail would lead to the other caravan, if both parties hadn't already met up again. They likely had, as they were far enough from the border that they wouldn't think any U.S. federals or even bounty hunters were clinging to their trail. This was Mexico, after all, and there was safety in numbers.

By now, they were either expecting to meet up with Hammond's party soon or looking for it. Which meant that Spurr had to keep a sharp eye out not only for wagon tracks but for a possible bushwhack. He'd be a hell of a lot less conspicuous if he weren't trailing Hammond belly down across the dun.

Later in the day they came to a jog of chalky buttes. Spurr knew from his map that the west fork of the Rio Yaqui, wet only part of the year, flowed through this area of central Sonora. He reined Cochise down, dismounted,

and tied both his horse and Hammond's horse in a clump of
half-dead cottonwoods around which sparse tufts of relatively green grass grew. He left Hammond hanging silently
across his saddle. The killer had stifled his screaming complaints lest he should attract Indians, banditos, or, just as
bad for both him and Spurr, Mexican Rurales.

Grabbing his Winchester, Spurr climbed a rocky trough
between two buttes, moving as quickly as he could but taking it easy, as he felt a familiar throbbing in his chest. He
pressed his fist against his breastbone, as though to quell
the complaints of the tricky ticker, and kept climbing.

He reached the crest of the buttes and found himself
staring into a hundred-foot gorge on the other side. A dark
stream about three feet wide and rippling softly across its
rocky, sandy bed, hugged the base of the cliff directly below
Spurr. The stream and the gorge continued to his right before curving away from him after sixty or so yards. Near the
bend, he spied movement and quickly doffed his Stetson
and ducked his head, nearly pressing his chin to the ground.

He gave himself about fifteen seconds, hoping he hadn't
been seen, then lifted his head but kept his rifle down so the
sun wouldn't flash off its brass frame. With only the top of
his head protruding above the crest of the gorge, he directed
his gaze to a horseshoe bend on the stream's far side. Someone stood on the edge of the stream, looking around, a carbine hanging by a rope lanyard down a tan back.

Down the back, long, coarse black hair hung.

Spurr's weak ticker chugged and gurgled, and he felt a
muscle in his cheek twitch.

Yaqui.

Feeling an instinctive fear of the formidable native Mexican warriors though he'd never run into one before, he looked
around quickly, and found more milling about fifty yards to
his left and downstream from him. There were roughly seven
in the group gathered around as many ponies, and a gallant-
looking cream stallion with a red tribal mark in the form of
a circle on its left hip.

Spurr drew his head back behind a boulder on his left,

shielding himself from the downstream warriors, continuing to hear his blood wash in his ears, and turned his attention upstream. A look of surprise flashed over his craggy, leathery features, and he narrowed his eyes.

He'd assumed that the Yaqui he'd seen standing downstream from him was a buck. But he saw now that the bare-legged, bare-armed Indian just now wading into the stream and kneeling down in it and beginning to slowly cup water to her arms, was just about as female as females got. He could see little but rough details, and they were enough.

Spurr felt his old heart hammer wickedly as he hunkered low and watched the girl, done washing her arms, suddenly lift her hands to her deerskin vest, which was all she wore on her torso. Throwing her long, rich mane of indigo hair back behind her shoulders, she opened the vest. Crouching low over the sliding stream that flashed in the waning sunlight, she splashed water to her chest and under her arms.

She was so far away that to Spurr's lusty eyes her breasts were vague jostling shadows between the flaps of her vest, but alluring just the same. To his old ears the splashing sounded like mere ripples on the river's surface.

When the girl had finished her brief bath, she stood and closed her vest, stepping back onto the shore and lifting her rifle, which she'd leaned against a rock, and swinging it by its lanyard over her shoulder. As she began walking over to where the Yaqui bucks were tending their horses, she stopped suddenly. Just as suddenly, she turned her head toward Spurr.

The old lawman gulped and mashed his chin into the dirt, cursing softly under his breath. He'd caught only a glimpse of the girl's dark eyes, but dark they were. And they had a sharp savageness about them. They were also likely as keen as a hawk's.

Had she seen him?

Vaguely, he wondered what the punishment would be for spying on a Yaqui queen's bath, and quickly vanquished the grisly possibilities from his mind.

After a half minute had passed as slowly as an hour,

Spurr lifted his chin and cast a look into the gorge. The Yaqui queen was twenty feet from where she'd been when she'd stopped, and was taking long, sexy strides toward the bucks, her hair rippling down her slender back.

Spurr heaved a relieved sigh and brushed a gloved hand across his forehead. Then he held his ground and watched until the bucks and the girl, who'd swung easily onto the back of the beautiful cream stallion, had turned their horses away from the river and galloped south across the desert. The seven bucks followed the queen in a loose pack, keeping a good thirty-foot gap between her and them, as though she were not to be sullied by their smelly, sweating male presence.

Spurr stared after the war party—and that's what they were, judging by their arms and the paint on several of the braves as well as on the horses. Finally, he blew another, relieved sigh, feeling his nerves leaping around like little snakes trapped beneath his skin.

With a grunt, he pushed himself to his feet, donned his hat, and headed back down the trough between the buttes.

He needed a drink.

9

WHEN HE RETURNED to the cottonwood, he thought Hammond was dead. The outlaw hung unmoving down both sides of his horse. Neither his back nor his shoulders were moving.

"Hey, Hammond," Spurr said, nudging the outlaw's head with a moccasin toe. "You ain't dancin' the outlaw two-step with El Diablo, are you?"

Hammond did not stir.

"Hammond?"

Spurr bent down, grabbed the outlaw's collar in his fist, and twisted his torso around so he could see his face between the flaps of the burlap scarf. Hammond's eyes were slitted, and they were sharp with rage.

"You son of a bitch," he bit out just loudly enough for Spurr to hear.

"You keep callin' me names," Spurr said, leaning his rifle against a tree, then sliding his bowie knife from its sheath, "you're liable to go to bed without your supper."

He reached under the dun's belly and cut both ropes that tied Hammond's wrists and ankles together. Then he reached up and grabbed Hammond's cuffed hands, and grunting with the effort, pulled the outlaw down out of the saddle none too gently.

Hammond hit the ground with an indignant grunt and groan. He rolled onto his side and raised his knees toward his belly.

"You've killed me, you son of a bitch," he rasped. "You done killed me."

"You've done killed yourself. And if I don't know by tomorrow where your friends are headed . . . and what they're leadin' me into . . . you're gonna be a lot more dead than this. Hell, you'll be rememberin' this day as a Sunday afternoon ride in the country with a yellow-haired girl!"

While Hammond lay on the ground, groaning and trying to work some blood back into his legs, Spurr unsaddled both horses, watered them, rubbed them down with a scrap of an old saddle blanket, and tied them back in the brush with feed sacks draped over their heads.

He gathered some wood while it was still light enough to see, piled it up in the trees and rocks, where a fire wouldn't be so apt to be spotted from the low country to the west, then grabbed his two canteens as well as Hammond's two. He didn't bother tying the half-conscious outlaw. Even if his hands hadn't been cuffed behind his back, Hammond was too beaten up from the ride to go anywhere.

"I'm lightin' out for water. Don't pine for me too loud. Yaqui in the country."

"Ah, Christ," Hammond said, rolling over to cast his beseeching gaze on Spurr, who'd started walking away with the canteens. "You can't leave me here alone, you bastard! Not cuffed like this. Not without a gun!"

"That's the price for killin', my boy," Spurr said and tramped on off toward the south, hoping to find a way down to the water. He hadn't run into much water so far, and he had to take advantage of whatever he did find.

It took him nearly a half hour to find a way down to the stream, but it was not a hard way down as the cliff wall dropped to nearly ground level about two hundred yards south of where he'd left the horses and Hammond. It was just after sunset when, sweating and footsore, he dropped beside the stream, set his rifle and canteens down, doffed his hat, and stretched out to plunge his face into the cool, refreshing liquid.

He took several deep swallows, thrashing his face around to rid his dry, sunburned cheeks and beard of the trail grit. When he finally lifted his chin, water dripping from his beard and sculpting his chin whiskers into the shape of a spade, he glanced toward the other side of the stream. He frowned, staring. Finally, he heaved himself to his feet, then, leaving the canteens but not his rifle lying on the shore where he'd dropped them, he waded across the shin-deep river to the other side and stared down.

Before him were the unmistakable tracks of a heavy wagon with double-wide wheels. A midsized freighter of some sort. Could the tracks belong to the California rack beds that had been stolen from Fort Bryce?

He looked around and found several more sets of tracks where the wagons had swung in from the northeast and stopped here for a time before swinging back away from the spring and continuing south across the desert. As he stomped around, he found several more sets of wagon tracks, but also the large, shod hoof tracks of mules and also those of horses and the footprints of many men.

He also found a rock ring mounded with cool but relatively recent ashes. Strewn about the ring were cooked deer and quail bones, airtight tins, and empty whiskey bottles.

The old lawman's heart began to wheeze and heave almost as much as it had when he'd been watching the Yaqui queen bathe in the stream.

He swung around and stared southward. The light was fading fast, but the burnt-orange rays still shone the indentations the wagons had made when, traveling abreast, they'd headed on off to the south.

The same direction the Yaqui had headed.

Were the Yaqui following the wagons?

"I hope so," Spurr muttered, still staring after the tracks. "Go ahead, my beautiful Injun girl. Go ahead and dog their heels then run 'em down like the purty little she-coyote you are. Make 'em scream."

Spurr scratched his beard, grinning, amused at himself.

But then he wondered what she'd do with all those guns and ammunition, and his belly flooded with bile. Many innocent folks would die hard, as the Yaqui were cutting a wide swath across Mexico—almost as wide as the one the Apaches were cutting across the American Southwest.

He hurried back across the stream, filled all four canteens, swung them over his shoulders, then tramped back up into the buttes. At the camp, Hammond was sitting against a cottonwood, his legs spread out before him, looking dour as he stared at the fiery sunset behind coal-black ridges. His head was canted back against the tree, and his arms hung slack at his sides. His red neckerchief glistened in the last rays of the tumbling sun.

Spurr stopped.

Hammond hadn't been wearing a red neckerchief.

A figure in the trees beyond Hammond swung toward Spurr as the old lawman dropped all four canteens, took his rifle in his left hand, and slipped the Starr .44 from its holster with his right. Automatically, he shifted his feet, putting his right shoulder toward the bearded Mexican who'd been going through Spurr's saddlebags but who'd now risen and stood holding his Spencer repeater out from his right hip, the maw aimed at Spurr.

The Mex, who was obviously a bandito, wore a ragged-brimmed black sombrero and a leather jacket and charro slacks adorned with silver conchos. Two cartridge bandoliers crisscrossed his chest. A loosely rolled, wheat-paper cigarette smoldered between his lips.

Hooves clomped behind the man, and Spurr saw another bandito moving into the camp with both Spurr's roan and Hammond's coyote dun in tow. He, too, was smoking a quirley, and when his dark eyes found Spurr, they widened as he gave a surprised grunt and stopped suddenly, reaching for one of the two Colt Navy revolvers holstered for the cross draw on his hips.

Something moved to Spurr's right, and he slid his eyes to see yet another man walking into the camp from behind it, a Springfield Trapdoor rifle resting on his shoulder, Spurr's whiskey bottle in his other hand. He was tall and wore a bleached tan walrus mustache, and he had his straw sombrero tipped back on his nearly bald head.

The three men stared grimly at Spurr as he held his cocked Colt on the man who'd been going through his saddlebags and who now continued to hold his Spencer on him. The carbine wasn't cocked, but the bearded man's gloved thumb was on the hammer.

"Those saddlebags ain't yours to go through, amigo," Spurr said tightly, softly. Shifting his gaze only slightly, he added, "And that's my whiskey. For all you know, the hombre whose throat you cut could have been a friend of mine. And you killed him. If we *was* friends, that might stick in my craw."

The three banditos stared at him with mute interest, wrinkling their foreheads. Likely, they hadn't understood a word of what he'd said. That was all right. Spurr had only wanted time to figure out which one he was going to kill first and last.

The bearded man holding the carbine on him glanced at the man holding the two horses, and then he turned his head back to Spurr, and he started to laugh. He laughed as though at the funniest joke he'd ever heard, though he kept the carbine he was holding on Spurr steady.

Spurr waited about ten seconds, and then he smiled. At the same time, the bearded man suddenly stopped laughing, and just as his thumb started to draw back his Spencer's hammer, Spurr shot him. He shot the man holding the whiskey bottle next, and then he shot the man holding the horses. He swung his smoking .44 back to the man who'd dropped and shattered his bottle and blasted another slug through the man's neck as he tried regaining his feet while blood oozed out the hole in his leather cartridge belt.

Seconds ago, Spurr had sensed more than heard someone moving up on his left, from the direction of the open coun-

try, and now he dropped to the ground and turned to see a
fourth bandito, who'd likely been off looking for the owner
of the big roan, kneeling beneath a mesquite and triggering
a Colt Navy. Smoke and flames jutted from the Colt's barrel,
and the slug spanged off a rock in the fire ring as Spurr triggered his last two shots and sent the fourth bandito spinning
around and screaming beneath the mesquite.

Spurr slid the empty pistol into its holster and levered a
shell into his rifle. He looked around quickly.

The bearded bandito and the one who'd stolen and broken
Spurr's only bottle were down and bleeding and not moving,
eyes glassy in death. Cochise and the coyote dun had run off
when the guns started blasting, and the man who'd been
nearest them was nowhere in sight. Blood splashed the rocks
where he'd been standing, and there were several scuff
marks leading northward from the camp and into the dark-
ening desert.

Spurr strode across the camp and into the scrub and
rocks. He climbed up and over a low rise. On the other side,
he spied the bandito stumbling, crouched forward, into
some rocks jutting out from the side of a chalky butte. Spurr
glanced down to see gobbets of bright, frothy blood staining
the desert gravel and creosote. The bandito was lung-shot.

Spurr jogged toward the rocks and stopped when a
round, brown, clean-shaven face and two brown eyes stared
out from a notch amongst the tangled boulders. A gun came
up in the bandito's hand, and Spurr dove sideways and rolled
as the younker's pistol barked twice, kicking up dust and
gravel behind the old lawman. Spurr rolled onto his chest,
leaned into his rifle, aimed hastily into the notch though he
could no longer see the kid amongst the bluing shadows,
and triggered three rounds quickly.

Rock dust flew. Spurr fired two more rounds, heard a
scream. He got a creaky knee beneath him, but it took him
several seconds to get the limb, which he'd bruised when
he'd hit the ground that seemed to get harder and harder
with every passing week, to cooperate and straighten.

"When's it time to retire, Spurr?" he asked himself

aloud, aping the words of Chief Marshal Henry Brackett, spoken three or four times every year upon Spurr's return from assignments looking more and more bedraggled.

He shambled forward, feeling as though spikes had been driven into his knees and hips and also feeling as though the shoulder he'd landed on had been partially dislocated, and continued on through the kid's nest in the rocks, when he saw the kid run out the other side, screaming shrilly in Spanish, "I'm blinded! I'm blinded!"

Spurr squeezed through the tight gap and stepped out the other side. The kid had fallen and was twisting around, showing his bloody face that must have been sliced up from flying rock shards, and was trying to jerk a hideout pistol out of a shoulder holster under his cracked, bullhide charro jacket.

"You blinded me, *pendejo*!" he shouted in English.

As the kid managed to snake a .36 Remington pocket pistol out of his coat, Spurr kicked it from his hand and aimed his cocked Winchester from his shoulder, gritting his teeth and narrowing one cool eye. "Couldn't have happened to a nicer little feller," he said and squeezed the trigger.

The kid's head bounced off the ground once, like a rubber ball thrown by an angry child, before it slammed back down and remained still, the ragged-edged hole in his forehead leaking blood, eyes blinking wildly several times. His silver-tipped boots jerked from side to side before they fell still.

Spurr looked around to make sure there were no more banditos out here trying to draw a bead on him.

Then he walked back into his camp, looking around at the dead men and the blood—there was even blood on his saddlebags, the contents of which the bearded bandito had spilled onto the ground beside the fire ring—and the broken whiskey bottle. Finally, he looked down at his dead prisoner Del Hammond, blood from the savage slice across the blond brigand's throat bibbing his shirt and denim jacket.

Spurr poked his hat brim back off his forehead and spat. Shaking his head, he walked out away from the camp and was relieved to see Cochise and the coyote dun grazing in the desert nearby, silhouettes in the pearl-blue wash of the Mexican dusk. He turned and looked to the south, thinking of poor Flora Hammerlich, tugging at his beard.

"I sure hope you're still kickin', little darlin'. Or I've come a far piece . . . and likely died . . . for nothin'."

10

CUNO PULLED HIS blue bandanna up over his nose and blinked against the dust kicked up by the freight wagon hammering along about fifty yards ahead of him. He glanced to his right and left, saw the other three drivers cracking their blacksnakes over the backs of their two-mule hitches.

They were rambling along a dusty playa, an ancient, alkaline lakebed, to try to make up the time they'd lost when they'd spent nearly three hours earlier that morning, Cuno's second day on the trail with the so-called soldiers and whatever they were hauling so desperately into southern Sonora, waiting for another contingent of wagons that had never showed.

Two more wagons, Cuno had heard, though no one told him much of anything about what they were doing out here. Two scouts had been dispatched to look for the missing team. If and when the two missing wagons showed up, there would then be a total of eleven, with twenty-two mules that it was getting harder and harder to find grass and water for.

Cuno had asked Bennett's second-in-command, Sapp, what they were hauling and where, and Sapp had only given him a dead-eyed stare. He saw no point in asking any of the others or probing Lusk further, as no one but Lusk had said more than five words to him since he'd accepted the job from Major Beers. Even Lusk now gave him little time when they stopped to eat and make coffee and to rest and water the mules and to wait for the wing riders to return from scouting the area they were traversing for trouble in the form of Indians or Rurales or even large bands of roving banditos, who could often be nearly as formidable as the Yaqui.

Everyone in this party of obvious cutthroats treated him like he was carrying the smallpox, regarding him, when they looked at him at all, with suspicion at best, hatred at worst.

It was further evidence, he thought, that while these men might have been soldiers once, they were soldier-outlaws now. What they were doing down here Cuno did not care. What they were carrying and who they were carrying it to, he did not care. He had nowhere else to go, nothing else to do. He had no one waiting for him at home, if he had a home, which he did not, and the money Beers was paying was nothing to scoff at. All he had rattling around in his pockets were a few lonely pesos.

These men may have looked on him with suspicion, treated him like they wanted to stick a sharp knife in his back, but they were the only company he had except Renegade, and down here even bad company was better than no company. He'd learned that two days before when he'd first been introduced to Sapp and Lusk and was about the width of one war hatchet blade away from snuggling with diamondbacks.

A rider materialized from the dust ahead of him, and Flora, the blonde who belonged to Beers, came galloping toward the wagon ahead of him. She shouted something to the driver of that wagon, then galloped on back toward Cuno, putting her calico gelding up near his lumbering team and jouncing wagon. She wore a red calico blouse, tight denims, and cream duster that flapped around her like wings. A .36 Smith & Wesson was thonged low on her left thigh. She jerked her bandanna down from her nose and mouth, and her face looked small and fragile beneath the brim of her slightly oversized Stetson.

"Beers says Trinidad Tanks is just on the other side of this dust bowl. We'll be pulling in. He says it's a tight fit, but it's got good grass and water."

Cuno nodded as he leaned forward, resting his elbows on his knees and holding the ribbons in one hand, the black-snake in the other. Beers obviously knew the area, as did Sapp. Likely, both men had been on the run down here at one time. "Thanks for the heads-up."

She kept her cool brown eyes on Cuno for about one more second then lifted the bandanna over her nose, turned her head forward, and touched spurs to the calico's flanks. She galloped off and Cuno glanced back to watch her; it was hard not to watch the blonde, pretty in a suntanned, tomboyish way. He turned his head forward, and as he did he thought he glimpsed her swing her own head around to look at him again as she galloped back to the next wagon.

Nearly an hour later, Cuno stood in his seat to hooraw his two mules up out of the lakebed, along which adobe and rock ruins of a long-extinct village once stood—there'd probably been gold and silver mines in the mountains around the playa—then turned it into a broad canyon mouth opening on the right. Dust sifted from the three wagons that had pulled in ahead of him. Those wagons pulled to stops where the canyon walls opened wide and the area formed a green park where a stream meandered through sycamores, willows, and cottonwoods.

An ancient church ruin stood amongst the trees, fronting the stream, birds winging in and out of its gaping front opening that had probably once been covered by stout oak doors. There was plenty of grass along the southern canyon wall flanking the church, and here the wagons were driven, splashing across the stream, the men berating their weary mules and cracking their whips over the teams' lathered backs, making sounds like pistol fire.

Cuno took his time with his team and with Renegade

who'd been trailing along behind his wagon. He watered
the animals in the creek, enjoying the memories the mules
conjured as he carefully, almost dreamily adjusted their
harnesses and hames and made sure all the buckles and
chains were secure before inspecting the mules themselves
for injury.

His father had taught him the value of a good mule team,
and their mules had become like family. Cuno had always
thought he'd have mules and his own freight business, and
he'd managed to run one for a time in Colorado until the
Utes had attacked the Trent ranch to which he and his partner, Serenity Parker, had run a load of winter freight to for-
tify the ranch against the looming high-country winter.

He'd lost Serenity, but he'd managed to save himself,
Camilla, Michelle Trent, and the Lassiter children from the
Utes before he'd gotten crossways with Dusty Mason and
ended up in the federal prison.

When he'd tended the mules and set them to graze, he
glanced around to see the other men building fires or heading
out with rifles to patrol the area against interlopers. Several
others gathered wood while the man who'd been designated
cook and his helper began throwing a meal together—likely
beans and dried jerky again, which seemed to be the caravan's staple, maybe rabbit if anyone had shot or snared one.
Snakes seen along the trail were fair game for the stew pot,
as well.

Beers and Sapp stood around a rock over which they'd
draped a map, and, smoking, they appeared to be discuss-
ing their route.

Cuno was vaguely curious about that route, but he could
live without knowing where he was heading. He didn't care
how lost in Mexico he became. He'd likely be down here
awhile. It was best to forget about home.

He glanced at the wagon he'd been pulling. He'd taken a
look through the front pucker, of course, but all he could
see were crates stacked tight against the wagon's sides and
tailgate. The crates were unmarked. Likely guns and ammo,
and he didn't care about that, either, so he turned his natural

curiosity away from it. He was a fugitive. He couldn't get into any more trouble than he was already in.

When he'd washed in the stream and filled his canteens, he went over to pour a cup of coffee from the cook's fire. Beers shouldered up to him for a moment and told him which watch would be his tonight. Aside from that, Cuno spoke to no one, and no one spoke to him. He parried a couple of dubious looks, then drank his coffee alone before grabbing his rifle and deciding to take a walk around, maybe inspect the church.

He walked along the stream for fifty yards, then followed an old path that led up through it via a small cemetery, long since abandoned and grown up with grass and shrubs. He entered the church through a small side door and heard the echoes of his boots off the cavernous walls and high ceiling.

The place had been gutted by time, spiderwebs hanging from the ceiling. The flagstone floor was cracked and buckled, and many flags were missing, showing the grit-laden clay beneath. There were no windows, only a door on each side and the large front door that gaped broadly, allowing the late afternoon light to angle inside, flooding the room with gray-blue shadows.

Cuno walked around, looking at the old walls and the ceiling, the pitted flags, feeling the eerie presence of ghosts from generations past, when the church had once served the village whose ruins remained along the playa, whose dead lay in dusty, sunken graves, long forgotten.

The large, sepulchral church gave him a sense of how ancient this country was compared to his own. All the misery it had known, all the people who had settled here, lived out their lives and died. All the wars. All the men like himself to whom it had offered sanctuary over the centuries. Men like himself maybe who had only wanted a decent life but had found themselves kicked around by random currents that were always swirling, kicking a soul this way and then that.

Oh, well. He'd find a woman here eventually. A good life. What choice did he have?

A woman's laughter tinkled beyond the far side door, as if dramatizing his thoughts. Flora said something, then laughed again. A man's voice pitched jovially, intimately, joined hers. The voice didn't sound like Beers's.

Cuno crossed the silent church to the far side wall and pressed his back to it about five feet from the open door. The voice had fallen silent but now the woman said angrily, "No, Dave. I told you—no!"

Dave Sapp's back must have been facing the church, for his voice was muffled when he responded, and Cuno couldn't hear him clearly. But he heard the belligerence in the man's voice.

Flora said something in a frustrated, fearful tone but keeping her voice down, and Cuno turned through the doorway and walked outside. There was a large cottonwood near the church, and the two were standing beyond this and some willows.

Sapp said as though through gritted teeth, "You think you can have it any way you want it—that it?"

"Let go of me, Dave, or so help me I'll scream for Beers!"

Cuno moved around the tree in time to see Flora jerk her arm out of Sapp's grip. She jerked around, but Sapp stuck out his foot and tripped her. Flora hit the ground with a gasp. Cuno stepped forward, between the girl and the tall, blond-mustached Sapp whose face beneath the broad brim of his tan kepi was swollen red with rage.

"I think the woman's finished with the conversation," Cuno said, knowing he was likely pounding the first nail in his Mexican coffin.

Sapp's eyes blazed at him. "You just stepped in the wrong pasture, honyocker."

"She's had enough."

"Knock it off," Flora said, pushing up on her elbows, keeping her voice down. "Both of you!"

Sapp showed his two silver front teeth as he ground his jaws and stepped toward Cuno. "You spyin' on us, boy?"

"I was in the church."

Sapp took another step, and suddenly the knife he'd had on his belt was in his hand, and he was crouching and moving toward Cuno fast, holding the knife as though to slice it across Cuno's belly.

"Dave!" Flora hissed, crabbing out of the way on her rump.

"Shut up," Sapp said, brows hooding his eyes savagely.

He wasn't holding the knife right. Cuno spread his boots, then kicked his right foot up. It connected with the underside of Sapp's wrist.

The brigand gave a startled grunt as the knife flew out of his hand. Instinctively, he whipped the injured wrist back, and then Cuno bounded forward and hammered the man's face with a right cross and then a left uppercut.

Sapp didn't know what hit him.

Dust flew as he spun around and fell hard, kicking up dirt and gravel. He pushed up onto his hands and knees and shook his head, throwing his thin, blond hair around before glaring at Cuno over his right shoulder.

Cuno held his fists up. He could feel the girl's eyes on him in shock as he sidestepped around Sapp, hoping the man would leave the trouble where it was. The last thing he needed was to be cut loose from the caravan this deep into Mexico, with Yaqui thick as buzzards on a gut wagon.

Damnit, why hadn't he just stayed with his wagon and his team and his horse and minded his own business?

"Stop," Flora said, pushing herself to her feet and regarding Cuno and Sapp anxiously before swinging a glance in the direction of the main camp, obviously hoping that Beers hadn't heard the commotion. "Both of you—stop it right now!"

"I don't think so, sweetheart," Sapp said as he leapt to his feet and lunged toward Cuno, faking a jab with his left fist. When Cuno didn't go for it, he still hurled a haymaker. He was no bare-knuckle fighter, likely just a saloon brawler.

He grunted as he spun, and then he yelped when Cuno smashed his right fist, knuckles out, into his ear.

Sapp turned his face toward him, and it was even redder

than before. Blood dribbled from the cut on the back of his ear. Fear flashed in the man's eyes as he realized he was fording the wrong stream. Then he glanced at the girl shuffling around them anxiously, and his eyes went hard once more.

Now there'd be no stopping him, Cuno knew. If the girl wasn't here, he'd stop. But he wouldn't stop now.

Cuno would have to finish it fast.

Sapp was too angry now to fight any better than he already had, and Cuno let him come. Easily ducking another haymaker and feinting away from a left jab, Cuno hammered his left into the man's belly, then drove his right fist into Sapp's jaw.

Sapp stumbled backward.

While Cuno had him off balance, he hit his other ear and then his jaw again, and while Sapp continued to stumble backward, falling, Cuno followed him, unable to stop himself now, the tension of the past several days and also his disdain for the men he'd thrown in with uncoiling within him.

Again and again he smashed Sapp's face, and when he was down, he hit him once more.

He straightened and backed up. Fire raged through him. Bells tolled in his ears. He was holding his jaws so tight he could hear his molars grinding.

Sapp lay on his back, knees slightly bent. He shook his head, planted his hands beneath him, and tried to push himself up, but he couldn't do it. He sank back again in the gravel, his belly expanding and contracting quickly as he breathed.

A familiar voice chuckled behind Cuno. He heard the trill of a spur and then Bennett Beers's voice: "You had enough yet, Dave?"

Faintly, Cuno heard Flora gasp as she jerked her head toward the man who'd put his stamp on her.

11

BEERS WALKED UP with two other men flanking him. He was puffing one of his long Mexican cheroots, and he held a brass-chased Henry rifle on his shoulder. Against the growing night chill, he wore a tan duster over his black frock coat, silk shirt, and string tie.

"Thought you didn't allow fighting amongst your men, Bennett," Flora said. "I heard a bunch of scuffling and cussing while I was gathering firewood, and walked over to see these two going at it like two hammerheads in the same corral."

Beers slid his devilish, blue eyes toward her, rolling his cheroot around between his teeth. "Hope it didn't ruffle your drawing-room sensibilities, my pet."

She looked at him sharply, flushing.

Sapp lifted his head and heaved himself up on his elbows. "My fault." His lower lip and both ears were bloody. "I reckon I was just teasin' the new dog a little to see what kinda fight he had in him." As he tugged on one of his silver-capped teeth as though it might have been loose, he cut his eyes to Cuno but could not completely conceal his disdain.

"Did you find that out, Dave?" asked one of the men flanking Beers, who studied his first lieutenant coolly through downcast eyes.

"I reckon I did." Sapp chuckled and raised his left hand. "Come on, kid—you done enough damage. Now give me a hand up."

Cuno grabbed his hand and pulled him to his feet, keeping himself tense and ready for anything. He wouldn't have put it past Sapp to try a sucker punch.

Beers cut his half-shut eyes to the girl. "That how it was, Flora?"

She wrinkled the skin above the bridge of her nose. "How else would it be?"

"I don't know. I just know I've told Dave a thousand times that we'll put up with no fighting amongst the men, as we have bigger fish to fry down here. And then I find him carryin' on, and . . . you're here, too." He rolled his cigar from one corner of his mouth to the other and let his pale blue eyes flick to the girl's ample breasts pushing out from behind her calico shirt.

She drew her shoulders forward a little, and self-righteous indignation flashed in her eyes. "What's that supposed to mean, you *bastard*?" She'd whispered it, bright eyes slitted, then brushed past Beers and stomped back in the direction of the camp.

Beers smiled in admiration as he watched her walk away from him.

"Good-lookin' girl," Sapp said, donning his hat and brushing blood from his lip as he shouldered up beside Beers. He threw an arm around the gang leader's shoulders and gave him an affectionate squeeze. "But that there's a little too *much* girl for me!"

He chuckled as he and Beers began walking in the direction of the camp, the two other men falling into step behind them.

Beers said something that Cuno couldn't hear, and all four men threw their heads back, laughing.

As they rounded the rear corner of the church, Sapp

stared over his shoulder at Cuno for about five menacing seconds, then turned his head forward and walked away with Beers and the others.

Cuno slept lightly that night with his weapons close to hand. He knew Sapp would make a play for him sooner or later, and he had to stay prepared.

The next two days were hard pulls across the Sonoran Desert—hot, dusty, grueling, and tedious even this late in the year when the days, with their blazing sun, were blessedly short. At night, Cuno slept only a few hours before he was kicked awake to take one of the several revolving scouts. Two Gatling guns were always posted, but he was usually sent to a rocky knob somewhere to keep scout with his rifle.

He didn't mind. He enjoyed being away from the others, as their company—if you could call it that—was growing as tedious as the desert rolling away in all directions toward distant, blue mountains in the south that appeared to grow only minimally closer. He'd be relieved to draw his time from Beers and light out on his own again. It had been nice having a pack to run with for a while, but he was once again yearning for the company of only his horse.

Renegade even smelled better than this lot of cutthroats. All except Flora, of course, who was as dangerous, he realized now, as she was comely.

On the group's third night out from the place where Cuno and Sapp had locked horns, Cuno found himself around midnight keeping watch from a boulder about ten feet down from the top of a tall escarpment of ancient, eroded lava. The campfire was a flicker of light behind him, beyond a knoll. From his vantage he could see a complete circle around the camp they'd made in a vast nest of black boulders strewn eons ago by an erupting volcano chain.

He heard the light foot thuds of someone walking toward him and looked down to see a shadow moving amongst the rocks that resembled a giant house of cards that had been knocked into a ragged pile. He knew it must be someone from the camp, but he wasn't out here to make assumptions.

Softly, just loudly enough for the person now just directly below him, he said, "Identify yourself."

The dark, slender figure stopped moving. He saw a tan hat move and a pale, oval face tilt toward him. "Flora. Identify yourself."

"Your knight in shining armor."

The girl made a scoffing sound. She didn't move for a time. Finally, she said, "Hold on." Then she moved around in the rocks until her shadow disappeared. He could hear her footsteps growing louder, and he could hear her breathing as she climbed the escarpment, grunting a little as she slipped over large, slender rocks.

He could smell the freshness of her just before she appeared before him, moving along the same small corridor he'd taken up here. There was a thumbnail moon to her right, and it shone in her hair tumbling down her shoulders.

She stood before him, looking down at him obliquely. He did not get up. Finally, she hiked a hip on a rock behind her, kicked her dangling leg.

"Fool stunt you pulled the other day."

"I didn't realize I was leaping into quicksand until I was nose deep."

"What's that supposed to mean?"

"It means your stunt was just as foolish."

"If it was any of your business." She looked around cautiously for a time. Sliding off the rock, she sat down three feet to his right, pressing her back to the stone escarpment. "You could have told Beers. Might have got you somewhere."

"Where?"

She hiked a shoulder. "Maybe into a higher pay bracket."

"You mean the others aren't getting two dollars a day?" he asked, pitching his low voice with sarcasm.

She didn't say anything to that, just stared at him stonily.

He already knew what she thought of him, so it couldn't hurt to probe her further, for the distraction, a way to pass the time, if nothing else. Besides, he enjoyed looking at her, even though, especially in her case, beauty was only skin-deep.

"One man not enough for you? Or you playing both ends against the middle?"

She raised her knees and pressed her palms against them thoughtfully. "Beers is a big man. That's why I threw in with him when we met in Tucson. He's got ambitions. But he's a liar and a cheat. I don't trust him."

"Think he'll cut you out when the big money starts getting spread around?"

"Who said anything about big money?"

Cuno doffed his hat, ran his hands through his shoulder-length blond hair. "I don't know—I figure all those guns and ammunition have to be worth a few buckets worth of Mexican gold."

Flora laughed, then covered her mouth—an unexpectedly girlish gesture. But her voice was genuinely cautionary. "Don't get too curious, bucko. Men disappear in Mexico all the time."

"You trust Sapp?"

She sniffed and threw her hair back from her shoulders. "I trust the way he looks at me."

"Right."

"A girl has to use what she has. It's an ugly business, being a woman in these woods, if you get my drift." She paused, studied the moon for a time, then rubbed her palms against her knees again. "Where'd you learn to fight like that?"

"Here and there."

"You didn't look like you had it in you, but I swear, you'd have killed Sapp if Beers hadn't come along." She stared at him. "What's got your neck in such a hump?" Pitching her voice with teasing, she said, "Worried about me?"

"That must have been it."

"How old are you?"

"Twenty-four."

"My age." Flora drew a deep breath, and a haughtiness

entered her voice. "Me, I'm worldly. At first I thought you were just a kid lookin' for gold or somesuch, but I think you might be worldly, too."

"You mean jaded?"

"Something like that."

"So, then . . ." Cuno cocked a brow at her, waiting.

She wrinkled her lips together as though in mild reproof. "We've been up here several minutes, Beers and Sapp are both snorin' in their blanket rolls, and you haven't even made a play on me."

"Hurt your feelings?"

"Nah. I'm just starting to wonder if you're not just a fool kid down here lookin' for gold and about to go home broke. If you go home at all."

Cuno chuckled. It was crazy, but he felt wild and reckless. Since he was here he might as well make an adventure of it. "What on earth could I possibly offer you, Flora?"

"Maybe I'm just a sucker for a man who tries to defend my honor."

"The first time I laid eyes on you, Flora, I knew you were many things. Honorable wasn't one of them."

"That's a helluva thing to say!" She leaned forward and slapped his face a stinging, ringing blow.

Cuno grinned. Her eyes blazed. He wrapped his hand around the back of her neck and pulled her to him. She was pliant in his brusque hold, and when her lips met his, they were open, and her tongue jutted into his mouth. She wrapped her arms around his neck and pressed her breasts to his chest, groaning as she kissed him, digging her fingers into his shoulders and biceps.

Finally, she pulled away from him, staring at him in the darkness. Her chest rose and fell. "Beers is . . . old."

She unbuttoned her shirt and tossed it away. She lifted her chemise above her head and threw it onto her shirt. Breathing harder, grunting, she leaned forward and started unbuttoning Cuno's shirt. When she had it off she dug her hands into his chest, squeezing and probing his powerful torso.

Finally, she stood and pushed her denims and underwear down to her ankles. Cuno slid his own pants down to his knees, and she straddled him.

They were like two wildcats going at it over a fresh kill.

When she finished, she sagged to one side, breathless.

She stood, dressed quickly, crouched over him, ran a brusque hand through his hair, and kissed him quickly, almost painfully. "You're gonna want me bad now, but don't expect anything like this to happen again." She scampered back the way she'd come, disappearing like a ghost in the darkness.

Cuno leaned back on his outstretched arms, drew a deep breath, and chuckled. He'd be damned if he didn't feel like a rug hung up and beaten on a clothesline.

He spent the rest of the next hour keeping watch from his niche in the rocks, then returned to the fire, nudged awake the man assigned to relieve him, then rolled up in his blankets beneath his freight wagon near where Renegade lay, asleep on his side.

Cuno was awake at first light and filling his coffee cup at the fire, when a man nearby said, "Hey, look there."

The several other men in camp now rising and tending nature and filling coffee cups turned to see one of the wagon drivers walking toward them, carrying another man over his shoulder. The man was the lanky redhead, Lusk. The man carrying him strode sullenly forward and eased Lusk onto the ground near the fire.

The others stepped back, muttering.

A bloody gash curved across the redhead's throat. Lusk's eyes were crossed and his tongue hung out a corner of his mouth.

Beers and Sapp had heard the commotion, and now they walked over to stare down at the dead man.

"Where'd you find him?" Beers asked Long.

"In the rocks over yonder, where we set up the Gatling gun. Lusk was slumped there, dead." Long cast his sharp, anxious gaze at the gang leader. "His Gatling's gone."

12

EVERYONE, INCLUDING CUNO, grabbed a rifle. Any man who wasn't yet wearing his shell belt and pistol donned them fast, then stepped into the cover of the wagons, a few sidling up to large boulders, looking around warily.

On the other side of the stream, the mule herd sensed the tension and stomped around and brayed, pulling against their single picket line.

Cuno stood beside his own wagon, his Winchester in his hands, and slid a look around the jagged crests of the scarps jutting around him. He could tell what the other men were feeling—he was feeling it as well. They were feeling as though bull's-eyes had been drawn on their chests or across their backs.

That it was the Yaqui who had killed Lusk and taken the Gatling gun there was little doubt. Only a Yaqui could successfully pull off a stunt like that.

Beers had a cocked Colt Navy in his hands as he peered over the tarp-covered top of the wagon standing about twenty feet from Cuno's. To a guard standing with a rifle atop an escarpment just opposite the men and wagons, the gang leader said, "Noble—you see anything up there?"

Holding his Winchester low across his thighs, Noble, a hatted silhouette against the dawn's lilac sky, turned his head this way and that, then turned it back to Beers. "Nope." He kept his voice low; it sounded eerie in the morning silence in the wake of what had happened to Lusk. "What's goin' on, Boss?"

"Lusk had his throat cut last night. His Gatling gun's gone."

Noble looked around once more, then turned his head toward Beers and said just as softly as before, "Yaqui?"

"We're gonna find out." Gritting his teeth, Beers looked at the others around him. There were roughly fifteen, including Cuno, Flora, and Sapp, as the others like Noble were still on the night scout, either hunkered in stationary positions or making a slow patrol on foot.

"You men spread out. I want that Gatling gun found. More important, I want the Injun who took it found! I want every last one of 'em found—you hear me?"

The men spread out. Cuno glanced at Flora. She returned the oblique look, then, holding her Winchester carbine up high across her chest, began moving out away from the wagons, looking around cautiously.

Cuno strode off in the opposite direction. In the light of what had just happened, and with the cold dawning of a new day, his and Flora's frolic of last night left a bad taste in his mouth. It had been careless and stupid. He felt no real allegiance to these men, but that didn't mean he should be horsing around while he was supposed to be keeping the night watch. It was easy enough to die in Mexico without acting like a tinhorn.

He scoured the area, feeling a prickling at the back of his neck, waiting to hear the sudden hiccup of a Gatling gun that could cut him to pieces in seconds. Finding no moccasin prints or any other sign of Yaqui, Cuno returned to the wagons. Nearly all twenty men were there, with three keeping watch on the near ridges. No one said anything, but they all looked scared. Cuno thought he could safely assume that none of the others had discovered Yaqui sign, either—much less the Yaqui themselves or the stolen gun.

The drivers were rigging up their teams while the outriders saddled their horses. Obviously, since the fire had already been doused, they were forgoing breakfast, and Cuno could see the urgent desire in the men's eyes to hit the trail, to hightail it out of this nest in the rocks that a Gatling gun could exploit so savagely.

Within a half hour, they'd threaded their way out of the jumbled slabs of lava and were heading across a rolling, rocky desert to the same southern ridges Cuno had been watching for the past several days. Beers and Sapp rode lead scout. The wagons followed in a line along the trail that was too meandering and rocky to make good time on. Several scout riders rode out to each side. Flora and a man named Kettleson rode drag.

Beers had dictated no certain order, but when the wagons had pulled out of the lava bluffs, Cuno had found himself second to last in the ragged line. As they traveled, gaps of fifty to a hundred yards opened between the wagons despite the drivers' intentions to stay close to one another, so that in case of an attack they could quickly form a defensive circle.

As the trail was rocky and hard to negotiate, and the mules typically fickle, it was hard to stick close, and when a thunderhead closed over the caravan from the west, Cuno found himself about sixty yards from the wagon ahead of him while the wagon behind him was closer to a hundred yards distant.

The sky darkened. A cold wind howled. Lightning forked. Thunder exploded, causing the ground to pitch. Rain spit for a time, then began hammering down at a cold, stabbing slant.

The mules brayed and balked. Trailing behind Cuno's wagon, Renegade whinnied and shook his head.

The rain continued to hammer and roar. Thunder sounded

like empty barrels rolling down a boulder-strewn hill. Lightning danced in the west, growing closer. Cuno stood up, put his head down, and whipped the reins over the team to keep them moving. A couple of times he had to use the blacksnake.

It took less than a minute for him to get as soaked as if he'd jumped into a river with all his clothes on. Water sluiced off the canvas enshrouding the wagon. It dribbled from his hair under his collar and down his back, making him shiver. All around him, silver puddles stood amongst the rocks and cactus, whipped to a froth by more rain. The damp air was heavy with the smell of brimstone and sage.

The rain hammered without any sign of letup until Cuno thought the up-and-down trail was going to become a river and wash him away. Ahead, another wagon appeared stopped in the trail, about a hundred yards in front of a narrow canyon mouth. The driver stood in the driver's boot, his back to Cuno, staring straight ahead. A rider was galloping toward him from the canyon mouth, which, Cuno saw now as he stared in slack-jawed wonder, was crinkling closed as a mudslide tumbled down the right ridge. The slide made a low roar above the pounding rain and intermittent blasts of thunder.

The horseback rider galloped up to the wagon in front of Cuno. Cuno couldn't make out his identity because of the rain and the water sluicing off the man's kepi. He'd also donned an india rubber rain slicker, and its collar rose to his jaws. The man shouted something to the other driver, but Cuno couldn't make it out above the rain and the thunder of the slide.

The man assaulted his bay's flanks with his spurred heels, and the horse gave an indignant whinny as it galloped back toward Cuno. The face of Dave Sapp appeared beneath the dripping hat brim, his eyes blazing anxiously.

"The canyon's closed! Swing this sumbitch around—we're headin' west, try to get around it!"

Again, he rammed his spurs against his horse's flanks and galloped back toward the wagon just now splashing up behind Cuno. The wagon ahead was turned to the right, and Cuno, sleeving rain out of his eyes, followed suit, having to pop the blacksnake over his team's back, as the sodden clay was grabbing the wagon's wheels like giant fists.

He made the turn and followed the other wagon along another trail that paralleled the steep wall of a mesa to the south, on his left. Several times he looked back to see the slide continuing to seal the canyon mouth as though with wet adobe. No one would ever again make passage through that chasm. He wondered if the lead wagons had been sealed in and covered or if they'd made it out the other side.

The rain splattered like quicksilver off the mules' backs. Their heavy hooves splashed in the trail's water-filled chuckholes. Cuno glanced over his shoulder. The last wagon was behind him. Coming up fast was another rider, and as she passed him without even glancing at him, he saw Flora's soaked hair pressed flat against her back. She kept her head down, hat brim drawn over her face, as she galloped on up the trail to disappear in the white fog of rain.

Shortly, the rain lightened a little, as did the thunder and lightning, and the mules relaxed somewhat in their harnesses. The trail rose and pulled to the left, and here the mules started balking again. They were wet and tired and scared, and they were threatening a strike.

Cuno went after them again with the blacksnake, and they pulled the wagon on up the rise and onto a bench. The rain continued but not too heavily for Cuno to see the village sprawling across the side of a mountain on his left and onto the bench before him.

He could see no people moving about or any lights in any of the shacks. The bulk of the village lay before him—all adobes hunched along both sides of the trail that was two ancient wagon wheel ruts filled with water. The structures around this central square were all grown up with weeds and cactus, and most appeared roofless, doorless ruins. A church in the central square sank into itself, dripping.

As Cuno pulled his team to a stop behind the wagon in front of him, a door opened on the right side of the street.

A stocky little woman stood in the doorway wearing a sackcloth dress and a blue calico scarf around her Indian-dark face. Her lips were parted, showing two brown teeth. She turned her head both ways, inspecting the newcomers, then slammed the door of her mud-brick shack.

Faintly, from elsewhere, Cuno could hear a baby crying.

Just then an especially loud thunderclap shook the wagon and caused the mules to jump. The rain began hammering once more, tumbling straight down from a large mass of blue-black clouds. Sapp galloped around the wagons, shouting above the rain, "Barn ahead on the right. Pull in!"

As he galloped back to the last wagon, Cuno hoorawed his fidgety team forward. The barrack-like adobe barn with an arched double doorway stood with both wooden doors thrown wide. Flora stood beside one of the doors, holding her carbine across her chest. A little man in peasant's pajamas and a straw sombrero stood on the other side of the opening, a corncob pipe in his mouth. Behind him, a calico cat hunched just inside the doorway, pressed taut against the frame as it watched the rain and flicked its tail, peevish.

Cuno pulled his rig inside the large, sprawling barn that smelled of musty hay. There were a few stalls on the left but the rest of the cavern-like place was open, with a hayloft stretching over a quarter of it.

"What the hell happened back there?" yelled the driver of the wagon parked to the right of Cuno's. He was a big, shaggy-bearded man called Hays who wore a corporal's tunic and buckskin trousers, and, like all the other cutthroats in Beers's employ, he was heavily armed with pistols and knives.

"You saw what I saw," Sapp said, riding in ahead of the last wagon and swinging out of his saddle.

Cuno climbed down from his wagon box and looked outside, beyond Flora, who stood in the open doorway, gazing inside the barn. The last outrider was riding up to the barn on a claybank gelding, and he sat his saddle oddly. As the horse stopped in front of the barn, Cuno saw why he was sitting that way.

Cuno grabbed his Winchester and, eyes riveted on the man atop the claybank, walked out of the barn and into the street, looking around cautiously.

"What is it?" Flora said.

Cuno jerked his head to the last outrider, who leaned farther forward now with the Yaqui arrow bristling from between his shoulder blades. The man rolled out of his saddle and hit the muddy street with a wet squishing sound. The claybank jerked with a start and sidled away, blowing and stamping.

Something whistled on the other side of the street. The whistling grew louder, and Cuno flinched as the arrow curled the air to his left before smacking the open wooden door behind him with a thud and a quivering shudder.

"Get inside!" Cuno told Flora.

The Indian who'd fired the arrow lifted his head above an adobe roof on the other side of the street. Cuno dropped to a knee, levering a cartridge into the Winchester's breech, and fired two shots, blowing up mud and sod from the hovel's roof a half second after the warrior pulled his green-and-ochre-painted face down.

"We got trouble!" Flora cried.

Sapp ran out of the barn behind Cuno and Flora and did a little dance as rifles thundered from gaps between buildings on the other side of the street and from other rooftops, the bullets ripping up mud in front of the barn and to both sides of Cuno. The young freighter picked out two more targets, and triggered two more rounds, but the Indians were hammering away in earnest now with both bullets and arrows.

He turned to see Flora dashing into the barn while Sapp grabbed the right side door and began pulling it closed. Cuno grabbed the other door as a bullet hammered it and an arrow embedded itself in the street a foot from his right boot.

He kicked the arrow out of his way and drew the door closed. Bullets plowed into it from the outside, making it shudder in its frame. When Sapp had his own door closed, he stumbled past Cuno, his sunburned face pink with fury above his muddy blond mustache, cursing shrilly.

"Thanks a whole bunch, Beers!" he shouted as though the gang leader were here. "Easy money down in Mexico!" He laughed loudly, for a second nearly drowning out the thunder of the rifles slinging lead against the barn's stout adobe walls. "Oh, it's easy, all right—*if you don't get hit by the fucking Yaqui!*"

13

SPURR REINED HIS big roan to a halt at the edge of the Mexican village from which heated gunfire crackled, adding a staccato undertone to the sporadic bursts of thunder that accompanied the steady rain falling from a sky the color of dirty rags. One hand on his holstered six-shooter, he led Cochise off the trail and into thick brush and strewn boulders.

From a knoll, he'd watched through his field glasses as the Yaqui followed the three wagons and three outriders until both parties had disappeared amongst the adobes. Now he tied the horse to an old wagon grown up with weeds and cacti and slid his Winchester from its ancient leather saddle boot even more pliant now after the rain.

"Stay here, Cochise." Spurr ran a hand along the horse's sleek, rain-soaked neck and made sure the knot he'd tied in the reins wasn't too tight. "I'll be back soon."

But he'd tied the horse loosely in case he didn't return. He wanted Cochise to be able to hightail it from here in the event that Spurr saddled a cloud. He wouldn't want the Yaqui to get their hands on the big, handsome roan. The Mexican Indians were notoriously cruel to their animals.

Spurr moved through the brush, heading toward the steep ridge on the village's north side. The guns were popping a good ways off to his right, on the far side of the village where the Indians had apparently pinned down their quarry.

Spurr wasn't sure of his plan here. Possibly mop-up duty after one side of the two factions had won the battle. He'd come down here looking for the daughter of an old friend of his, and she was his primary concern, but he had no idea if she'd ended up with this contingent or the one that entered the canyon before the mud walls had collapsed around it in the driving rain.

If he could, he'd like to retrieve or destroy the stolen weapons and ammunition before either they got where they were going or the Yaqui got their hands on them. But his fight wasn't with the Yaqui, only the men who'd sacked the fort and stolen the guns. Barring his ability—he was only one old lawman, after all—to do anything about the guns or the men who'd stolen them, however, he'd be satisfied with rescuing the girl and taking her home.

Was that really the only reason he was down here?

The question pricked at him like the cockleburs that clung to his wet trouser legs now as he left the brush and sidled up to a building that fronted on the *pueblito*'s main drag. The question was vague, like a ghostly whisper in his ear, and he was only half conscious of it, half nettled by it.

Why were you really down here, Spurr? Do you really think you can do anything to save Abel Hammerlich's daughter—one old man against a veritable army of cutthroats and a pack of rampaging Yaqui? Was there some other reason for this ride or had you gone crazier than a vampire bat on a moonlit Halloween?

Spurr let the question evaporate as he edged a look around the front of the building to his right and stole a look down the *pueblito*'s deserted, waterlogged main drag. Smoke lifted from several chimneys, but all the doors and shutters that Spurr could see were boarded up. Not even a dog moved. The rain splashed puddles pocking the old, stone-paved street.

The Indians and the Anglo cutthroats were exchanging gunfire farther up the street, around a slight northern bend. Spurr could hear occasional shouts amidst the shooting and see smoke puffing from the front of a big adobe structure on the road's right side. Squinting, he could see the moccasin-clad feet and tan legs of a dead Yaqui lying facedown on the street's opposite side, the rest of the body hidden by a rain barrel.

Holding his rifle up high across his chest, Spurr ran, crouching, across the street. He continued limp-jogging northward for a hundred or so yards before swinging right, intending to give the shooters a broad berth until he could see who was winning the battle. Fifteen minutes later, he was crouched behind an abandoned stable flanking a large, pale church capped by a blocky bell tower rising from a red slate roof.

Between him and the church, two Yaqui warriors with hideously painted faces were carrying a Gatling gun away from a mustang pony while the Yaqui queen whom Spurr had seen bathing in the creek watched with an imperious air, grunting orders and pointing at the church's bell tower. When the two warriors, each carrying an end of the brass-cased Gatling, one with a long cartridge bandolier draped over a shoulder, swung toward a small wooden door in the church's back wall, the queen reined her cream mustang around, slammed her moccasins against its flanks, and galloped off through a gap in the buildings.

Spurr scratched his beard as he stared at the half-open door. A wistful expression pulled at his eye corners.

He hunkered low, waiting, looking around to make sure he wasn't being flanked by the wily Yaqui. Finally, he heard what he'd been waiting to hear—the rat-a-tat-tat of the Gatling gun in the bell tower. A man yelled sharply from the far side of the street. As the Gatling continued hammering away, sounding eerily loud in the still air with the steadily falling rain, Spurr moved out from behind the stable and jogged, skirting mud puddles, to the door at the back of the church.

He stopped in front of the door, lowering his Winchester and raising his Starr, more effective in close quarters. Pushing the door open, he stepped inside quickly and to one side. The light from the open door cast the inside of the church in a dull, milky dusk. Candles were lit at the church's front, to his right—two large standing racks of them. A young, round-faced priest in a brown robe and rope sandals knelt before the candles on the far side of the church. His hands were entwined before him, a rosary chain dangling, and his shaved head was bowed. His lips moved as he muttered prayers, squeezing his eyes closed.

Spurr looked around at the crude wooden benches. There was no one else here.

The Gatling gun sputtered, stopped, then resumed its caterwauling, the blasts muffled by the church's stout ceiling. Spurr glanced at the priest once more—the man continued moving his lips desperately, head bowed—then headed toward a narrow stone stairway rising at the front of the church, left of the closed double doors.

At the bottom of the stairs, Spurr looked up into the bell tower through an open cellar-like door. He couldn't see much but wafting powder smoke and gray sky.

"Forgive me, Father," the old lawman muttered, clicking the Starr's hammer back as he began climbing the steps, "for I am about to sin."

He climbed the steps quickly, or as quickly as his old heart would allow, hearing the Gatling gun's ever-loudening belching. Above the opening and to his right, the gun was set up on its wooden tripod, the barrel blasting over the bell tower's low wall. One of the Yaqui was crouched over it, cranking the wooden handle and whooping and yelling, the empty casings clinking onto the bell tower floor. The other warrior crouched over his Winchester, triggering lead toward the big building on the other side of the street.

The old lawman stopped a few feet from the top of the stairs. The Gatling gun fell suddenly silent as the Indian who'd been cranking it froze and rolled a dark eye back. He turned his head toward Spurr. His paint-ringed eyes jerked wide with shock. With a yowl, he started to swing the Gatling's muzzle toward the lawman.

Spurr's revolver roared twice. His .44 slugs blew both warriors against the bell tower's far wall, at the base of which they piled up, limbs entangled, jerking and dying. Spurr climbed the last five steps into the bell tower. One of the braves was reaching for a saddle-ring Colt on the floor near his face.

Spurr shot him again, then looked down into the muddy street beneath the church.

Five Yaqui braves were crabbing belly down across the muddy street toward the livery barn. One more was approaching the barn from Spurr's left while another knelt by a trash pile and fired a Winchester at the barn's wall, likely aiming at a window though Spurr couldn't see that side of the barn clearly from his vantage. They'd been using the Gatling for covering fire while they'd stormed the barn, but a good half of the seven were craning their neck to peer incredulously up at the bell tower.

Spurr was between a rock and a hard place, but he'd put himself there. The men in the barn and the Indians were his enemies, and he was tempted to let the battle play out.

But what if the girl was in the barn with the Anglo cutthroats?

And what if the Yaqui got a hold of the guns and ammo? There would likely be a blood bath in these parts like few had seen since Juarez and Prince Maximilian had locked horns in the late '60s.

Spurr holstered his pistol, crouched behind the Gatling gun, dropped the muzzle a few inches, and turned the crank.

Bam-bam-bam-bam-bam-bam-bam!

The five Indians directly beneath the church screamed and tried climbing to their feet as the .45-caliber rounds hammered through them, spraying red onto the muddy street. They hadn't had a chance in their positions. Neither did the other two left of the barn.

Bam-bam-bam-bam-bam-bam-bam!

One managed to squeeze off two rifle rounds, the slugs

hammering the wall in front of Spurr, but then three bullets shredded the brave's deerskin vest and black calico shirt as they lifted him straight up off his feet and threw him several yards back, where he tumbled into a trash pile with a rattle of rusty airtight tins. The other Yaqui had been trying to run away when Spurr's burst drilled through his back and butt and threw him into a goat pen behind the livery barn.

Silence.

Spurr kept the Gatling's muzzle down. He looked at the bandolier feeding its breech. There were only eight or nine bullets left. But he had the Starr and his rifle, and he had the rifles and pistol of the two Yaqui lying dead around him, if he needed them.

A face appeared in the small window left of the livery barn's closed, bullet-shredded double doors. The head wore a tan cavalry kepi. "Who's out there?" the man shouted.

Spurr bit his lip. Then he grinned and chuckled, hoping he'd sound like at least one man in the cutthroat party. "Ha-ha! Miss me, boys?"

He kept his head low, so that just the feathered crown of his hat shown above the tower's lower wall.

"Hardwood—that you?" said the man with his head in the open window.

Spurr chuckled again and patted the Gatling's smoking muzzle. "This belly buster cleans up right well. Wouldn't mind havin' one o' my own."

The man in the window continued to stare toward the bell tower. Spurr couldn't make out any details of his features except a shaggy blond mustache. That meant he couldn't make out Spurr's features, either, and the men in the barn may or may not fall for the bluff.

There was only one window at the front of the barn, and behind it Spurr spied movement in the barn's heavy shadows. The old lawman waited, lifting his head and removing his hand from the Gatling's crank but not wanting to show too much of himself until everyone in the barn was outside.

The left side door swung open, its hinges whining in the rainy silence. A man lay slumped and bloody just inside the barn, and the blond-mustached gent in the tan kepi stepped over him and outside, carrying a rifle in his right hand. Several pistols showed behind the swinging flaps of his yellow rain slicker.

Spurr was happy to see that he and the three other men who followed him out, one with a bandanna wrapped around the top of his left arm, were more interested in the Yaqui strewn in the street before them than their savior in the bell tower. They looked around cautiously, the rain dripping off their hat brims, as they held their rifles on the dead braves, as though expecting one or two to come to life and resume triggering lead.

The street was as vacant as before. Smoke curled from a couple of shacks lining the main drag, but none of the *pueblito*'s citizens had ventured outside. They'd likely seen the Yaqui, and there was nothing a Mexican feared more.

Spurr was about to crouch over the Gatling gun and wrap his hand around the handle when he hesitated. Another man just now stepped out of the barn—a stocky young man with longish blond hair falling over the collar of his faded blue chambray shirt. He was a little under six feet, but broad-shouldered, with heavy arms and big hands, and he wore a tan slouch hat. A green neckerchief was knotted around his neck.

His sun-reddened face, covered with several days' growth of blond beard, was broad and handsome, his blue eyes alert and without the cunning and meanness of the others who'd ventured out ahead of him.

Deep lines spoked the old lawman's eyes. He mouthed the name. *Massey?*

When the others had spread out, the stocky blond standing more cautiously back near the barn than his trail brothers, holding his rifle up high across his broad chest, Spurr crouched over the Gatling gun once more and wrapped his hand around the wooden handle. The pivot pin squealed as he aimed the maw at the men in the street. They all stopped in their tracks and jerked anxious looks toward the bell tower.

Spurr didn't have to raise his voice very loudly to be heard in the dense, damp silence. "Names's Spurr Morgan, deputy U.S. marshal, and you fellas best throw down your guns unless you want me and my six-barreled friend here to blow you to kingdom come!"

They all stared, dumbfounded. Even the kid who looked like the fugitive Cuno Massey, whom Spurr and Sheriff Dusty Mason had chased from Colorado into Arizona.

The man with the blond mustache broke into sudden motion, shouting, "Goddamnit!" He jerked his Winchester to his shoulder.

The others brought up their own weapons, and Spurr began cranking the Gatling gun once more. First the blond-mustached gent went down, screaming, and then the three beside him, none of the four having time to trigger a single shot before the Gatling gun's eight of nine remaining bullets cut them apart and piled them up not far from the Yaqui.

Spurr held the Gatling gun's maw on the stocky blond, who hadn't moved but stood as before, near the barn and with his Winchester on his right shoulder. His chest and face had tensed, and he seemed to stand there, shoulders back, waiting.

Spurr studied him, one eye narrowed.

"Well?" the stocky younker said. "What're you waiting for?"

"I'll be damned," Spurr said. "Throw that gun down, Massey."

The young man's eyes widened beneath the brim of his slouch hat, and he jerked his head up. "Look out!"

Spurr had felt the presence of someone else in the bell tower about a second before. Now he reached for his pistol as he swung around to see the dark figure with long wet hair pasted against slender, bare shoulders dive toward him, shrieking and thrusting a large bowie-like knife down toward Spurr's chest.

Spurr knocked the girl's knife hand away with his left forearm and smashed his pistol against her temple. As the girl flew over to where the other two Yaqui lay dead, Spurr fell back against the tower's front wall, cracking the back of his head against the wall so hard stars blossomed in his eyes.

He tried to draw a breath but could get no wind in his lungs. As he noted a searing pain in his chest, as though he'd been kicked by a stout cow pony, his eyelids drooped, and the world went black.

"Ah, shit," he heard himself mutter, faintly. "Here's that cloud."

14

CUNO STARED IN shock at what suddenly appeared, aside from the Gatling gun resting with its barrel angled up, an empty bell tower over the church. He'd seen the girl leap at the old lawman, and he'd seen them both go down. Now, neither of them moved.

Cuno looked around at the dead Yaqui and the dead cutthroats, trying to wrap his mind around all that had happened. Of the wagon crew, he was the sole survivor.

No. Not the only survivor, he remembered now as he heard the thunder of horse hooves behind him.

"H-yahh!" Flora shouted as she slapped her rein ends against her calico's withers and exploded out of the barn, nearly plowing into Cuno as she swung right to head west along the main street. Cuno got his feet back under him and watched as horse and rider bounded up a muddy hill, gobbets of wet sand thrown up by the horse's hooves, and disappeared down the other side. She reappeared a few seconds later, dwindling quickly into the western distance.

What the hell—she wasn't Cuno's concern. She hadn't spoken more than five words to him since their wild tussle atop the escarpment.

He racked a shell into his Winchester's breech as he stepped over the bodies littering the street, pulled one of the church's double doors open, and stepped inside. Voices sounded above him, and he lifted his head to see a hole in the ceiling, at the top of a stone stairs to his right. He climbed the stairs, clicking his Winchester's hammer back and holding the rifle up and out from his hip.

In the bell tower, he found Spurr on the floor, resting back against the tower's front wall. A young priest in a brown wool robe knelt beside him, digging a flask out of his robe pocket and handing it over to Spurr with a sheepish expression on his broad face. Spurr's own face was pale and gaunt, and his chest rose and fell heavily.

"Much obliged, Padre," said Spurr, lifting the small flask to his lips.

To his left, the girl sprawled across the two Yaqui braves who'd been manning the Gatling gun. She had a wicked-looking cut in her right temple, and she wasn't moving, but her chest rose and fell slowly, regularly, her gaping, tight-fitting deerskin vest revealing the deep, alluring brown valley between her breasts.

"Rest easy, senor," the padre told Spurr, "and it will pass."

"It'll pass when I'm dead, Padre." Spurr winced and took another pull from the flask. "My ole ticker's about done for." He looked at Cuno. "Fancy findin' you here."

"You get around."

"We both get around."

"What's a U.S. lawman doing in Mexico?"

Spurr shook his head impatiently. "The girl with you?"

"Flora?"

Spurr's eyes brightened with interest. "That's her."

"She was. Rode out of here like a donkey with its tail on fire."

Spurr frowned, befuddled. "Why in the hell did she do that? Didn't she realize I was law?"

Cuno chuckled as he off cocked his Winchester's hammer. "I reckon that's why she did it."

Spurr continued to frown at Cuno as though the young freighter were speaking in a foreign tongue. He was about to say something else when the Yaqui queen moaned and lifted her lovely breasts behind her vest with a short, gasping intake of air.

Spurr narrowed an eye at Cuno. "You ain't gonna try to kill me, are you?"

"I reckon I wouldn't have to try." Cuno glanced at the Winchester in his hand, then returned his cool gaze to Spurr.

He'd seen the old lawman once back in Arizona a couple of months ago, and while the man had hunted him a long ways, he found himself harboring no ill feelings for him. He was just doing his job. Cuno knew what that was like— just trying to do a job. Besides, Spurr had let him go.

"But if I wanted you dead, I could have let her do it," he said.

"Then do me a favor." Spurr reached behind his back for a set of handcuffs, which he extended to Cuno. "Cuff her before she lays into us like the wildcat she is."

Cuno glanced at the Indian girl, who was trying to lift her head but was squeezing her eyes closed painfully. He took the cuffs and went over and grabbed one of her wrists. She fought him weakly, still half unconscious, and after he'd gotten the cuffs on both her wrists, she relaxed a little, as though the struggle had exhausted her.

Relaxed, her face was incredibly beautiful, with rich full lips, a strong chin, and a long imperial nose. A medicine pouch dangled from a braided rawhide thong around her neck, as did a necklace of grizzly claws. Her skin was the color of varnished cherry, her long coarse hair like the tail of a coal-black horse.

Her eyes opened suddenly, and she became a demon—a beautiful, chocolate-eyed demon glaring up at him, wanting to kill him, torture him slowly. But then her lips stretched back from her teeth painfully once more, the flames left her eyes, and the lids dropped over them. Her body relaxed, and she lay still.

"Fire Eyes."

"What's that?"

"That's what I'm told the border toughs call her."

"Acoma," said the padre, taking a small sip from his flask and acquiring a slightly sheepish flush. "She is well known as a fierce fighter in these parts, determined to win back her tribal lands or die trying." The priest studied the girl with a mix of fear and appreciation. "She tries very hard. The peons think she is a demon from the spirit world, sent here to test their faith. I think they might be right."

He turned to Spurr, who was also studying the Yaqui queen. "Are you better now, senor?"

"Call me Spurr. And help me up, would you?" Spurr began pushing off the wall, and the padre slipped his flask into his robe and helped the old lawman to his feet. Spurr flexed his left arm and hand, then lowered the limb and took a deep breath of the damp air, the rain just a mist now and continuing to bead his thin-bearded face. "I reckon your brandy put some spark back in my blood. Thought I was a goner there. That'd have been simpler. Oh, well."

"Now what?" the padre asked.

Spurr looked at Cuno and then at the girl. "Yeah, now what?"

"You need to rest, Spurr. Please—I have a casa behind the church. You are most welcome there though I confess my furnishings are humble."

"I appreciate that, Father. I'd like to spend the night and . . ." He looked at Cuno. "I wanna hear about Miss Hammerlich. And I want answers to a few more questions swirlin' around in this tired old brain, so if you're thinkin' of runnin' out on me, you got another think comin', boy. You're with me till I say otherwise."

Spurr groaned and leaned heavily against the padre, and Cuno grabbed his other arm. Spurr glanced at him, "Forget me. Bring Fire Eyes. I don't want her gettin' away to cut our throats later tonight."

"That she would try," the priest agreed as he began leading Spurr down the steps.

Cuno gave a wry snort as he turned back to the girl. He'd do the lawman's bidding, because he didn't have anything pressing at the moment, or anywhere else to be, for that matter. And he supposed he owed the man for turning back with Mason near the Mexican border and not causing Cuno to have to kill him.

Cuno leaned his rifle against the wall, then crouched and drew the queen up over his shoulder. She groaned and stiffened and rolled her head but otherwise did not fight him.

When he had her positioned comfortably enough, he grabbed his rifle with his free hand and carried her on down the stairs. He followed Spurr and the padre out the rear side door and along a twisting path toward the high northern ridge. It was a five-minute walk during which Cuno saw no one, though smoke lifted from plenty of chimneys and goats and chickens milled in their pens that reeked of hay and ammonia.

The aroma of beans and chili peppers wafting in the damp air made Cuno's empty belly gurgle. A few rain-damp curs scrounged around privies and trash heaps, and one loose sow snorted around a dried-up corn and pumpkin patch.

The padre's shack sat alone near a low, sheer-sided dike about a hundred yards from where the main ridge rose sharply in the south. It was a small, square, brush-roofed stone shack with a wooden front gallery and a dozen chickens pecking in the hard-packed yard. A chicken coop, a small, trenched garden, and a privy flanked the place. A spring bubbled out of the side of the hill and formed a creek that curved around the shack's right side, fringed with willows.

"Come inside, senor," the padre said, his rope-soled sandals flapping against the ground, chickens clucking their disdain for the intruders. "You may rest in my bed, small and lumpy as it is."

"Just a straw pallet would do me fine, Padre."

"Nonsense."

Behind the two men, Cuno stopped with the unconscious Yaqui dangling down his back. "Where you want her?"

The padre pointed at the front gallery that was propped on stones. "Set Fire Eyes there. Tie her to a post, if you wish. I see no reason to keep her, however. She is Yaqui. They are savages. It might be best for all of us, including her, to take her out back and shoot her." The padre regarded the unconscious girl fatefully and crossed himself.

"You're prob'ly right, Padre," Spurr said. "But I reckon I'm weaker than you folks down here and couldn't shoot the girl like I'd kill a rabid dog." He glanced at Cuno, jerking his head to the gallery. "Cuff her to the post good and tight. I'll figure out what to do with her tomorrow."

While the padre led Spurr into the cabin, Cuno eased the girl onto the porch floor, resting her back against the post that sat at the top of the gallery's three steps and supported the sagging roof. He removed her cuffs, then wrapped her arms around the post behind her and cuffed her wrists.

Her head sagged, hair tumbling down both sides of her red-brown face, obscuring it. But as Cuno straightened, she lifted her head and opened her eyes that shone amber in the dying light. She pulled at the cuffs till Cuno thought she was going to break the post, but then she stopped and, gritting her teeth, said in a menacingly low voice and in Spanish-accented but clear English, "I am going to gut you and twist your insides around your neck. *Keel you slow!*"

"Wouldn't blame you a bit."

Spurr poked his head out the open door. "Boy, fetch my horse. Just off the main trail into town. Big roan."

Cuno stared at him.

Spurr shrugged. "Call it payback for savin' your hide back there."

"I saved your hide."

"But I saved yours first. Them Yaqui were movin' in quick!"

Spurr turned away from the door and disappeared inside.

Again, Cuno snorted. His belly gurgled. He could do with a meal.

He glanced at the stream running down from a stone trough someone had mortared around the lip of the spring, embedding a single silver cross in the mortar. Water would do for now. He walked into the grass and willows, knelt, and took a long drink of the cold, sweet water. He hadn't had a drink in hours. Inside the livery barn, he'd been sure he was going to die—probably slowly—at the hands of the Yaqui.

The situation had looked especially grim when the Gatling gun had opened up in the bell tower and hammered forty-five slugs through the rotten door and sent them zinging around inside the barn's brick walls. While the idea hadn't frightened him overmuch, it had made him thirsty though his canteens were empty. Funny the things you think about when you think you're about to die. He'd really wanted a last drink of water, as dying thirsty seemed especially uncomfortable.

He took another long drink, rubbed some of the fresh water across his damp, sweaty, grimy face, then grabbed his rifle and tramped off in search of the old lawman's horse, chuckling again at the oldster's nerve but feeling no acrimony. There was something about the old lawman—his wry toughness despite his obvious health problems—that reminded him of his own frontiersman father, one of the toughest old devils Cuno had ever known.

As he walked through the town, meandering around mud puddles, the light faded from the slate-gray sky, like a lamp slowly being turned down beneath an old dishtowel. There were a few people out now, one dippering water from a rain barrel, one feeding his three penned cattle, both regarding him somberly. He found the big roan where Spurr had told him he would. It was a surprisingly sleek and fine, big-boned animal with some obviously noble Spanish blood in him—in sharp contrast to its knotted-up, craggy-faced, bandy-legged owner.

At first the horse resisted Cuno's lead, then, when Cuno had offered a few lumps of sugar from his shirt pocket, the horse trailed him willingly as he led him along the meandering main street where more and more people were beginning to appear, mostly standing around outside cantinas or brothels. They all stopped talking as he passed and swung their heads around to follow him down the street with their wary, incredulous gazes.

As he approached the big, mud-brick livery barn at the far end of town, the old man whom he'd assumed owned the place was walking around the dead white men and Yaqui littering the street, his corncob pipe in his teeth. Cuno tied the roan to a handle of one of the barn's open doors.

"You kill the Yaqui," the livery owner said, wagging his head as he puffed his pipe. He looked at the dead Indians sprawled before him and continued shaking his head. "Very bad. Very bad. More will come. They will be very angry."

"Talk to the old lawman about that."

Cuno stepped over the dead outrider, a man called Hansen, whom the Gatling gun had shot through the door, and stopped just inside the barn. He turned around quickly and walked over to where the dead cutthroats lay. All except for Sapp, that was. He could see the tamped down mud and blood splatter where Beers's second-in-command had fallen, but the man himself was gone.

"Where's Sapp?" Cuno looked at the old man smoking his pipe. "Where's the man who fell here?"

The old livery owner didn't say anything, but he cut his eyes toward the livery barn behind Cuno. The younger man turned, raised his Winchester, levered a shell into the breech, and slowly approached the opening. If Sapp was alive, he'd be trouble if he knew Cuno had helped the old lawman.

Cuno stepped into the barn's musty darkness, saw the three saddle horses at the front, including Renegade, and two wagons still hitched to the mules. None of the stock had been hit by the Gatling fire, but the beds and canvas covers of both wagons had taken a few shots. They must have been carrying dynamite or gunpowder, because Sapp and the others had kept regarding the wagons warily after the Gatling had started hammering bullets through the front window and the brittle front doors.

None of that concerned Cuno now. What had attracted his attention was the gap between the two wagons, where the third wagon had sat.

It and its team were gone.

Cuno looked down and followed the fresh wheel tracks with his eyes. They wagon had backed over Hansen—the impression of one wide wheel shone across the man's broad back clad in a black wool shirt—and into the street before turning westward into the open desert.

Cuno studied the tracks for a time, then, realizing it was no concern of his if Sapp had made it out alive, he retrieved Renegade from the large pen at the front of the barn, looked the horse overly quickly for any possible bullet wounds, then led him out into street where the old livery owner studied him incredulously.

He looked to the west. Why was it that he had no urge to follow Flora and Sapp and rejoin the rest of the caravan?

He turned to the liveryman. "What's in them two wagons is yours. You might find something in there to help stave off a Yaqui attack, if one comes."

He swung up onto Renegade's back and headed into a break between the church and another building, trailing the old lawman's roan.

15

IT WAS NEARLY dark when Cuno rode into the yard of the padre's shack, scattering the chickens that the padre was scrambling around, trying to herd back into their coop. He was being helped by a little dog, part Chihuahua, who ran frantically around the yard, yipping and nipping at the chickens' tail feathers and sending them flying.

The padre yelled at the little dog in Spanish. The little dog ignored him, a devilish glee in its eyes.

The shack's windows were lit, silhouetting Fire Eyes sitting where Cuno had left her against the post, and the old lawman sitting back in a wicker chair between the front door and the window to the right of it. Spurr held a steaming cup in one hand, a cigarette in the other.

"Well, I'll be damned," the old lawman said in his gravelly voice, faintly slurred from the brandy he'd obviously laced his coffee with. "I figured you must have taken my horse and lit out for South America."

Cuno stepped down from Renegade's back and tossed his reins over the ironwood porch rail. "Nah, you didn't neither."

Spurr pursed his lips as he studied the young man.

Cuno tied the big roan to the porch rail as well, then unbuckled the latigo beneath his belly. "How you feelin'?"

"Fit as a fiddle. Coffee and tanglefoot and a cigarette rolled with this peppery Mexican tobaccy is the best medicine known to man." Spurr drew deep on the quirley, causing the coal to glow against his seamed, broad-nosed face. He held the smoke in his lungs, savoring it, then released it slowly and looked at Renegade. "Nice horse you got there."

Cuno pulled the saddle off the roan's back and set the saddle over the porch rail. "You got four fine hooves here yourself. You federals must make better wages than I figured."

"Got ole Cochise there off a wild horse trapper in the Pryor Mountains, Wyoming Territory. Got some old Spanish blood in him, and the pride of a noble line." As if in response to his rider's compliment, Cochise lifted his head high, blew softly, spreading his chest, and twitched his ears.

Cuno slung Cochise's bridle over the horse's saddle, then began unleathering Renegade. He glanced at Fire Eyes, who sat now with a wool blanket draped across her shoulders. The padre had wrapped a white gauze bandanna around her head. It glowed against her smooth, dark skin, blood spotting the wrap across her temple. She sat with her back straight, shoulders pulled back, breasts out. Her eyes were wide and unblinking, her jaws set hard with mute defiance.

"Looks like the queen is feelin' better, too," Cuno said.

"I think so. She done called me just about everything I ever been called in English and Spanish and threw in some Yaqui I couldn't understand for good measure." Spurr chuckled. "That's the thanks I get for convincing the padre to wrap her head."

"What're you gonna do with her?"

"Hell, I don't know. If I leave her here, the Mexicans will kill her." Spurr glanced at the padre now closing the door of his coop on the last, clucking chicken, the little dog standing on its back feet to observe the festivities. "It's sort of like havin' a rabid puma in a cage. If I turn her loose, she'll likely go back to her bloody ways. I'd best feed her a bullet, but I'll

have to work up to it." Spurr took another sip of his coffee.
"Shame to kill a girl so purty, but the rules play out different down here."

Fire Eyes stared straight ahead, at neither Spurr nor
Cuno but straight across the edge of the gallery. Her chest
rose and fell slowly, heavily. Her anger was almost a palpable thing hovering over the cabin.

"Come and sit down over here," Spurr said.

Cuno racked his tack near's Spurr's on the porch rail.
"That an order?"

"Hell, yes," Spurr barked as the padre approached, carrying a dead chicken, the little dog following close on his
heels. "You're a fugitive from American justice, damnit, so
don't go actin' all snooty. I let you go at the border because
Mason seemed to think he made a mistake, but I can still
haul you back in chains."

The padre glanced at both men warily, then mounted the
porch between them and held up the chicken. "Stew and
tortillas, amigos! And perhaps a little pulque, uh? It will
soften the hardness between you." He went on inside, and
the dog's toenails clicked on the hard-packed earthen floor
behind him.

Cuno had held on to his blanket roll, and now he draped
it over Fire Eyes's nearly bare shoulders against the growing, penetrating night chill.

She shook her head and shoulders fiercely, and the blanket dropped to the ground beneath the gallery.

Cuno sighed and picked up the blanket. He tossed it over
the rail near his saddle and looked at Spurr, who sat watching him closely, his eyes reflecting a little of the amber lamp-
light emanating from the window behind his right shoulder.
Cuno met the look with a grave one of his own.

"You ain't taking me nowhere, old man. Even if you
were good enough."

"Oh, I'm good enough, and if I didn't come down here
after Beers and Sapp and the rest of them turncoat savages,
I'd just do it!" Spurr lifted the quirley to his lips, scrutinizing

Cuno closely as he made the coal glow brightly against his face. "How'd you come to throw in with them, anyways?"

Cuno ducked under the rail and sat down at the edge of the gallery, leaning his back against a roof support post opposite Fire Eyes.

He crossed his arms and his ankles. "They gave me a hand with the Yaqui a few days back." He stared at the silently fuming Yaqui queen sitting five feet away from him. She turned her head away sharply to stare out toward the creek. "Then they offered me a job. I had nothing better to do, and my pockets weren't exactly bulging with pesos."

"Where's your girl?"

"She's no longer my girl."

"Did you know what they were hauling?"

"I had a pretty good idea."

"That didn't bother you?"

"Why the hell should it?"

Spurr sighed and leaned back in his chair, stretching his stiff back. "Those men were soldiers at Fort Bryce. They sacked the place, killed half the men there, including the fort commander, Major Hammerlich, before running off with seven wagonloads of arms and ammunition. And Hammerlich's daughter, Flora."

"Don't worry about Flora." Cuno turned to his head toward Spurr. "Go home, Marshal. Flora doesn't want or need your help. And going after Beers and Sapp is only gonna get you planted all the sooner."

"I'll be planted soon, anyway." Spurr leaned forward, elbows on his knees, and took a last deep drag from his quirley, then flicked the stub into the yard, where it hit the ground and bounced, sparking before fizzling out in a puddle. "You think Flora threw in with 'em willingly? That ain't like the girl I once knew."

"You must not have known her very well."

Spurr scratched the back of his head and made a face. "Where they headed?"

"I don't have the foggiest id—"

"Montana del Loco Oso."

Cuno and Spurr both looked at the girl sitting across from the younger man. She had her head turned toward Spurr.

"The guns and dynamite," she added in surprisingly good English, "are to be sold to a Federale general, Arturo Cuesta, for use in blasting a tunnel through Crazy Bear Mountain, a sacred sierra to the Yaqui. The most sacred in all our land. The rifles will be used to kill the Yaqui warriors who try bravely to keep that pig, Cuesta, from blasting our precious mountain and making our god of war so angry that he will abandon our people and allow us to become slaves of the vile Mexican invaders. They would make us toil for nothing but food and water in mines on our own land!"

Cuno shared a long incredulous look with Spurr, then asked, "Why's this general want to blast a hole through your mountain?"

She turned to him, nostrils flaring, showing her teeth like an angry cur. "So that he can build a railroad through the mountain to connect a gold mine to Mexico City. If you hadn't killed my warriors, Senor Spurr, I would have had the guns in those three wagons to use against the others and to give to my people to fight Cuesta."

Spurr just looked at her, as though he were trying to work all that through his brain. Cuno was working it through his own brain. He should have known that anything he got caught up in down here was going to be complicated. And bloody.

But, hell, he'd just been driving a wagon that someone else would have driven if he hadn't.

"How'd you find out about the gun shipment?" Spurr asked.

"We knew that Cuesta was looking for a big supply of guns and powder—a supply not easily found in Mexico these days. We knew he would look to America for such a supply, though it is not the government's policy to sell guns to Mexico at this time. So we intercepted telegrams he sent from an outpost near his own private train near Montana del Loco Oso, to a gringo outlaw, Major Beers, at Fort Bryce."

Spurr raked a gnarled, brown hand down his face. "Where's this mountain?"

Fire Eyes smiled but there was no warmth or humor in it. "Free me and I will tell you. I will even lead you there."

Cuno stared at the girl as she stared at Spurr, her upper lip raised slightly above her fine, white teeth. Spurr's question was the same one Cuno would have asked: "You gonna cut my throat tonight?"

"All of the warriors I brought with me here are dead— thanks to both of you and the Yankee gunrunners." She swallowed and lifted her noble head slightly. "I am not too proud to admit that I will need your help cutting off the caravan before it arrives at its destination." Red flames danced in her eyes once more. "When we have run General Cuesta away from our mountain, however, I cannot promise I won't kill you, senor, with pleasure."

The slap of sandals sounded in the open doorway behind Spurr. The padre stood there, his little dog on his heels. "Supper is served, amigos!"

Spurr glanced at Cuno and then turned to regard the smiling, half-drunk padre weaving in the doorway. "Set a table for four, will you, Padre?"

Flora brushed a lock of wet hair from her cheek as she galloped over the shoulder of a low bluff toward a gaping canyon mouth below on the other side. It was nearly dark, but the sandstone ridge shone burnt umber in the last light angling beneath the low clouds, and the canyon was blue-black between the walls.

Flora glanced behind her at the village that was little more than the size of a thumbnail from this distance and steel blue in the gathering darkness. No one appeared to be following. She turned her head forward, swiped another lock of damp hair from her face, then suddenly drew rein and slid down from her saddle. She ran up the slope on her left and leapt onto a pile of jumbled boulders and stood, thirty feet up, staring back over the broad canyon behind her.

No one was coming. There was only the slowly dissolving desert and the rain that continued to tick lightly against her hat brim. Flora dropped to her butt, raised her knees, and wrapped her arms around them.

Her mind was swirling while her heart raced. First the Yaqui and their sputtering Gatling gun that drilled bullets through the barn walls and windows until Flora thought for sure one of the casks of gunpower or crates of dynamite would blow her to kingdom come. Then, just when she thought they'd all been saved by someone from the other caravan contingent, Sapp and the others were cut down in the street with the dead Yaqui!

Flora hadn't seen who'd taken over the Gatling gun, but he'd sounded like a white man. Possibly a soldier from Fort Bryce, which would mean there'd been more soldiers, possibly a whole company of soldiers detailed from Fort Huachuca. Fear hammered at Flora, and she pressed her forehead against her knees so hard it began to hurt.

This could't be happening. The plan couldn't unravel like this. She would not go back to the States. She would not give up the guns and ammunition. She and Beers had made a deal with General Cuesta, and she was going through with it, and she was going to be rich with more Mexican gold than she'd need to hide out in Mexico for the next twenty years.

Flora deserved that money. After all she'd been through, dragged from one remote military outpost to another after her mother died back in Pittsburgh when Flora was only six. Since then, when she'd had to start living with her father in the West, she'd never lived anywhere but a remote military compound beginning with Fort Lincoln in Dakota Territory after the death of Custer. She'd been bounced around to eight different forts since then, each one drabber than the last. She deserved to finally be free of such colorless, cheerless places and the hard, cheerless, militant men—including her father—who populated them.

Her father . . .

Flora chewed her upper lip and felt the tickle of satisfaction, remembering him lying on his office floor, crouched over his belly, trying to hold his intestines in with his arms and his hands. He gurgled and groaned and, lower jaw hanging, looked up through his round-rimmed spectacles at the man, Beers, who had shot him from point-blank range.

Then he had slid his shocked, agonized gaze to Flora, who stood there laughing and pointing a jeering finger at him—the man who had held her captive for so many years, kept her practically chained to his private quarters, allowing her to speak only to certain men and only officers of course, the more boring the better. When her father hadn't been looking, she'd managed to slip away from the house and mingle with the enlisted men, and they'd at least had a sense of fun, and they'd passed her a bottle now and then. That's when she started growing more daring, acquired a taste for strong drink and bawdy conversation, and began to see what was possible beyond her father's picket fence.

She'd managed to escape the house for longer periods from time to time, and sometimes she saddled a horse and rode away from the fort. But those freedom treks had been few and far between, and mostly only when her father had left the fort on military business.

Otherwise, she'd been a prisoner. A prisoner forced to take piano lessons and to be tutored in literature, but a prisoner, just the same.

Until dashing, cunning-eyed Major Beers came along and became Colonel Abel Hammerlich's second-in-command. Flora, better schooled than her father ever could have imagined in the ways of men, had known Beers was a law dodger right off. And later, after Flora and the major had concocted their plan with Dave Sapp, also a man on the run, Beers had gut-shot Hammerlich while smoking one of his stogies before knocking a lamp onto the floor, offering his arm to Flora, and the two sashayed out into the main compound of the burning fort, where the wagons and saddle horses stood waiting.

It had been a great plan. But now a total of five wagons were lost. Nearly half the contraband gone. That meant that even if Flora made it back to Beers, their profits would be severely cut.

Beers.

Flora looked around. Night was falling fast. She did not know this country. How would she ever find the rest of the caravan?

Fighting panic, she climbed down off the rocks and swung onto her horse's back. With one more backward glance, she touched spurs to the calico's flanks, and horse and rider bounded on up the trail. They galloped down the hill and followed the trail into the canyon mouth. The canyon was dark and dank, and bobcats cried in the brush and rocks off both sides of the trail. Flora shuddered.

After a half hour of hard riding, she found herself surrounded by steep ridges and with a flooded arroyo before her, blocking the trail. The water was only an inch below the clay bank lined with mesquites and catclaw, and it swirled menacingly, looking like foam-edged tar in the near darkness.

The flood was moving too fast out of the mountains for her to chance crossing it. She looked to both sides. The arroyo formed a straight line before her, cutting her off.

Flora felt a sob ripple up from her throat. She choked it down, hardened her jaws against it. She'd plotted to kill her father, sacked an entire cavalry fort, killing dozens and stealing a hundred thousand dollars in army weaponry. She couldn't turn chicken-livered here. Simply, she'd need to look for a place to camp, then head off in search of Beers at first light the next morning.

She chose her direction quickly, reining the gelding off the trail's right side. She walked the horse slowly, looking for a place where she could build a fire to stave off the coming cold. A ridge ahead and to her right looked promising, and fifteen minutes later she was unsaddling the bay under a lip of sandstone. The ground here was relatively dry, and there was plenty of dead wood in the brushy cut at the ridge's base.

She found enough dry wood and tinder for a fire and set coffee to boil. She hunkered next to the fire, the calico picketed close by for security—the horse would surely warn her of predators—and nibbled some jerky she'd found in her saddlebags. Consciously, she tried to stave off the fear rippling through her.

Odd how, after all her years on crowded military forts and wanting only to get away on her own, she found being alone out here, lost, the most horrifying experience of her life. Part of her almost yearned for her bed in her father's house at Fort Bryce.

She sipped her coffee, wishing she had some of her father's brandy to put in it.

The calico lifted its head suddenly, worked its nostrils, and whinnied.

"Shit!" Flora kicked dirt on her fire and reached for her pistol.

16

FLORA CLUTCHED THE .44 Merwin Hulbert
pocket pistol in both hands in front of her chest and pricked
her ears, listening. For a time she could hear only the sputtering of the smothered coals and a faint breeze scratching
the weeds around her. Then the clatter of a wagon grew
slowly louder, as did the clomps of heavy hooves.

The wagon was coming along the trail from the direction of the village. The clattering grew louder until a man's
distance-muffled voice said, "Hoah."

The clattering stopped after a final squeaking of wheel
hubs and the clinking of trace chains.

Silence.

The driver had no doubt stopped in front of the flooded
arroyo. He'd be even less able to cross the flooded ravine
than Flora had been. Would he remain there in the trail or
go back?

"Shit!" came the angry cry from the direction of the
trail.

Flora squeezed the pistol in her hands and frowned. The
man had cursed in English. Could it be one of the Anglos
who'd taken down Sapp and the others? Possibly a cavalry-

man maybe moving one of the wagons, or maybe all three of the wagons were approaching the arroyo. If so, this place would be swarming with soldiers in minutes!

On the other hand, he might only be a freighter. There were likely more Yankees in northern Sonora than just her gang and those following her.

She continued to listen but heard nothing from the trail. Finally, her curiosity nipping like a rabid dog, she rose slowly and, tightening her coat about her shoulders, began walking down the slope and into the cut at the bottom. There she moved even more slowly, crouching, following the cut toward the trail until she could see the vague, pale shape of the covered wagon sitting about a hundred feet ahead of her.

She stopped and looked around, listening. A few stars flickered through the cloud cover. They offered the only light. Flora continued walking carefully, setting each foot down in turn, squeezing the Merwin Hulbert in front of her belly, until she came to the wagon.

She studied it closely, saw that it was one of her party's medium-sized freighters, its cargo covered with a damp, dirty, cream tarpaulin. A chill rippled through her, and her breath came short. She felt as though she were seeing a ghost. The gang members who'd joined her in taking shelter in the village were all dead.

Who had driven the wagon here?

She looked around, not wanting to move too much and give herself away. Where was the driver? Had he tramped into the brush somewhere, possibly to make camp?

She glanced up trail, seeing no movement, hearing no sounds of oncoming wagons. Finally, she moved up to inspect the mules, both of whom studied her closely in turn, obviously recognizing her as she recognized them, for they snorted and nickered but gave no warning cry. One blew loudly, and she froze, drawing her shoulders together, looking around.

The wagon's driver's boot was empty.

Flora walked around the front of the mules and started back toward the wagon, cocking the pistol and extending it straight out in front of her. "Hey, you—driver," she said, trying to put some steel into her voice but hearing it quiver. "Where are you?"

She walked over to the driver's boot, scruitinized it from this closer vantage, then started walking back along the side of the wagon. Something smashed into both her shins, and she gave a horrified cry as the world turned upside down, and the ground came up to smash her hard. The pistol popped, a red flash in the darkness. The bullet smacked the side of the wagon, and the mules lurched forward, both braying now indignantly.

Flat on her back, Flora groaned and sucked a breath, feeling the cold, wet gravel beneath her, grinding into the back of her head. Her mind spun—she was too confused to feel fear. Then a face appeared above her. A familiar face with a dragoon-style blond mustache hiding his lips. Flora blinked. A chill swept her. Dave Sapp scowled, his jaws hard, eyes pinched.

"Thought I recognized your voice," he said, his own voice raspy, his silver teeth winking in the ambient light. Blood stained his blue wool tunic over his right shoulder. That arm was in a sling fashioned from a red bandanna.

"D-Dave . . . !"

"Don't 'Dave' me, you little bitch. Where were you when that son of a bitch started crankin' that Gatlin' gun? Cowering back in the barn somewhere? Maybe ready to make a deal with the son of a bitch to keep you alive?"

"How . . . how . . . Dave . . . ?"

"That first bullet clipped my ear. The second one tore through my shoulder. I made like I was dead, and him and your pal, Massey, didn't check. Seems they knew one another."

"I know. I heard." Flora pushed up on her elbows. "Oh, Dave—you don't know how relieved I am to see you."

"I bet you are, you poor, frightened little thing."

Flora stayed down and glanced at Sapp's left fist, which he held clenched at his side. His feet were spread a little more than shoulder width apart. He was mad, fuming mad, and if she didn't want her face bashed in, she best stay where she was.

"Look, Dave—I didn't see no reason to walk out into the street with you, because—"

"Because you might've gotten shot with the rest of us."

Anger fired through Flora, then, and ignoring the man's offensive stance, she grabbed her pistol and heaved herself to her feet. "Listen, fool!" She stepped back, raised her pistol, and drew the hammer back, aiming at Sapp's belly. "Just because I wasn't dumb enough to believe the fella in the bell tower was one of us, deciding instead to play it cautious-like before I got a good look at him, is no reason for you to get your panties in a twist. So, I made it out of there without getting my head shot off!"

She gritted her teeth, shifted her feet, and aimed the pistol at the man's head. "What're you gonna do about it?"

Sapp stared at her, chewing his thick, blond mustache, a wariness drifting into his eyes.

"I did what anyone would have done in my position—I got out of there first chance I got," Flora continued, raging. "What was I supposed to do—stay there and face that Gatling gun all by myself?"

Sapp held up his hand, palms out. "All right, all right! Put that damn gun down before you hurt yourself."

Flora gave a chuff and depressed the hammer but kept the pistol aimed at the lieutenant's belly. "Don't think you can soften me up and take this away from me, Sapp. Just cause you can't see 'em don't mean I don't have more like it, and a tiny little knife I keep filed to a sharp edge."

Sapp raked a laugh, then winced and clutched his bloody shoulder. "Where you camped?"

"Up yonder."

"Help me get the wagon off the road. Then I hope your nursin' skills are as good as your bad-girl skills, 'cause you're gonna have to burn this shoulder closed."

Flora looked at the wagon, feeling relief they'd lost only

two more freighters instead of three more. That meant more money in her pockets. And she was also relieved to not be spending the night alone out here . . .

Just to keep Sapp on his heels, she curled her upper lip with menace. "Don't think you can order me around, you son of a bitch," she said, shoving her pistol down hard into her holster.

She reached up into the driver's boot to release the wagon brake before tramping up toward the front of the mule team and leading it into the brush.

The bowie knife's silver blade glowed red, throbbing like a miniature sun, as Flora lifted it out of the fire's flames and pressed it against the ragged, bloody wound in Sapp's left shoulder.

The lieutenant chomped down hard on his leather glove, throwing his head back and tensing until the muscles in his neck stood out like ropes.

"P.U.!" Flora exclaimed, holding the hot knife against the wound, the smoke wafting away from it rife with the smell of scorched blood and skin. "That stinks worse than anything I ever smelled before!"

Sapp mewled and groaned, his chest quivering.

Flora held the knife against the wound, looking with unabashed delight up into Sapp's agonized face. When he started to jerk his shoulders around and lower his head to glare at her, she pulled the knife away from the wound.

"There you go, that oughta do it," Flora said. "Don't say I never did nothin' for you, Dave. That's a nasty business, cauterizing a bullet wound."

Sapp let the glove drop out of his mouth as he stared down at her, leaning against a rock at the edge of their camp beneath the sheltering western ridge. "Flora, I do believe you enjoyed that."

"I reckon I just enjoy helpin' those in need. Probably should have been a nurse, if my old man would have let me be *anything* but his chambermaid." Flora held the knife in the fire's flames and watched the blood sizzle along the blade. "I reckon that's what I should be doin' 'stead of runnin' around down here in Mexico with you curly wolves."

His body shuddering from spasming pain, his shoulder still sizzling, Sapp grabbed her arm and pulled her toward him and kissed her. "I think you like running around down here in Mexico with us curly wolves, Flora." He kissed her again, hard. "Purely, I do!"

She groaned against the pressure of his strong hand and pulled away from him, but it was with a jeering laugh that she said, "Don't strain yourself, Dave. You're in no condition to try sparkin' me. Besides . . ." She held the knife up and slowly, lovingly cleaned the blade with a burlap cloth. ". . . I'm spoken for. Once we've sold the guns to Cuesta, Beers and me are gonna get hitched in Mexico City."

Sapp laughed painfully as he turned his head to inspect his shoulder. "You think so, do you?"

"Sure," she said with feigned insouciance. "You aren't jealous, are you, Dave?"

Sapp stood and pulled up his balbriggan top, then drew on his blue wool army shirt, moving easily to avoid straining his shoulder. "What if I said I was, Flora?" He stood and faced her as he buttoned the shirt. "What if I said I wanted you for myself?"

Flora slid the knife into its sheath—she'd stolen both from a whiskey trader while the man had been passed out one afternoon in the noncommissioned officers' quarters at Fort Bryce. She'd fleeced the Merwin Hulbert from an Apache scout, her proudest conquest. Leaning back against the rock Sapp had been resting against, she entwined her hands behind her head and crossed her ankles.

"Well, to that I'd say, what do you have to offer?" Flora tittered. "I mean, besides what Beers offers on a nightly basis."

"I 'spect I can offer you more than what Beers is offerin' you, little girl." Sapp withdrew a bottle from his saddlebags, popped the cork with his teeth, and spat the cork into the fire as he sat down beside the dancing flames. "A whole lot more." He tipped back the bottle, took three long swallows, and grinned. "Want me to show you?"

"Keep it in your pants, mister. This little girl is interested in more than trouser snakes." The image of the stocky blond pilgrim, Massey, floated behind her eyes, and disappointment twinged in her lower belly. She'd enjoyed her time with him, brief as it was, and she'd been hoping for more, though she'd wanted him to come around for it. She'd wanted him to need her, because there was nothing quite like having a man need you like a sip of water in a parched desert.

That was one good thing that life had taught her—the glorious feeling of being desired.

But, regarding Massey, it hadn't been only the physical stuff she'd been thinking about. She'd thought maybe she could bring Cuno into her plans for Beers . . . for after they'd met and been paid by General Cuesta. She supposed it was best she found out about him now—how easily he could be turned from one side to the other—rather than later. That he was no more trustworthy than Beers, whom she was certain would throw her out like an empty bottle as soon as he'd had his fill of her, and no doubt take her cut of the gold.

It was hard to find a man you could trust any farther than you could throw him uphill against a cyclone. Unfortunately, however, she needed one. The West was a big, lonely, dangerous place without one, though having one was often like sleeping beside a whole nest of diamondbacks.

Sapp took another deep pull from the bottle and leaned on his good arm, wincing at the pain in his left shoulder. "What sparks your fancy, Miss Flora? Just name it, and"— he snapped his thumb—"it's yours."

Flora leaned forward and grabbed the bottle out of his hand. "Don't play me for a fool. You're just horny tonight, Dave."

"I'm horny every night, Flora. And it ain't easy, watchin' you and Beers drift off to your private little camp in the brush, like you do."

Flora tipped the bottle back. The whiskey raked across her throat like sharp nails, and she choked but took another pull, knowing that the more she drank the easier it was to keep it all down. And the warm feeling it would give her. After her second pull, she handed the bottle back to Sapp and ran the back of her hand across her mouth. "That shit's worse than the swill at Bryce!"

"That there come from Tucson!"

"It's still shit."

"Never mind the whiskey." Sapp scuttled over and sat beside her, leaning against the rock. She could feel the warmth of him against her arm and hip, and she found herself liking it despite the horse and sweat smell of the man, and the smell of harsh Mexican tobacco. "Let me tell you about my plans for the future."

Flora glanced at him in mock surprise. "Imagine that— a man with plans!"

"No foolin' now, Flora. I aim to take my cut of the gold and head up to Montana. That's where I was born and raised and still have some family. Well, one uncle, anyways. He runs a ranch and wants to expand it and bring more cattle up from the Nations and even run some blooded horse stock. Maybe Thoroughbreds."

"Those are some mighty tall plans, Dave. I never figured you for the settlin'-down sort."

"You ain't known me all that long, Flora. Me—I aim to make something of myself before it's all said and done. This army wasn't no place for me. To tell the truth, both me an' Beers joined up to avoid a posse in Abilene."

"No!"

"Sure as hell we did. But we had a work ethic, so we moved up fast in the ranks."

"And officers are sorta in short supply on the frontier," Flora added, willing to put up with only so much bullshit.

"All right, all right. Now, it's a nice night out here—ain't it? No reason to be nasty."

"Sorry," Flora said, taking the bottle. "It's just in my nature."

"What I'm tryin' to say, Flora, is . . . I'm gonna need . . . want . . . a woman to join me up in Montana. I don't mean just to cook and clean and to tussle with at night—but a woman to, you know, raise a family with. Spend my life with."

Flora tried to look genuinely surprised and pleased. "Why, Dave! That's so sweet. But . . . what about Beers? You ain't thinkin' I'd play an angle on him with you, are you?"

"You don't think he ain't playin' an angle on you?" Sapp looked at her askance, one eye squinted. "Come on, Flora. Just between you an' me, the longest Beers ever stayed with one woman—and I know him better'n anyone, as we hid out together for three years right here in the Mexican desert—was six months. And she was a whore, and we was stuck all winter in the Sierra Madres with nothin' to do but play cards, drink whiskey, watch the rain and snow fall, and, if you'll pardon my tongue, fuck."

"Six months, huh? Don't you think he might've loved her just a little?"

"Hah!"

Sapp took the bottle back, took another pull, and sighed as he stared thoughtfully into the fire. Neither he nor Flora said anything for a long time.

Then Flora leaned forward to toss another mesquite log on the fire, and said, quietly, timidly, "Where is this ranch you're talkin' about, Dave? Where in Montana? Is it purty country?"

"Purty country?" Sapp handed her the bottle. "Hell, it's on the Yellowstone River, in the shadow of the Absorky Mountains. Country don't get no purtier'n that."

Flora took another drink and smacked her lips. It was going down easier now. And she was feeling as though she'd been wrapped in purple velvet.

"What about Beers?"

"You let me worry about Beers."

"You know what, Dave?"

"What's that?"

Flora threw her leg over him, straddling him and grabbing his shirt collar in her fists. "I think you'll do, Dave."

Sapp chuckled, winced at the pain in his shoulder.

"That hurt?"

"Just a little."

"Don't worry." Gently, she slid her butt down the length of him until she was straddling his knees. She leaned forward and began unbuckling his cartridge belt, smiling up at him coquettishly. "Flora knows just what you need."

Sapp chuckled as she opened his pants and stuck her hand through the fly of his balbriggans.

Finding what she'd been seeking, she smiled up at him again, devilishly. Then she lowered her head.

"Oooh . . . th-that's good," Sapp said, rolling his eyes up. "That's real, real . . . good."

17

.

ASLEEP ON THE padre's front gallery, Cuno felt something touch his side. Instantly, even before he'd opened his eyes, his right hand reached for the Colt .45 in the holster he'd placed beside him. He closed his hand around the ivory grips, but he could not pull the gun from its holster.

A moccasined foot pressed down on it hard.

Cuno blinked. His heart hammering, he trailed his bleary gaze up from the moccasin to a narrow, copper-brown ankle and slender shin and then up past the knee to a well-turned thigh, smooth as whipped butter and broad and taut with horse-riding muscle, to a scrap of unadorned deerhide skirt. From there he saw the vest, the bare shoulders, the grizzly claw necklace, and the medicine pouch nestling in the deep cleavage.

He trailed the long, slender neck up to the regal face with the long, clean nose and chocolate eyes that stared down at him without a trace of emotion.

Cuno tensed, nerves firing, as though he were about to have his throat cut.

"The old man," she said softly, tonelessly, canting her head toward the cabin. "He says to wake you. The sun is up."

"Oh, he does, does he?"

"He says you're going with us."

In the same pitch and tone, Cuno said, "Oh, he does, does he?"

The door opened behind Fire Eyes, and the haggard old lawman's stooped frame filled the low doorway, a stone mug smoking in his gnarled, age-spotted brown hand. "Rise an' shine, sprout. I need a deputy, and you're it!"

Cuno groaned as he sat up and ran both hands roughly through his hair, trying to clear the cobwebs. "You're memory's as sour as your ticker, Spurr. I'm an escaped convict from a federal penitentiary and a fugitive from justice."

"Let's not split hairs."

Spurr crouched and held the coffee mug out to Cuno, then turned back into the shack. When he returned, he had another mug of the black, steaming brew in his hand, and as he walked over to the edge of the gallery steps, he blew on it and sipped and smacked his lips. "That's good coffee. You get to be my age and in my condition, you get so's you appreciate a simple cup of coffee on a cool Mexican morning."

Cuno took a sip, half consciously taking note of the taste, then heaved himself to his feet and stomped into one boot and then the other. Spurr looked at him. "So, what's your answer?"

"I didn't know it was a question. Sounded like an order to me."

"Come on, kid—I know you well enough to know you don't take orders from no one. I need a deputy. A partner. Whatever the hell you want to call it. Someone to back my play."

Cuno took another sip of his coffee and stared off across the sloping yard and through the scattered sage and pinyons toward the back of the church, which he could just make out in the dim light of the predawn. "What is your play, anyway?"

"I want to intercept that wagon train before it gets to this General Cuesta the Yaqui girl told us about. And I want justice for my old buddy, Abel Hammerlich. Which means if I can't haul any of those other killers back to the border, I'm gonna try like hell to haul her back."

Cuno looked at him in disbelief. He snorted a laugh. "You're one man. If I go, we're two men. Against a good fifteen, and the Mexican Federales."

"What other pressing business you got down here?"

"Livin'."

"Take it from me, kid," Spurr said, clamping a hand over Cuno's right shoulder. "Just livin' is overrated. It's *how* you live that counts."

Cuno gave another snort and took another sip of the coffee.

"I done already took out three wagons and five badmen." Spurr winked. "That's upped our odds."

"Two wagons and four badmen."

"What?"

"One of 'em must've been playin' possum, because when I went over to the barn to get my horse, one man was gone." Cuno looked at Spurr pointedly. "One man and one wagon."

"Well, hell, kid—why didn't you tell me this yesterday?"

Cuno hiked a shoulder and finished his coffee in two long gulps. "Didn't think much about it yesterday. Hell, I guess I was still sort of on the other side. To tell you the truth, old man, all this sort of has my mind spinning. I came down here to get away from trouble. Then I join up with them and run into you, and now you want me to throw in with you to go after *them*!"

Spurr grinned. "It's an exciting life you got, kid."

Cuno was rolling his blankets and muttering to himself. "So, what do you say?"

Cuno donned his hat and wrapped his shell belt around his waist. "I reckon it wouldn't be right to let a senile old codger ride off to get himself killed. I'll throw in with you, but just till you see the odds are stacked tit-high against us and agree to turn your wrinkled old ass for home."

"Good 'nough. Come on inside. The padre's cooked us

up some eggs and frijoles. We'll shovel some down, saddle up, and hit the trail in a half hour."

Cuno set his blanket roll near his saddlebags, which he'd draped over the porch rail. His rifle leaned against a near porch post. He looked around the yard, which the gray light was slowly revealing.

"Where's Fire Eyes?"

Spurr looked around, then, too.

"Who knows? Maybe she got tired of all our palaver."

"Think she ran out on us?"

"Doubt it," Spurr said, looking around the yard. "She woke me a half hour ago by putting a cold bowie knife to my neck." He chuckled. "She's in a hurry to get on the trail, I reckon. Might already be scoutin' it." He arched a brow at Cuno. "Not sure where she spent the night. Out here with you, maybe?"

"I'm alive, ain't I?"

"Right."

Spurr ambled on inside the shack.

A fine drizzle began to fall just after sunup, and a thin ground fog moved like white snakes amongst the brush and cacti.

In the gray, wet morning, Cuno and Spurr followed the wagon tracks away from the livery barn and into the western desert. Unshod hoofprints scored the trail before them, between the two fresh wheel furrows. Fire Eyes's tracks.

"That girl has pluck," Spurr said. "Ridin' out here all alone. Any man with a gun would shoot a Yaqui, even a pretty one like herself, on sight."

They followed the tracks through a canyon and to the edge of an arroyo, where they became confusing and overlaid, as though the wagon had left the trail and then turned onto it again. The arroyo was about half full of swirling, clay-colored water.

Renegade whinnied a shrill warning. Cuno palmed his .45 and clicked the hammer back. He stared across the arroyo, in the same direction in which Renegade was staring, twitching an ear. Spurr slid his old, brass-framed Winchester from its boot and levered a shell into the chamber one-handed.

From ahead, a horse snorted. There were the soft clomps of hooves on wet gravel. Finally, the cream stallion came around a bend about forty yards away, and Fire Eyes rode toward them, swaying easily on her blanket saddle, a bow and quiver of arrows poking up from behind her head, a Winchester carbine hanging from a rope lanyard down her other shoulder. She wore a short bearskin jacket over her vest, open to reveal her belly button just beneath the lower edge of the vest.

Fire Eyes stopped the cream and stared toward them, characteristically cool and reproving. "They camped there," the Yaqui queen said, casting her glance toward the ridge flanking Spurr's right shoulder. "Then crossed the arroyo early this morning—while you two lay half dead in your blankets."

Cuno and Spurr shared a wry glance.

Fire Eyes batted her moccasins against the cream's sides and moved forward at a spanking trot, her stygian hair bouncing straight up and down. "They have joined the others." She disappeared for a moment as she entered the dense willows lining the arroyo then reappeared as she dropped into the arroyo, splashed through the knee-deep flood water, causing it to splash up against her bare legs, then bounded up the other side.

She stopped in front of Cuno and Spurr, shifting her dark eyes between them. Beads of water, like molten copper against her tan skin, dribbled off her legs. "We can cut them off before they arrive at Cuesta's headquarters. They must follow a wagon trail through a canyon two, maybe three days away. We will move faster, get ahead of them, and throw rocks down on top of them." She wrinkled her nose a little, and Cuno felt a vague pang of desire deep in his young man's loins. "*Big* rocks . . . and *crush* them!"

She reined the cream around them. "Come! I will need help!" As she turned the cream off the trail to Spurr's right, heading south along a secondary arroyo that meandered along the base of the sandstone ridge, Spurr slid his Winchester into its sheath. "Come on, kid. The girl needs our help."

"This I have to see."

As they rode along behind Fire Eyes, who seemed to be holding her own horse back so she wouldn't lose the two gringo white eyes, Spurr said, "Kid, I bet that girl's hell in the sack."

"You better hope you never find that out, old man."

Spurr shook his head, laughing, and booted Cochise into a lope across a broad, open flat stretching out between widening ridges.

Gradually, the day cleared, and the humidity gave the desert a heavy, peppery smell. The men rode hard behind the Yaqui queen, who often disappeared for an hour or so at a time, so that Cuno and Spurr had to track her to keep from losing her. Occasionally, she'd appear on a distant hillock, beckoning, then rein the gallant cream down the other side of the hill and be gone again, like a dream upon waking.

"Damn," Cuno said, late in the afternoon when they were back to following the tracks of her unshod horse, in a bowl surrounded by vast sierras, "I thought I had one of the best horses on the frontier. That cream of hers must have a heart as big as a rain barrel."

"Old Cochise has plenty of bottom himself," Spurr said, patting the roan's sleek neck. "But them Yaqui horses are made of sterner stuff—I'll give them that. And so is she. I haven't seen where she's yet stopped to eat. She only stops at water tanks, and she must know every one out here."

She reappeared an hour later, trotting toward them from the west, when the sun was touching the western ridges. She was a silhouette against the large, buttery orb, until she drew rein a few yards away. She'd tied her bear coat to the cream's back, with a skin sack of sparse camp possibles. "We camp in a canyon straight ahead. There's a one-armed saguaro. Just beyond it. A spring in there."

She reined her horse around to head southwest. "Now,

hold on," Spurr said. "Where in the hell you goin' there, missy? You too good to ride with us?"

She turned the cream back toward them, the yellow-eyed beast rising up on its hind legs, its silky mane fluttering in the warm breeze and saffron light. "Many banditos here. I am checking out a camp they use. If they are here, they will know we are here, and they must be dealt with."

She reined the cream around once more and batted her heels against its flanks. "Yeah, well, how are you gonna deal with 'em all by your ownself?" Spurr said only loud enough for Cuno to hear as he scratched the back of his head, watching her gallop off.

Cuno narrowed an eye at his old partner. "I do believe you're in love with the girl, Spurr."

"Ain't you?"

"Sure."

Cuno touched spurrs to Renegade's flanks, trotting ahead across the fading desert.

They found the one-armed saguaro a half hour later. The canyon opened just beyond it, between two shelving mesas and near the adobe remains of an old mine shack, with tailings and rotten wood Long Toms strewn across the slope behind it. When they'd gone in and found the spring and set up camp, Cuno filled his canteen at the spring. Spurr was bringing in an armload of firewood, which he dropped beside the charred rocks forming a ring obviously used by many past travelers.

Spurr groaned, cuffed his hat back off his forehead, and sank down on a rock, adjusting the Starr on his hip. Behind the sun and windburn, his face was pale, cheeks hollow. Cuno walked over and handed him the canteen.

"No, thanks." Spurr waved off the flask and crouched over the saddlebags at his feet. He withdrew a bottle he'd bought from the padre. "This'll do."

Cuno set some catclaw twigs in the fire ring, and with his pocketknife he filed some shavings off a paloverde branch around the catclaw. "You look whipped."

"I feel whipped. That squaw sets a smart pace."

"This is her country, Spurr. Not ours."

Spurr popped the cork on the bottle and squinted at Cuno. "Wanna chew that up for me?"

"I think you'd best head back to the border."

"You do, do you?"

Cuno struck a lucifer to life on his thumbnail and touched the flame to the tinder, watching the flame catch the shavings and catclaw, and grow slowly, a slender ribbon of white smoke rising with the smell of the burning wood. When the fire looked like it was going to go, he leaned back on his heels. "What're you after, anyway, Spurr? What're you really after down here, this far out of your jurisdiction?"

Spurr took another pull from the bottle, throwing his head back and washing the liquid around in his mouth before swallowing as though he'd just ingested a rare elixir. "I told you what I'm after. I'm after that girl. Was gonna rescue her, now I'm gonna tan her hide and take her back to Arizona to stand trial for bein' an accessory to the murder of her old man." His eyes were bright and rheumy from the drink as he pointed around the bottle at Cuno. "And as many of them cold-blooded killers as I can throw a loop around."

Cuno regarded him skeptically. The flames were crackling as they engulfed the catclaw and paloverde shavings. Cuno set some larger shavings on the burning pile and added a few sticks. "Well, then you're just as crazy as I first suspected. Even with Fire Eyes guidin' us and probably getting in a few good licks of her own, we don't have a chance."

"If you're so damn sure of that, why'd you come?"

"I don't know. I reckon for some fool reason I thought you'd see the error of your ways after a day or two out here, and you'd do what any sane man would do and head back to the border. And I'd have the satisfaction of seeing it."

"And what would you do?"

Cuno hiked a shoulder and looked around at the rocky canyon walls and the blue sky greening toward dusk, the lengthening shadows of the shrubs tumbling over the rocks and clumps of buckbrush. Loneliness was a cold breath in his lungs.

He drew himself up against the dizzying rush of emptiness. "Well, I wouldn't be heading to the border, I'll tell you that. I won't be heading that way for a good, long time, if ever. I have no intention of being led in chains back to that rat farm you call a federal pen."

"If you play your cards right, I might put in a good word with a judge. I know Sheriff Mason would, too."

"Thanks." Cuno dropped a few more, larger branches on the fire, then rose and grabbed his Winchester. "I'll take my chances down here."

"Lonely damn place for a man alone—no family, no girl, nothin'."

"North of the border ain't much better." Cuno levered a cartridge into his rifle's breech, then set the hammer to half cock. He began striding up the canyon. "I'm gonna go shoot us something for supper." He took another step, swung back around. "And as far as why you're really here, old man, I know as well as you do."

"You do, do you?"

Cuno shook his head. "I ain't goin' that far."

He turned away again, and as he walked up the twisting canyon, whose walls closed and then widened around him, he tried to keep his mind off his dilemma. There was no point in thinking about anything that had happened, or was going to happen. He figured he'd thrown in with the half-mad lawman because he had nothing better to do.

That was as good a reason as any. He'd likely get himself killed, or let the old man get him killed, but he'd never been less afraid of death. He wasn't ready to die, but he wasn't afraid of it, either.

He'd walked up a feeder canyon when he spied a jackrabbit sitting beneath a paloverde tree not far from a moldering deer carcass. Swerving to the right, he crouched behind a rock and watched the rabbit munching grass, its head half turned away from Cuno and downwind. He drew a bead, squeezed the trigger, and gritted his teeth against the rifle's screeching report echoing off the canyon walls.

The shot would be heard for miles around, but it was too late to mess with a snare.

Cuno ejected the spent cartridge, walked over to the dead rabbit, and began cleaning it with his pocketknife. A small stone rattled down the canyon wall to his left. He whipped his head around to see a great mountain lion crouched atop the rocky ridge, staring at Cuno, its ears laid back.

A hard rock fell in Cuno's gut, and for an instant, fear froze him. The cat gave its tooth-gnashing shriek, brown eyes flashing demonic yellow, its tail curling up viciously. Cuno dropped the knife and the rabbit and grabbed his rifle, but by the time he'd gotten a cartridge levered, the cat was a gray-brown blur diving toward him from the rocky ridge, extending its long, thick body and giving another wail.

Cuno raised the rifle defensively, as though to shield himself from the beast. The cat plowed into him, knocking his onto his back so hard, smacking his head on the gravelly ground so resoundingly, that for several seconds he felt ensconced in warm tar. There was a floating feeling.

Was he dead?

He blinked his eyes, and as they cleared, he saw the cat's eyes flashing yellow at him. The lids were slowly drooping closed, and the pupils were narrowing to black pinpoints. The wet tongue, flecked with white foam, came to rest in a corner of its open mouth, the cat's fangs looking steel blue in the last light.

The smell emanating from the open mouth was like old urine and rotten meat.

Wrinkling his nose, Cuno canted his head to the left. The fletched end of an arrow protruded from the cat's thick, gray-brown neck. Cuno turned his head the other way and saw the razor-edged, strap-iron arrow point, coated in blood, protruding six inches from the cat's shoulder. Blood oozed out around the ash-wood shaft and started to dribble slowly down through the cat's fur.

He could feel the heart fluttering in the beast's chest, but the cat was a deadweight pinning him to the ground.

He got his knees and arms under it and heaved it off his side, then slid his legs out and gave it a kick. A brown figure dropped straight down off the opposite ridge and landed on the canyon floor with a solid thud. Still holding her bow, Fire Eyes strode toward him and looked down with the expression of an overwrought schoolteacher.

"Rifles make too much noise," she said tonelessly.

Cuno stared up at her, his heart still hammering, feeling genuinely chagrined.

He sat up, looked at his half-skinned rabbit and then at the big cat. The rabbit appeared little larger than one of the painter's broad paws.

"Thanks for supper," he said.

Saying nothing, Fire Eyes pulled a bowie knife with an elkhorn handle from her belt sheath, dropped to her knees, and went to work butchering the wildcat.

Fighting off the hot flush in his cheeks, Cuno retrieved his own knife and helped her.

18

BENNETT BEERS MOVED to the lip of the gorge through which a slender creek flowed amongst willows, cottonwoods, sycamores, and more green grass than he'd seen since he'd left Missouri so many years ago he'd lost count. He could hear a slender stream dropping out of a spring in the ridge wall, and he could hear Flora moaning and groaning as she washed herself.

He couldn't see her from this angle, but she'd told him before she'd left the camp that she was coming over here and she wanted him to make sure none of his "low-down" men followed her.

He'd made sure.

Beers grinned slyly, stretching his dark mustache, as he started down the game trail that twisted down the steep, sandstone embankment. He followed the trail around a thumb of rock arching out over the gorge, and then he gained the canyon's bottom and stopped.

Flora stood before him, beneath another ledge of rock about ten feet out from his. She was naked, and water dribbled down over her blond head and slender shoulders. It curved down her back and fanned out across her slender hips and buttocks that were as creamy and pink as fresh-whipped butter.

Flora raised her hands to work the water through her hair, pivoting slightly on her hips so that Beers glimpsed the tender half curves of her breasts.

Beers stood admiring her for a time, wanting to hold on to this image of her for later, when he wouldn't have her anymore, and then he reached up behind his head and snatched the five-inch Arkansas toothpick from the sheath behind his neck. He moved slowly forward so that his low-heeled cavalry boots would not make a sound on the wet rock. He stepped up behind Flora, then drew his left hand out around her to clamp it over her left breast and, holding her taut against him, slid the toothpick's freshly sharpened blade about one inch from her smooth neck.

"Oh!" Flora said throatily, jumping.

"Hello, my sweet—enjoying your shower?" Beers whispered menacingly into her left ear, letting the five inches of stone-sharpened Damascus steel press against her neck just this side of actually scoring it. With his other hand, he squeezed her breast savagely.

"Oh—ow—Bennett—what the *hell*?"

"Just wanted to let you know that Sapp told me the kind of chicken-hearted connivery you two was up to last night on your little campin' trip."

"What?"

"Sure." Beers gritted his teeth as he spit the words out against Flora's jaw, holding her fast against him with his left hand. "He told me what you two decided on, and he confessed you gave him a tumble, to sorta seal the deal. Told me that, he did, just before I stuck him like a pig and he crawled around squealin' while he bled out in front of the rest of the men. Ruined supper for a few of 'em. Made it sweet for them that never liked him in the first place, figured he might be a goddamn, pink-panty-wearin' four-flushin' bastard!"

Flora did not struggle, but held her body tight, every muscle ridged, and angled her neck away from the knife Beers held against her neck. He felt her throat work as she swallowed—or maybe it was her pulse—shoving the blade out just a hair.

In a strangled voice, panting, she said, "Bennett . . . for chrissakes . . . I don't know what the hell you're talking about. If Sapp said anything like that, he's gone plumb loco, and he shoulda been put out of his misery. Him and me shared no blanket last night, and if he told you we did, he's a goddamn braggart and bald-faced liar. Why, I'd no sooner let that pig grunt around between my legs than I would a horny *javelina*!"

Beers drew his hand from her breast, his knife away from her throat. She turned and looked up at him, her face red with shock and terror, veins standing out in her forehead.

"Just checkin'," Beers said, reaching up to slide the knife back into its sheath.

"What?"

"You heard me."

Flora crossed her arms on her breasts, the thin waterfall tumbling onto the rocks behind her. "You mean—you were lyin' about gutting Sapp?"

"I wouldn't gut Dave. He's my right-hand man. If I found out you two been biblical, hell it's you I'd gut like a pig. I'd wait till our mission was over, and then I'd shoot Dave through his lyin' heart, but"—Beers winked—"I'd dig him a nice grave and say a few words over him. Can't blame a man for wantin' to give you a roll, Flora honey. In fact, I don't know if I'd trust a man that didn't . . . or a man that wouldn't if he had the chance."

"You bastard," she said in a monotone, flaring her nostrils at him. "You don't trust me."

"Don't take it personally," Beers said, walking out away from the waterfall and sitting down on the lip of the ledge, where he could feel a soft, cool spray against his neck. "I don't trust anybody."

Beers swung his feet over the ledge, dug into his silk shirt pocket for a long, black Mexican cheroot, and stuck it between his teeth. He fired a match on his shell belt, and as

Flora sat down beside him, wrapping a blanket around her shoulders, he touched the flame to the cigar, puffing smoke.

"You know you can trust me, though, don't you really, Bennett?" She looked up at him meekly. "Tell me you were just foolin', all right. You had me plum scared out of my wits!"

"I trust you probably about as much as you trust me, Flora. I'm no fool. I know a man like me ain't trustworthy. But I know you, Flora. I know how you were around the fort, drivin' your poor pap mad with your cavortin' with the noncoms. I don't know if you were just hotter'n a stick of detonated dynamite or if you just wanted to drive him crazy. Maybe kill the poor son of a bitch."

"Poor son of a bitch?" Flora exclaimed. "I told you what he did to me. Tried to keep me enslaved in that house of his, like I was his damn chambermaid. And I could tell you other things he did, too, Bennett, if I didn't think it would turn your stomach against me."

Bennett chuckled as he stared out at the tree-lined creek the waterfall trickled into via its natural stone aquaduct, the leaves shimmering in the pink evening light. A great stone bridge stood over the canyon to his right, built by the conquistadores over two hundred years ago and still used by the peasants in the area.

Faintly, Beers could hear the mules of his caravan braying for supper a hundred yards up the canyon on his left. The party had stopped for the night a few hours after Flora and Sapp had met up with Beers's five remaining wagons at a fork in an old Indian road.

Bennett didn't believe a word the girl said about her old man's improprieties. He'd soldiered closely to Abel Hammerlich for nearly a year, and while he'd hated the man's sternness and painstaking attention to detail, he'd been no different from any other fort commander. Most of all, the colonel had been no pervert.

"What's so funny?"

Beers gave her a sidelong look. "A girl as pretty as you

should learn as soon as she's out of swaddling clothes to fend off any man, including her father. If she had to."

Flora bunched her lips. Veins bulged in her forehead, just above her nose. She whipped her hand back, then brought it forward. It smacked Beers's face so loudly it echoed. "You don't believe me!"

Beers laughed, drew a big arm around her shoulders, and kissed her. She struggled against him, finally broke away.

"Bastard!"

"Oh, come on, Flora!" Beers said with a laugh. "You been waggin' your ass so long, I think you're startin' to believe your own bullshit." His face sobered instantly, his steel-blue eyes turning hard as stones in their deep sockets mantled by thin, black brows. "And if you ever hit me again, I'll kill you."

Flora stared at him, gulping. Finally she ran her hands up and down her pale, damp thighs, fidgeting, then broke into a laugh. "Ah, come on, Bennett. You an' me gotta lighten up. I do believe we've both started to take ourselves too seriously!" She squeezed his arm, then pressed her cheek against it, curling her bare legs and snuggling against him as she changed the subject. "The men piss-burned about losin' those two other wagons, are they?"

"They'll get over it."

"We mighta gone back for 'em. Lord knows we got enough weapons to stand against any amount of men the army might have sent down here."

Beers shook his head and blew a smoke plume out over the canyon. "Not worth the delay or the risk. We're due at Cuesta's train day after tomorrow. Besides, we can make up the money we lost with them wagons by robbin' a few banks in the gold country west of here on our way down to Mexico City."

Beers turned to Flora and studied her creamy, naked body beside him. She was shivering, as the air was turning cool. "Darlin', I do believe you're chilly."

She snuggled tighter, giving an alluring little groan,

against him and pressed her soft lips to his neck, about the same place he'd held that Arkansas toothpick to hers.

"Need me to warm you up some?"

Flora lifted her face toward his, her eyes bright, and nodded slowly. Beers reached around behind her shoulders to grab a fistful of her wet hair and pulled it back, lifting her chin. He kissed her. She snaked her arms around his neck and returned the kiss, moving her body enticingly against his.

"I'm glad you and Dave is both still my friends," he said quietly, smiling into her face.

"I'm glad, too, Bennett. You're my only *friend*," she said, "from here on out. Oh, we're gonna have a lovely life in Mexico City!"

Beers picked her up in his arms and carried her down to the brush lining the creek, where she'd left her clothes and blankets. She pressed her head to his chest and closed her eyes, enjoying his big, warm arms wrapped around her, holding her close, but thinking what a thrill she would have soon, when she used his own knife on him.

Later, as they were both dressing in the greenish, fast-fading light of dusk, a pistol crack echoed from the direction of the camp upstream along the creek. Beers, buttoning the fly of is whipcord trousers, jerked his head in that direction and narrowed his eyes.

"Somebody taking target practice?" Flora said. Pitching her voice with dark irony, she added, "Or they fightin' again?"

A man's muffled shout sounded, and then more gunfire crackled from upstream. Beers's pulse hammered in his ears—they couldn't lose any more wagons!—and he reached for his gun belt where he'd tossed it into the brush just before lowering himself between Flora's supple thighs and quickly wrapped it around his waist and buckled it. Seconds later, he and Flora were sprinting upstream, their rifles in their hands, leaping deadfalls and rocks.

Pistols and rifles continued hammering for several minutes beneath angry shouts that echoed around the canyon.

Then there was the tooth-gnashing rat-a-tat-tat of a Gatling gun opening up—one short burst followed by a long one and then another short one.

"Shit, they have one of the guns!" Beers bit out as he and Flora continued to run upstream.

Just before they came to the leftward bend in which their camp had been setup, Beers stopped, sucking air. "Flora, you head around to the left and get down behind them rocks. Stay there till I tell you it's safe to come out. I'm gonna cross the stream, try to get behind that Gatling gun."

"Banditos, you think?" Flora said, her voice pitched with exasperation as she began running through the willows toward the canyon's southern ridge.

"I don't know what the hell to think," Beers said with a growl as he began splashing into the stream. "Hell, this is Mexico!"

19

THE SHOOTING HAD stopped by the time Beers had gained the base of the escarpment on which his men had set up a Gatling gun to watch over the camp from the north. Keeping the scarp between himself and the camp just on the other side of the stream, he looked up the knobby wall toward the top, from which a Spanish-accented voice was now shouting, "Throw down your pistols and rifles, amigos, and we let you live! We will even give you some tequila for your long ride back to the border! If you do not obey my command, however, my twenty men will kill you like dogs!"

"Twenty men?" Dave Sapp shouted from the direction of the camp. "Bullshit—you don't have twenty men out here!"

The Gatling gun hiccupped. In the following silence, the man atop the scarp shouted, "Twenty men and one Gatling gun. You wish to live or die?"

There was another silence. Slowly, Beers began climbing the backside of the scarp. It was a steep climb, but there was a natural corridor amongst the rocks and plenty of foot- and handholds.

He was halfway to the top when Sapp shouted, "You want our wagons, come and get 'em!"

Pistols and rifles began thundering from the other side of the stream. The Gatling gun began opening up once more, and Beers quickened his pace, gaining the top after a minute of hard climbing. He could see the back of the Mexican crouched over the Gatling gun—a bulky silhouette in the twilight—the gun spitting its empty cartridge casings over the stocky Mexican's right shoulder.

Behind the man, one of Beers's men, Kiowa Ames, lay unmoving in a pool of his own blood. His neck was a black, nasty mess of gushing blood.

Beyond the man shooting the gun, Beers saw the silhouettes of about five men crouched amongst the willows on the near side of the stream, rifles flashing as they fired across the stream toward the camp around which the wagons had been circled.

"Twenty men, my ass," Beers said, sneering, as he stepped over Ames and reached up to slide his Arkansas toothpick from the sheath behind his neck. Crouching behind the man shooting the Gatling gun to avoid the return fire of Beers's own men, he moved up on the man until he could smell the sweat and leather stench of him, then grabbed the man's long braided pigtail and jerked it back.

The man screamed as his head came up and back, and Beers put his head up right close to the Mexican's, grinning into his shocked eyes. "Fandango's over, amigo." He slid the toothpick slowly across the man's throat.

The Mex grunted liquidly.

Blood squirted straight out before him, splattering the smoking Gatling gun, and within seconds he began convulsing. The tension left his body, and Beers released his pigtail. The Mexican slumped to the ground near Aimes.

Beers cleaned his toothpick on the man's wool coat, frowning, studying the stocky Mexican more closely. He was dressed in deerhide and buckskin, with bandoliers crisscrossed on his chest. He had a broad face, cheekbones tapering to a jutting jaw, and a spider tattoo on his left cheek. His half-open, dead eyes were green.

Rage was an insant blaze inside the outlaw leader.

"Why, *you* . . . !"

Beers slipped the toothpick back into its sheath, then crouched over the Gatling gun, edging the barrel down toward the gun flashes and crouching, silhouetted figures on the near side of the stream. He began furiously turning the crank.

Bam-bam-bam-bam-bam-bam-bam-bam-bam!

Screams rose from the willows. Through the weblike haze of the Gatling's smoke, Beers saw the figures jerk or slump or leap or twist around, and fall. In less than fifteen seconds, he silenced all the guns on his side of the stream.

Beers kept his head down as he stared off across the Gatling gun toward the wagons on the other side of the creek. No guns flashed over there.

Finally, Sapp said out of the near darkness, "Boss?"

Beers lifted his head. "They're dead. Get over here, Dave!"

He wheeled, stooped over the dead bandito, and lifted him over his shoulder. Grunting under the weight, he walked past the Gatling gun and heaved the body over the edge of the scarp. After two seconds there was a loud, crunching thud.

He looked toward the camp, saw Sapp and two other men wading across the stream glittering pearl and violet. Flora was angling toward him from his left. Beers cursed, turned, and descended the escarpment the same way he'd climbed it.

He was standing over the dead outlaw when Sapp, Bill Finnegan, and C. J. Corcoran were walking up, slouch-shouldered with chagrin.

"Sorry, Boss," Sapp said. "Somehow they got Tack to the south of us and Aimes to the north, and caught us by surprise. How they got through the pickets I sent out, I can't fathom."

"Your pickets are most likely dead—just like Tack and Aimes. Any others?"

"Just two wounded. They can both still skin a team, though. Good thing we had the wagons in a circle."

Beers kicked the rounded side of the dead man sprawled belly-up at the base of the scarp. "Recognize him?"

Sapp crouched over the dead man, then knit his brows as he looked up at Beers. "Carlos Riata?"

"That's right. One of the most feared banditos in all of Sonora. Story has it he does killing and thieving jobs for the Federales, when they don't want to be implicated themselves and start another revolution."

"Well, Jesus Christ. No wonder he slipped up on us quiet as a damn coyote."

"Fortunately, he didn't sneak up on me," Beers said.

"Nor me," said Flora, giving Sapp a hard look of reprimand.

Beers kicked the dead Carlos Riata hard in the side and cursed. "And it's no damn coincidence he targeted us."

Sapp winced, said darkly, "You think Cuesta sent him?"

"Why not have your highest-paid bandito rob us rather than pay us off fair? You ever know an honest Mexican?"

Beers cursed again, then brushed past Sapp and Flora and the others and took long, angry strides toward the stream. "That double-crossing son of a bitch just double-crossed the wrong goddamn gringo!"

The next day, around noon, Renegade threw his left front shoe.

As Cuno, Spurr, and Fire Eyes rounded a broad bend in the trail they'd been pushing hard on, trying to make their rendevous at the Fuerte River gorge well in advance of the gunrunners' wagons, Cuno heard the clink of the shoe rolling off the side of the trail and piling up against a rock.

Cuno pulled back on Renegade's reins, scowling down at the cracked shoe, and cursed. Spurr and Fire Eyes checked their own horses down and blinked against the dust catching up to them. Cuno groaned, stepped out of the saddle, knelt down, and picked up the shoe in his hands, squeezing it as though to break it again in frustration.

"That's the trouble with shoes," said Fire Eyes in her characteristic imperious tone, flashing her haughty eyes. "They come off."

"Girl's got a point," said Spurr.

"You two go on. I'll head back to the village we just passed. There's probably a blacksmith there who can forge a new shoe."

"All right," Spurr said with a nod, adjusting his hat and turning his head forward. "Break a leg, kid."

He booted Cochise on up the trail, and he and Fire Eyes soon had their horses loping once again, eating up the trail they followed across a parched flat where only small tufts of cactus and white rocks seemed to grow. Earlier that morning, they'd crossed the saddle of a small mountain range and were heading for another sierra growing taller ahead of them on the shimmering southern horizon.

A half hour later, they passed along the edge of a giant, round crater, a good hundred yards in diameter and no doubt carved by a falling meteor—Spurr had seen other such sites in Arizona and New Mexico Territories—and entered an area of scalloped lava rock rising from both sides of the trail, like the totems of some alien civilization.

A large hawk was perched on one, about fifty yards off the trail to their right, fluffing its feathers and watching them stonily. When they'd ridden well beyond the bird, it screeched behind them, and Fire Eyes instantly drew back on her reins, frowning at the oddly shaped formations tilting around her, some no taller than her horse, some a hundred feet high and serving as a pedestal for others.

Spurr glanced at the Yaqui queen and drew rein, frowning. "What is it?"

She looked around nervously, dark eyes darting about in their sockets, lines of consternation cutting across her forehead. She stiffened as her gaze held on something off the trail to their left. She had just started to swing her rifle down off her shoulder when a voice said in Spanish, "Hold it right there, or we gun you both where you sit!"

Spurr followed the man's voice as well as Fire Eyes's

gaze to an H-shaped formation not far from the trail. The man was staring between the two upper bars of the H and aiming an old Civil War model Springfield Trapdoor rifle at Spurr and Fire Eyes. He wore no hat, and his black hair was cut in a straight line over the top of his forehead.

He shouted orders in Spanish, and suddenly the rocks were raining men dressed in dusty, dove-gray uniforms and wearing wagon-wheel sombreros. They all held old rifles and had pistols on their hips in covered black holsters. Some wore two or three cartridge belts around their waists; some wore them crisscrossed on their chests. They were a ragged lot, dirty and sweaty, red-faced from the sun, but the uniforms they wore were of the rural Mexican police— Rurales.

"Ah, shit," Spurr said tightly, stretching his lips with a frustrated grin.

As men scrambled around them from both sides of the trail, the man who'd spoken came down out of the rocks— a stocky gent a little under six feet, in his late thirties or early forties, clean-shaven, and looking all business. The others—there were ten Rurales in all, a few looking well under twenty and fidgeting around inside their too-large uniforms—stood within ten feet of Spurr and Fire Eyes, cocking and aiming their rifles from their shoulders.

Spurr offered a stiff smile and raised his hands to his shoulders, palms out. He'd been afraid he'd run into a Rurale, so he had his story all written out in his head.

"*Hola*, amigo," he said now in his limited Spanish to the man striding toward him, looking angry. "No need for all this pomp and circumstance. I'm a lawman, like yourself." He'd seen the lieutenant's bars on the shoulders of the stocky gent's gray tunic, one pocket of which was torn and hanging. "Name's Spurr Morgan—Deputy United States Marshal Spurr Morgan out of Denver, Colorado Territory. I'm here on official business, and don't worry, it's all been given the stamp of your own government in Mexico City. You probably ain't gotten word yet, but I'm sure a letter's in the mail."

He chuckled, trying to put the serious-looking officer at ease. It didn't work. The man stopped just off Cochise's left wither, scrutinizing Spurr through one narrowed eye before narrowing the other at Fire Eyes. He canted his head to one side, frowning, then strode slowly around Spurr's horse to stop in front of the cream stallion that was nodding its head nervously.

The man said nothing for nearly a minute. Fire Eyes stared straight ahead, chin lifted proudly. She could have been sitting there by railroad tracks, waiting for an overdue train.

Finally, the lieutenant stiffened and took one step back. "Fire Eyes!" His tone was not so much recognition as accusation. He raised his rifle to his hip and hung his lower jaw in shock. "*Si, si*—it is you, isn't it? My god, what are you doing out here with this old gringo?"

Fire Eyes only let her gaze flick to the man before hardening her jaws and staring straight off over the heads of the men aiming their rifles at her.

Spurr felt as though he were sitting on a mound of fire ants.

"Fire Eyes here," he said, gesturing at the woman beside him, "is my official guide. I'm after a passel of bank robbers trailing here from Arizona, and she was kind enough to offer her services. Now, I'm sure you have a bone or two to pick with the little gal, but she's promised to mend her ways, so I do hope you'll see fit to gaze beyond them bones for now. This is an important mission I'm on, and like I said, I do have the blessings of *both* our countries."

He couldn't let the Rurales know what he was really doing here, as he wasn't sure how closely allied they were with the Federales led by General Cuesta.

The stocky lieutenant backed up another few steps, shifting his rifle between Spurr and Fire Eyes, his eyes shiny now with what appeared to be both fear and exhilaration. His men's eyes looked the same, the young ones riveted on Fire Eyes, Spurr figured, not only because of her comely figure but because of her notorious status here in Sonora. If he hadn't realized it before, he realized it now—she was a living legend, albeit a feared one.

And would likely be quite a trophy for the man who could throw a loop around her.

"You first, senorita," the lieutenant said tensely, his nostrils expanding and contracting anxiously, "throw your weapons down. One at a time. Slowly. I warn you to try none of your Yaqui tricks! I assure you that neither I nor my well-trained platoon will hesitate to blow you off your handsome stallion!"

Spurr said with a defeated air, "Now, look here, Lieutenant . . ."

"Silence!"

The lieutenant held his rifle between Spurr and Fire Eyes. His men were sweating and shifting their rifles between both their targets.

Fire Eyes sat her saddle stiffly, staring into the far distance even as she let her rifle slide off her shoulder and hit the ground with a rattling thud. Curling her upper lip, she lifted her quiver lanyard up over her head, and let it and her bow drop to the ground near Spurr.

She continued staring into the distance with mute disdain, as if these diseased dogs were not worthy of her gaze.

The lieutenant, staring at her almost fondly, smiled. "The rest!"

Fire Eyes pressed her lips together then lifted her right moccasin and slid her bowie knife out of the sheath sewn into the top. She dropped the knife near her rifle, then sat stiffly, haughtily unmoving once again.

"Let me assure you, Senorita el Diablo, that my men will search you thoroughly, and if you are hiding any more weapons, you will be dragged rather than allowed to ride to our outpost in Cala del Coyote."

The lieutenant turned to Spurr but said nothing. He was beginning to fully realize whom he'd just captured, and he was feeling smug. He merely flicked his glassy eyes at Spurr's pistol commandingly. The old lawman, knowing the time for talking was over, that he'd met his match and was badly outnumbered, slipped the Starr from its sheath and let it drop to the ground.

Sliding his bowie knife from the sheath on his left hip, he dropped the knife down beside his pistol. He shucked his Winchester, but rather than drop the old, prized weapon, and possibly break the stock or foul the workings, he tossed it out to the Rurale lieuenant, who caught it with his free hand and lowered the butt to the ground.

The lieutenant smiled, shifting his eyes between his prisoners and thrusting his chin up, shoulders back officially. "I am Lieutenant Carlos Nova, and you are both under arrest—you, sir, for aiding a fugitive of Mexican justice, and you, senorita, for many, many things over the past five years, including burning rail lines, common stock thievery, and the wanton killing of Mexican citizens."

His smile brightened but somehow also grew more sinister. "Let me assure you that both crimes are punishable by death by firing squad! *Sooner rather than later!*"

20

"EASY!" SPURR SAID as one of the Rurales grabbed Fire Eyes's left arm and jerked her out of her saddle. She hit the ground hard on her shoulder and hip but didn't let out a peep. She merely rolled over and climbed to her knees.

Spurr, who had just stepped down from Cochise's back, saw the lieutenant's fist coming toward him too late. The fist slammed into his belly, and he dropped to his knees, sucking air and cursing.

Nova ordered three men to hold their rifles on Spurr, and then he walked over to where two other Rurales pulled Fire Eyes to her feet and prodded her over to the lieutenant, who grinned as he swept the Yaqui queen's body with his lusty eyes.

"Hold her arms," he told his men.

Each man grabbed an arm. Fire Eyes stared straight ahead, proud as an eagle, and didn't make a sound while Nova ran his hands across her breasts and belly and then down her legs, ostensibly looking for more weapons, which he did not find. He ran his hands over her again, grunting,

glaring at her, wanting to evoke some response. But Fire
Eyes held her jaws taut, eyes cool, ignoring him.

"Did you like that, *puta* bitch?" the lieutenenat spat out,
holding his face six inches from hers. "Did I arouse the
whore in you, uh?"

Finally, he evoked a response. She jerked her head to
face him, and spit a gob of saliva on his lips. He jerked back,
running a tunic sleeve across his mouth, then drew his left
arm back over his right shoulder before swinging the back
of his hand hard across Fire Eyes's left cheek. The blow
threw her back violently, and her hair danced in her eyes,
but the two men holding her arms held her upright.

"That's enough, goddamn your sorry ass!" Spurr said
through gritted teeth, still convulsing against the lieutenant's
blow to his solar plexus and trying to draw a full breath.

The two young corporals in front of him edged their rifles closer to his head, threatening. Spurr cursed them both
in Spanish, no longer caring what happened, a younger
man's fury taking over. Fire Eyes was a cold-blooded killer
in the Mexican's eyes, true enough, but in Spurr's view she
had a right to be, just as the American Indians had a right to
their own offenses, though Spurr had fought against them in
his prime and had killed some, though not without regret.
They had been warriors fighting one side of a bloody war,
and he'd fought on the other. It was the same in Mexico.

"If he makes another sound," Lieutenant Nova ordered
the men holding their rifles on Spurr, "shoot him." To the two
men holding Fire Eyes, he said, "Put her on her horse. Tie her
tight—hands and ankles."

An older sergeant with long, grizzled gray hair falling
down from his sweat-stained straw sombrero walked over,
and with the back of his hand slid a wing of Fire Eyes's
black hair away from her face. "What do you say we have a
little siesta, Lieutenant?" The sergeant ran his long, hawkish
nose against the girl's neck, sniffing her lustily. "She's so
damn quiet—I bet I could get a scream out of her!"

He and the other men laughed.

Nova shoved the man aside. "No, Pablo. Many a man has

died howling from a hideous, burning disease after bedding a Yaqui whore such as this." He looked at the two younger men holding Fire Eyes. "Tie her now. Tie them both to their horses, and then we head out. If we ride hard, we should reach the outpost by sundown, and I can send a rider to fetch Major Dominguez from Hermosillo. He will be very pleased at our conquest and will invite half the Rurale force in Sonora to the firing squad! Hurry, now! Move, I said!"

"Get your goddamn hands off me," Spurr said through gritted teeth at the Rurale trying to pull him to his feet. The man stepped back and aimed his rifle at Spurr's head. Spurr heaved himself up and, as Fire Eyes was literally thrown up onto her cream's back while one Rurale held the horse's reins, Spurr grabbed his saddle horn and pulled himself into the leather.

His and Fire Eyes's hands were tied to their saddle horns. Their ankles were tied to their stirrups. Several Rurales had been sent to fetch the others' horses, and soon they were all mounted up and heading southwest across the desert, Spurr's and Fire Eyes's horses led by their bridle reins.

Spurr ground his teeth in frustration. Likely, this had blown his chance at taking a crack at the gunrunners. Fire Eyes was probably thinking the same thing, though it was impossible to tell anything she was thinking by the stoic set to her features, black hair bouncing on her shoulders. He had a feeling she felt the disgrace of their situation, as well. As did Spurr. How had they ridden so easily into that trap?

Lieutenant Nova set a hectic pace, riding at the head of the ten-man pack. They crossed a low divide and forded a river—probably the same river the gunrunners would be following through Fiero Canyon, Spurr mused, absently watching the water splash up across his stirrups—and then followed a climbing valley floor over another divide. Finally, they turned onto a wagon road finely churned by heavy traffic. Ahead, sprawling down the side of a dun, rocky slope, lay a good-sized village of white adobes glowing in the late-day light.

Smoke from cook fires wafted over the slope. Dogs

barked. Somewhere, a baby cried. Chickens scattered as the procession entered the town and followed the main street up a hill and curving to the right. Peasants sprawled before cafés and cantinas, indolent in the time between siesta and the rollicking Mexican evening.

Nova reined his grulla mustang to a halt before a sprawling, brush-roofed, three-story adobe. The flags of both Mexico and the state of Sonora flapped from the same wooden pole in the front yard. Wicker chairs sat on an adobe porch mounted on stones, and on the two balconies above.

As Cochise stopped in the street before the Rurale headquarters, Spurr looked around. They'd attracted a growing crowd; brown-faced peasants in their traditional white pajamas or deerskin breeches and serapes were wandering toward the headquarters with murmuring interest. They'd no doubt recognized the legendary Fire Eyes and were coming in for a closer look at the Yaqui demoness.

Again, frustration clawed at Spurr. His only hope was the kid, Cuno Massey, but what could the younker do against nearly a dozen Rurales? Spurr found himself hoping he wouldn't try. He had a feeling that once word had spread of Fire Eyes's capture and the ensuing celebration he and she would be stood up against a wall of the Rurale headquarters and shot without further ado.

Death in Mexico. Well, why not Mexico? He'd hoped for a grave where someone could find it and maybe toss a few wild roses on it every now and then and build up the rocks to keep the coyotes from dragging his bones around.

Damned foolish mistake he'd made, riding into that trap. Chief Marshal Henry Brackett should have forced him into retirement several years ago.

As a small crowd continued to gather, the Rurales dismounted, and Spurr and Fire Eyes were cut loose of their saddles. Their cuffs were kept on, and Nova led them up the porch of what appeared an old hotel.

The grizzled Rurale sergeant, Pablo, followed Fire Eyes, pressing an old Remington revolver against the small of her back. Spurr followed the sergeant, himself followed by three other Rurales, all now aiming their own rusty Remingtons at him while the rest of the men milled amongst the crowd, sticking their chests out, gloating, or began leading away the sweaty, dusty horses.

The inside of the Rurale headquarters was an old hotel lobby, with a long desk to the right, flanked by pigeonholes and key rings. There were stairs at the rear of the high-ceilinged room, several tables, desks, and chairs, and four strap-iron cages against the wall to the left.

"Right this way if you please," said the lieutenant, grinning over his shoulder at the Yaqui queen as he wended his way amongst the desks, stumbling over a sandbox pocked with brown tobacco quids.

One of the men behind Spurr prodded the old lawman painfully with his rifle barrel. "You don't stop that," he said, glaring at the younker, "I'm gonna take it away from you and shove it up your ass."

The long-faced kid looked at him blankly, curling up his mouth corners, from beneath the wide brim of his straw sombrero.

Spurr had just turned his head forward when the sergeant pressed his nose against the back of Fire Eyes's neck. They were just passing a cluttered desk with, amongst other things, a clear bottle and a glass on it. Fire Eyes wheeled around in a blur of fast motion, grabbed the bottle off the desk with her cuffed hand, broke it over the desk's edge, and, screaming like a bobcat, rammed the broken bottle into the sergeant's belly.

The sergeant yowled and doubled over, drawing his hands over his gut. Fire Eyes drove her right knee into his face, and as the man flew back toward Spurr, blood geysering from his broken nose, the old lawman wheeled, shoved the pistol out of his back, and slammed his cuffed fists as hard as he could against the corporal's face.

He heard the kid's jaw crack as the kid squealed, dropped the Remy, and staggered sideways. Hearing Fire Eyes raging behind him, furniture breaking, and the lieutenant shouting, Spurr threw himself to the floor, rolling off a shoulder and trying to claw up the corporal's revolver with his cuffed hands. He'd just gotten the revolver up and was about to cock it when several gray-uniformed bodies barreled onto him. A rifle butt appeared, growing quickly larger as it careened toward his head.

Then a shattering tidal wave of pain washed over him, and the room went dark and silent for he didn't know how long before a loud clang invaded his tender brain. He opened his eyes slightly, stretching his lips back from his teeth to find himself in one of the cages. The young Rurale who'd been prodding him with the pistol was turning a key in the lock of the cage door, glaring at Spurr.

The kid's right eye was swelling shut.

Behind him, two men were carrying the sergeant whom Fire Eyes had nearly gutted toward the stone steps at the room's rear. The sergeant's face was a bloody mess. His moans echoed loudly off the cavernous adobe walls.

At the same time, Lieutenant Nova was poking a Schofield pistol through the door of the jail cage next to Spurr's, in which Fire Eyes lay flat on her back on the cracked stone floor, arms and legs akimbo. Her lips were cut and swollen, and she had a nasty bruise and another, deeper cut on her left eyebrow. Her vest was torn, exposing nearly all of one tan breast.

Her chest rose and fell heavily as she breathed.

"I would drill a hole through your worthless Yaqui head right now if I did not want to make a spectacle of you later!" the lieutenant shouted. He depressed the Schofield's hammer, pulled the pistol out of the door, and holstered it. He turned to Spurr.

"Big Yankee lawman. How big you feel now, uh, Yankee lawman?"

He laughed, turned to the two corporals flanking him, shouted orders at them in Spanish to sit in chairs in front of the cages and to not take their eyes off either one of the prisoners until they were relieved. Then he walked over to the desk from which Fire Eyes had pulled the bottle, sank down in his swivel chair, and laced his hands behind his head with the air of a man most satisfied with his day's accomplishments.

Spurr sat up, sucking a breath through his teeth. He reached into a shirt pocket, found the little burlap pouch in which he kept his nitroglycerin tablets, and popped one in his mouth. He rolled the pill around on his tongue and looked at Nova staring at him smugly.

"Don't s'pose I could get a shot of whiskey to wash my pill down with?"

Nova only stared at him.

"Figured as much," Spurr said and swallowed the pill dry.

21

A LEANING WOODEN sign appeared along the side of the trail, beside a leafless sycamore. Cuno gigged Renegade up closer until he could see it in the failing evening light: CALA DEL COYOTE.

Cuno looked up the trail at the shimmering yellow lantern lights. The hillside across which the pueblo was sprawled was cloaked in darkness, but he could make out the lights and the pale adobe shacks nestled in rocks and brush. Up higher on the hill was the obligatory church with bulging bell tower.

The smell of a cookfire threaded the still early evening air. He could hear the murmur of a crowd from somewhere up the hill, somewhere in the heart of the town.

Cuno lowered his gaze to the trail freshly pocked with the shod hoofprints of a dozen or so horses—the same horses he'd been following since Spurr and Fire Eyes's tracks had been absorbed by them. Where the tracks had intersected, there'd been many sets of boot tracks, including Spurr's and Fire Eyes's moccasin tracks, and the scuff marks that indicated a tussle.

Cuno had no idea who Spurr and the Yaqui queen had

ridden off with, but there was no doubt they hadn't gone willingly. They hadn't headed southeast, toward the canyon where they'd intended to attack the gunrunners, but to the southwest. And over the past few hours, they'd likely missed their opportunity to follow through with Fire Eyes's plan of ambushing the gunrunners with a rockslide.

No, Spurr and Fire Eyes had been taken here, to Cala del Coyote, against their will.

By whom?

Cuno touched spurs to Renegade's flanks and rode slowly up the gradually curving hill. He looked around for a place to hide his horse, as a gringo riding alone into town on the fine skewbald paint would draw unwanted attention, and found a nest of rocks around an abandoned brick stable. He gigged Renegade inside the crumbling stone walls, dismounted, and threw the reins over a fallen ceiling beam. He started to slide his Winchester from its saddle boot, then stopped.

The rifle would look conspicuous. He'd scout the town first, try to locate Spurr and Fire Eyes, then return for the rifle later.

He gave Renegade some water out of his hat, then patted the horse's neck and headed up into the town, staying off the main trail but taking footpaths that zigzagged around buildings. He slipped between two adobes facing what appeared to be the main drag and stopped at the alley mouth.

A wide dirt street opened before him. Adobes of all shapes and sizes, some with broad gaps between them, stood along both sides of the street. There were a few people milling around at this end of the town, but he could see more lights up the street on his right. Voices rose from that direction, as well—the collective, low roar of a celebrating crowd.

Cuno headed in that direction, moving slowly, staying to the intermittent boardwalks and galleries, smelling the astringent liquor brewed in these parts, the pepper strings drying on porch posts, and the spicy menudo emanating from a café on the other side of the street. He passed an alley

mouth and heard the grunts of a *puta* and her jake going at
it like dogs beneath some outside stairs.

Cuno walked on, feeling more and more conspicuous in
his gringo trail garb when everyone else here was dressed
either in peasant pajamas with sandals or the colorful attire
of the vaquero, with broad felt sombreros often gaudily
stitched in red or silver. He could have used a sweeping
black mustache, as well.

Keeping to the shadows, he approached the area teaming
with activity—cantinas lit up, women laughing, and men
talking loudly. At the center of the activity was a large,
barrack-like, brush-roofed structure with a flagpole in the
front yard. Men in dove-gray uniforms milled about with
women on the front porch as well as on the two upper-story
balconies.

Peasants were moving around the front yard or sitting
slumped on the front gallery steps, sharing bottles or wooden
cups or standing before the place, gazing into the two broad
front windows left of the gallery and chattering and gesturing animatedly.

Cuno stood in the shadows against a wooden wall, heart
thudding. He knew right away he'd located Spurr and Fire
Eyes. Cuno knew little of Mexico, but he was aware that the
gray-uniformed men were officers in the rural Mexican police force. Fire Eyes was doubtlessly an attractive trophy in
more ways than one.

He sqatted down on his heels and rubbed his bottom lip
with his index finger, staring at the two front windows on
the other side of the street. Somehow, he had to know for
sure.

He'd been hearing loud snores since he'd approached
what he figured to be a livery barn. Now he straightened
and turned to stare into a break between the barn and a low,
stone cantina inside of which a girl was laughing uproari-
ously, nearly drowning out the strains of a mandolin.

About twenty feet away from the alley mouth, two figures slouched in the shadows, both snoring, one snoring
raucously. One sat with his back against the cracked can-

tina wall, arms crossed, chin to his chest. On his head was a ragged, low-crowned sombrero with a braided eagle feather band.

Cuno crouched over the man, carefully lifted the hat from his head and set it on the ground. Less carefully, but not waking the thoroughly soused Mexican, he removed the man's serape and dropped it over his own shoulders. He left his own hat on the ground, donned the ragged sombrero, letting the hide thong dangle beneath his chin, and stepped cautiously out of the alley mouth into the street.

Keeping his head down, he made his way as inconcpicuously as he could through the crowd, staggering a little as though drunk, and after a time made his way into the yard where the smell of tequila and beer and strong Mexican tobacco was especially thick, as was the perfume of several *putas* lounging about with the celebrating Rurales. He shouldered between two peasants speaking in hushed voices while peering almost fearfully through the front window nearest the gallery and cast a glance through the flyspecked window himself.

The room beyond was large and square with a high ceiling, with several desks and four jail cages to the left. Two uniformed Rurales sat facing the cages in straight-backed chairs, rifles across their laps. In the cage nearest the front wall, Spurr sat on the edge of a cot, leaning forward, elbows on his knees, smoking and eyeing the two guards derisively. He looked especially haggard, frustrated, defeated. His lips were moving, but Cuno couldn't hear what he was saying though he doubted it was complimentary.

In the cage next to him, Fire Eyes sat on a cot, her back against the wall, one knee up and a wrist draped almost casually over it. Her lips were swollen, and there was a nasty gash on her right brow. She stared straight ahead in stoic defiance of her incarceration.

Several times since Cuno had begun milling about the crowd, he'd heard "Ojos del Fuega"—"Fire Eyes"—or simply "Fuega" spoken in hushed, shocked tones. He jumped now as loud pops rose behind him, and he whipped his head

around, hand closing over his pistol butt, to see two silhouetted figures stepping back from a line of crackling, flashing
firecrackers.

The men and whores laughed and clapped. Someone
threw out another line of sizzling firecrackers, and Cuno
used the diversion to make his slow but purposeful escape
down the north side of the street.

He crossed the street, slipped into the break between two
buildings, and made his way back to his horse. Pensively,
his heart beating slowly but insistently, he shucked his Winchester from the saddle boot. He gave Renegade another
soothing pat as the horse sniffed the serape suspiciously,
then stepped over the crumbling stable wall and made his
way back toward the Rurale headquarters.

He moved into the break between the stable and the
cantina, slumped down near the two deeply unconscious
Mexicans, stretched his legs out, crossed his ankles, and
lay the rifle across his lap. From here, he had a good view
of the street and the celebrating crowd.

Someone fired a pistol into the air, and someone shouted
something in Spanish that Cuno couldn't understand.

They'd likely celebrate all night.

Cuno dropped his chin and lowered the sombrero over
his eyes, waiting them out.

22

CUNO ONLY HALF slept, keeping one ear cocked, gauging the tides of the celebration that rose and fell with the endless hours. The cold seeped up out of the ground and into his butt and legs and back, and he felt his muscles tighten and turn to stone.

A couple of times he stood and walked around before slumping down against the stable once more. He had to keep an eye on the Rurale headquarters, waiting for a chance to try to spring Spurr and Fire Eyes. It probably couldn't be done, but he had to try.

He hadn't realized he'd slept before something woke him, and he jerked his head up suddenly with a grunt. The silence around him now was startling, and he swung his gaze across the alley mouth to the street. A man's voice sounded. Hoof thuds rose, growing louder until, in the predawn dimness, five riders angled into Cuno's view from the right and drew their horses up before the hitchrack fronting the Rurale headquaters sitting dark and silent on the other side of the street.

The newcomers all wore dove-gray uniforms and high-topped black boots. The beefy lead rider had some decorations on his tunic, and though it was hard to see in the dim light, Cuno thought he looked older.

The men spoke in Spanish as they tied their horses. There were four flanking the lead rider, who was much heavier than the others, his belly bulging almost obscenely. He wore two red stripes down the side of his uniform pants. As he and the others crossed the gallery and entered the headquarters, a dull yellow glow grew in one of the second-story windows.

Cuno climbed to his feet, silently berating himself for not waking earlier, when he might have had a decent chance to pluck Spurr and Fire Eyes from their trap. Now he grabbed his rifle, looked at the two Mexicans passed out where they had been before but snoring much more quietly now, and whipped off the serape and sombrero and dropped them down beside the man he'd borrowed them from. He picked up his own hat and donned it as he hurried out to the street, where he stopped and scowled at the Rurale headquarters.

Several windows glowed now, including the two large ones at the front. Cuno could see shadows moving around inside. Loud laughter thundered, along with the sound of a man clapping his hands once.

Cuno looked around. Seeing no one else on the street, he jogged across to the headquarters and pressed his shoulder against the front wall, left of the two front windows.

The voices continued, and now Cuno saw a stocky, middle-aged, black-haired lieutenant in the main room with the men who'd just entered, and a couple more, younger Rurales. The lieutenant was yawning and tucking his shirt into his pants while the fat newcomer, who wore a colonel's insignia on his tunic shoulders, stood before the door of the cage holding Fire Eyes, his boots spread, hands clasped behind his back. Cuno didn't understand enough Spanish to know what the man was saying, but he could tell by his demeanor he was very pleased by the capture of the Yaqui queen.

Cuno couldn't see much of Spurr because of the Rurales blocking his view. But as the fat man waved a hand at the cell door, and one of the younger Rurales moved forward with a key, Spurr leapt to his feet. "Keep your pig hands off her, Colonel!"

Three young Rurales aimed their rifles at Spurr while another opened the cell door, and the colonel, his fat face stretched with a lusty, oily smile, stepped back away from the door to let the younger men enter. Four younger Rurales bounded into the cell, as though into a lion's cage, and fairly hurled themselves at the cot.

Fire Eyes's head came up, fists and moccasined feet flying. She screamed like a trapped puma, fighting the young Rurales for all she was worth. As the colonel threw his head back, laughing, Cuno ducked below both windows and took long strides to the end of the gallery, stepped over the rail, threw one of the headquarters' two front doors open, and stepped inside.

The four Rurales had managed to each grab an arm or a leg and were hauling Fire Eyes out of her cell while she squealed and bucked and tossed her head furiously. The fat colonel and the dark-haired lieutenant were turned sideways to Cuno, their heads swiveling to watch the young Rurales carry the girl toward the stairs at the back of the room. What they had in mind was obvious.

Spurr had his face pressed up to the door of his cell, hands wrapped around the bars, shaking the door as if to rip it off its hinges as he barked rabid insults at the girl's attackers.

He was the first to slide his eyes toward Cuno. He stopped shouting and shaking his cell door, and as his gaze met Cuno's, a faint smile etched itself on his mouth.

The fat colonel, talking loudly with the lieutenant, turned his head slightly toward Cuno, started to turn away, then turned back again, his dark eyes incredulous. As the lieutenant followed his gaze, Cuno loudly racked a shell into his Winchester's breech and pressed the stock against his right hip.

That stopped everyone in the room, including the four Rurales hauling the struggling queen toward the stairs. Aside from Fire Eyes, everyone stopped talking. Then, as she turned her head toward Cuno, she stopped squealing and fighting.

Silence hung as heavy as a wagon-sized boulder suspended by a thin rope over the room.

Cuno's Winchester broke the silence, the resounding roar causing the whole room to jump and the colonel to scream and fly backward and sideways into the lieutenant, who took the next bullet just under his left ear and went down hard under the weight of the heart-shot colonel. Cuno cocked and fired the Winchester from his hip, squinting against the puffing powder smoke, the empty casings careening from the smoking breech.

The Rurales screamed and wailed and stumbled or twisted around or were punched back into desks or walls, dropping their rifles or pistols and making agonized faces as blood oozed from their tunics. The four men holding Fire Eyes had dropped her as soon as the shooting had started and reached for the pistols on their hips. They'd been the easiest to take down.

They were piled up around Fire Eyes now, two dead, two wailing and writhing as they bled. One of the others, lying back down over the lieutenant's desk, was flopping his arms and legs as though trying to stand. Cuno lowered his empty rifle, shifted it to his left hand, palmed his Colt .45, and silenced the man on the desk with a shot to his temple.

Quickly, Cuno stepped over the dead men and around the swirling blood pools and grabbed the keys where one of the dead Rurales had fallen. Fire Eyes had scrambled onto one knee, her brown eyes red and wild behind her hair, and glanced around at the dead men and then at Cuno. She still looked trapped and feral, breathing hard.

Cuno said, "Watch the stairs."

Then he turned to Spurr's cell and poked the key in the lock as the old lawman gazed at him through the bars. "Can't leave you two alone for a minute, can I?"

"I do believe I'm getting old, kid."

"Hell, you were old twenty years ago."

Cuno jerked the door open, and Spurr ran over to an unlocked rack on the front wall where his rifle had been placed and from the barrel of which his shell belt, knife, and Starr .44 dangled. Gunfire exploded behind him, and he whipped around to see Fire Eyes crouching at the bottom of the stairs, one of the Rurales' pistols in her hand, a fresh smoke cloud around her head.

Two half-dressed Rurales were rolling down the stairs, lifeless as dolls.

As Fire Eyes grabbed her own rifle, which had been leaning with her arrow and bow quiver against the lieutenant's desk, and slung their lanyards over her shoulders, Cuno ran to the door and looked up and down the street.

"All clear. I'm guessin' your horses are in the barn across the street. I would have saddled 'em, but the night got away from me."

Spurr was hastily buckling his shell belt. "Join the celebration, did you? It was quite the fandango—wouldn't have minded bein' part of it myself."

There was a flurry of footsteps and voices from above them, and dust sifted from the rafters as the other Rurales scrambled around, dressing, some moving toward the stairs and shouting in Spanish that echoed around the stony stairwell. Fire Eyes gave a harsh Spanish retort and fired her own rifle from her hip, the bullets plunking the wall of the second-story landing.

Fire Eyes laughed raucously then spat more lashing Spanish. That silenced the men upstairs, likely convincing them that descending the stairs wouldn't be a good idea.

Spurr had moved up beside Cuno and was looking around the Rurales' five nervously dancing horses at the street, where the dawn shadows were slowly fading. No one moved. Bird chirps were the only sounds.

"Let's get out of here," Spurr said, glancing over his shoulder at Fire Eyes and then crossing the gallery and dropping into the street.

He and Cuno walked cautiously across the main drag, turning and waving their rifles around, keeping an eye on the second and third floors of the Rurale headquarters. Fire Eyes followed close behind them, and as Spurr opened the barn's left side door, Cuno said, "My horse is back along the trail. I'll cover you while you saddle yours."

As Fire Eyes slipped into the barn behind Spurr, Cuno dropped to a knee and aimed his Winchester at the ominously silent headquarters. Behind him, he could hear the squawk of tack and the clink of buckles as Spurr and Fire Eyes quickly rigged their mounts.

A third-story shutter inched back away from a window, and a rifle barrel angled out of it. Cuno waited a half second, until he could see the silhouette of a head, and then he fired two shots quickly. The man gave a low grunt and disappeared while his rifle dropped out of the window and clattered onto the second-floor balcony.

Cuno heard the clomp of hooves behind him. Spurr and Fire Eyes were leading their horses up behind him, Cochise prancing and shaking his head, the cream stallion nodding and snorting. Cuno threw the second door wide, then stepped halfway out into the street, carefully covering the headquarters with his rifle as Spurr and Fire Eyes swung up into their saddles.

"Come on, kid," Spurr said, glancing anxiously at the headquarters while throwing out a hand toward Cuno.

"He rides with me," Fire Eyes said haughtily, throwing out her own right hand.

Cuno quickly glanced from Fire Eyes to Spurr then back again, then grabbed the girl's hand as he leapt up onto the stallion's rump behind her. Spurr chuckled and touched heels to Cochise's flanks, and the big roan and the handsome cream galloped off along the twisting, still-silent main street, the thuds of their hooves echoing like pistol shots in the silent early moring.

When they came to the stable where Cuno had left Renegade, Cuno slipped off the cream's back, led Renegade out of his confines, and mounted up. Spurr and Fire Eyes were already galloping down the trail and out of the town.

Well rested, though fidgety from his night in the stable,

Renegade had no trouble catching up to them. Fire Eyes overtook Spurr and said, "Follow me!" She angled off the left side of the trail and into the rocky desert between two sandstone ridges turning rose in the morning sunrise.

A javelina squealed and ran into a mesquite thicket.

"Where we goin'?" Spurr said, reining Cochise along behind her.

Cuno turned Renegade in the same direction, nudging his heels against the stallion's flanks. They were heading nearly directly west now, the sky lightening to their left.

Fire Eyes said over her shoulder, "We are going to need help keeping those guns and dynamite out of Cuesta's hands." She smiled shrewdly. "And I know just the people to help."

Spurr scowled and glanced at Cuno galloping off his left stirrup. "How come I'm feelin' like I just jumped out of the fryin' pan into the fire?"

23

AGAIN, CUNO AND Spurr had trouble keeping up with the wild-assed Yaqui queen. She and her horse seemed tireless. There were no springs out here—at least none that Cuno and Spurr knew about, and none that the queen stopped at—so several times they stopped to pour water into their hats for their horses and to take a few spare sips themselves.

Fire Eyes was staying at least a hundred yards ahead of them, and sometimes that gap opened to a quarter mile. By midday Cuno was beginning to believe that the Yaqui queen and her tireless horse were supernatural. She slowed her pace only to make sure that Cuno and Spurr were still behind her.

Up one canyon and down another they traveled, in some of the most waterless, rugged country Cuno had ever seen. If there was anything growing on any of the knobs and ridges they were riding between, he couldn't see it. The only life was the occasional hawk or small flock of turkey buzzards crowding some moldering animal corpse.

Around one thirty, judging by the sun, Cuno and Spurr galloped over a gravelly knob and saw the queen standing beside her cream about fifty yards ahead, at the entrance to a narrow canyon opening between two towering sandstone ridges. She was holding a bandanna out to the horse, rubbing its lips.

"I'll be damned if she and that damn creature aren't tired!" Spurr said as he and Cuno continued on down the knob.

"Don't get your hopes up."

They reined up before the queen, who tossed her head toward the narrow entrace to the canyon behind her, then reined the cream around and batted her moccasined heels against its sides. "Stay close now!" she said with an air of frustration.

She did not ride hard but kept the cream at a spanking trot. A hundred yards into the narrow defile, the wind- and water-sculpted sand rising to their horses' fetlocks, she reined up suddenly and waved her arm sideways across the top of her head. Cuno followed her gaze to the top of a finger of solid rock. A figure stood there, silhouetted against the bright desert sky. Cuno could see tan breeches, a red sash, and a red bandanna holding long black hair tight against the brave's head. He held a rifle in one hand down by his side, and after a few seconds he lifted it straight up above his head.

He touched his sash, turned to face the opposite direction, and then raised his other hand. The sun flashed off the signal mirror in his hand.

Fire Eyes heeled the barb on up the meandering canyon, keeping the horse to a trot. Cuno and Spurr flanked her, looking around warily. Cuno felt the hair on the back of his neck stand up. He sensed a primal menace. The fear was like hot lead seeping into his bones. He resisted the urge to reach forward and slide his Winchester from his saddle boot, instinctively feeling eyes on him and knowing that the move could get him killed.

He looked at Spurr. The old lawman was riding stiff-backed, grinning as though he were watching dancing girls undress on the stage of some frontier opera house.

"What the hell are you smiling about?" Cuno asked, unable to mask his annoyance.

"I always grin like that when I'm about to load my drawers."

As they wended their way through the canyon, Cuno saw several more armed pickets standing amongst the rocks. They watched expressionlessly as the Yaqui queen and her gringo partners trotted past them.

Finally, they rounded a curve and the canyon opened into a large, pie-shaped bowl with a creek running through it diagonally. Brush huts were scattered along both sides of the creek, and smoke from several outdoor cook fires rose. There were several large rope corrals containing a colorful selection of mustangs amongst the groves lining the creek.

Here and there, animal hides were stretched between standing poles. Bulky, raisin-faced old women ambled amongst the huts and the fires and the stretched hides that several were in the midst of curing. Small children ran amongst them.

As Fire Eyes reined the cream to a stop beside a large jacale partly dug into the side of a low, sandy hill, an old man stepped out of the hut. He wore a breechclout, fur moccasins, and a wolf fur cape, with a soiled blue bandanna wrapped around his forehead. He was gray and withered, his face long and angular, the sun-dried flesh hanging from his bulging cheekbones. One of his eyes was the color of an eggshell, and a jagged scar ran over the socket.

Fire Eyes sat her cream before him, and the old man scrutinized the girl's partners incredulously, lips parted to reveal only one yellow front tooth. At the same time, a younger man walked out of a jacale opposite the old man's. A small brush arbor fronted the young man's lodge. A colorfully dressed old woman sat cross-legged on a blanket on the earthen floor, sort of rocking back and forth, a striped blanket draped across her shoulders. As the young man muttered something to the old woman, he turned to dip water from an olla hanging from an arbor beam, then followed the old woman's gaze to the newcomers.

The young man, who wore a calico blouse and deerskin leggings, had Fire Eyes's fine features. He was almost as pretty, and he was long-limbed and muscular without being bulky. If he wasn't the girl's brother, Cuno thought, he was at least a cousin.

Now he dropped the dipper back into the clay water vessel and strode out from the jacale. He had a Navy revolver wedged inside the waistband of his deerskin breeches, and an antler-handled knife was sheathed low on his thigh, just above his knee.

As he approached the newcomers, he shifted his gaze from Fire Eyes to her two unlikely companions and back again, and then he said something in Yaqui—sort of spitting the words out and curling his upper lip and flaring his nostrils. His eyes shone hotly with the same passionate amber as did Fire Eyes's, and Cuno forcefully resisted the urge to reach for his Winchester.

Fire Eyes rejoined the man's exclamation in the same tone, and the argument continued for nearly five minutes, both Cuno and Spurr sitting their saddles tensely, hands glued to their thighs near their holsters but both knowing that if hell started popping, there would be no shooting their way out of this heavily guarded canyon. The young man was speaking Yaqui to Fire Eyes, but his fierce gaze was shifting rapidly between Cuno and Spurr.

Fire Eyes had the last guttural word, leaning out over the cream's left wither. The young man then turned to the old man and shouted something, waving one arm, but the old man did not respond. He turned and shuffled back into his jacale. Meanwhile, a crowd of old and young women and small children and several braves the young man's age had gathered in a semicircle around the strangers.

They regarded the white men with bald disdain.

Finally, the young man whom Cuno took to be Fire Eyes's brother wheeled and stomped back into his own jacale.

Fire Eyes turned to her guests and said with the anger of her recent exchange still burning in her eyes. "You will be welcome here." She jerked her gaze toward the creek. "Make your camp by the stream. There is grass for your horses. Food will be brought to you." Then she added, even more crisply than before, as though convincing herself, "You will be welcome here."

"Well, it's good to know we're welcome here," Cuno said as he and Spurr rode past several jacales and staring children toward the creek. "Especially since I don't reckon I've ever felt *less* welcome anywhere. And I've been unwelcome a lot of places."

Spurr chuckled. "Sometimes, kid, you just gotta let go and be a tumbleweed in a cyclone." He glanced over his shoulder as Cochise picked his way through the rocks, sage, green grass clumps, and willows that widely sheathed the stream flashing in the trees just beyond. "Just the same, I know I'll be sleeping with one eye open tonight."

They dismounted near the water but let their horses cool, unsaddling them and rubbing them down, before allowing them to drink. They arranged their gear around a stone fire ring, gathered wood though most of the deadfall around them had been gleaned, and built a small fire. They were lounging around, sipping coffee and smoking quirleys as the sun sank and the canyon filled with cool shadows, when a boy of about twelve years old came through the brush with an armload of split pine and cedar.

He said nothing as he dropped the wood near the stone ring, turned, and scampered away. Later, a round-faced girl about the same age, in a doeskin dress and wearing a blue bandanna, came from the same direction with a basket covered with burlap. She shyly set the basket down near where Spurr lay against his saddle and ran back toward the heart of the Yaqui village.

Spurr lifted the basket to see two wooden bowls steaming up at him—a thin, dark stew with some kind of shredded meat in it, and white flecks of something that looked like wild onions. He handed one bowl to Cuno, then took one for himself. No spoons had been provided, so they sipped from the bowls, sitting back against their saddles and staring suspiciously down at the steaming grub.

Cuno glanced at Spurr. "Reckon they might try to poison us?"

Spurr shrugged. "What's better—dyin' by poison or starvation?" He sucked some meat and broth into his mouth, and Cuno followed suit. The broth had little flavor aside from the onion, and the meat, which must have been some kind of bird—possibly sage hen or quail—was tough and stringy, but it went down well and fast. Cuno felt rejuvenated. Spurr set his own bowl down and belched.

"Well, we ain't dead yet—so that's a good sign." He grabbed his whiskey bottle and popped the cork. "Libation?"

Cuno had just poured himself a fresh cup of coffee. "Don't mind if I do."

Spurr was splashing whiskey into Cuno's cup when Cuno spied someone moving toward them through the brush, angling away from the jacales and a remuda of mustangs frolicking in the misty, blue twilight. Fire Eyes held a clay jug to her breast. She wore a short deerskin jacket trimmed with coyote fur and deerskin leggings. Her long, straight black hair appeared freshly brushed, so that violet streaks glinted in the blue light. The cuts and bruises on her face were healing and nearly unseen in the dim light.

She moved toward the gringos' camp with her slow, rolling-hipped, insouciant stride. Her feet were as light as stardust. The beating the Rurales had given her had taken nothing out of her, Cuno was happy to see.

Both he and Spurr stood as she approached—a white man's tradition that was likely not recognized here, as she gave them both a faintly puzzled look before glancing at the whiskey bottle in Spurr's hand, and saying, "That is not a real drink." She extended the clay pot in her hands. "This is a real drink. Pulque. My father makes it."

Spurr set the bottle down, looked into the pot at the milky brew, and sniffed. The vapors made his eyes water and his throat constrict.

"Yeah," he said. "That does indeed look like a real drink."

He glanced at Cuno. "A drink to make you feel like someone drove a railroad spike through both ears . . ."

Politely, though he was not aware of the Yaqui custom concerning drink, he extended the pot to Fire Eyes. She accepted the pot, tipped it to her lips, and took a good pull before handing it back to Spurr and running the back of her hand across her mouth. Spurr drank, then, too, and his eyes bulged and watered a little, and his throat worked extra hard, but he otherwise did not make a spectacle of himself. Cuno took a sip of the brew, then, too, and after the initial punch and firey burn from lips to toes, the liquor cast a soft haze over his eyes, easing the tension in his bones and muscles.

Fire Eyes sat down on a rock on the other side of the fire. Spurr sank back against his saddle with the clay pot, and Cuno sat on a log.

"What's the plan, Fire Eyes?" he asked the girl. "We appreciate the hospitality an' all, but what're we doing here? It's obvious we ain't exactly welcome."

"That was my brother you saw earlier. Tushikinhi. It means Red Water in your language. The old man is my father, the chief of the Agave clan. I have not seen them for a time. A wedge came between us when I decided to form my own clan and to make war myself, in my own way. My father and brother were insulted . . . especially when I gained the respect of other clan chiefs."

She lifted her eyes from the fire. "But we have discussed the stolen guns and the dynamite and General Cuesta's plan for Montana del Loco Oso, and we have agreed to work together." She shifted her gaze from Cuno to Spurr. "To work together with you in defeating the gunrunners and Cuesta. We will ride from here at dawn tomorrow. I have learned from my brother that Cuesta is awaiting the guns at the foot of our sacred mountain."

"How many warriors you have?"

"Fifteen have agreed to join me, including my brother."

"That gonna be enough?"

"It should be enough if I can get into Cuesta's camp first

and kill him. The others should be much easier to kill after the general is dead."

Cuno and Spurr shared a dubious glance.

Cuno laughed at the matter-of-factness with which she espoused such a grand intention. "What makes you think you can get into Cuesta's camp and kill him before he kills you?"

"For the oldest reason in the world, *mi* amigo." Fire Eyes stared into the thickening darkness beyond Spurr. "General Cuesta is in love with me."

Cuno and Spurr just stared at the mysterious woman sitting on the other side of the fire. They were both so amazed by the information she'd just shared that they didn't hear the tread of light feet until the newcomer was only twenty yards away. Cuno turned to see a short, rounded figure in a long bear robe step into the firelight—a young woman with a heart-shaped face and freshly brushed black hair spilling over her shoulders.

"Who's this?" Spurr said, climbing to his feet a little clumsily.

"This, in your language, is Chokecherry," Fire Eyes said. "She will keep your bones warm tonight, old man."

A faint smile touched the Yaqui queen's eyes.

"Oh—no kiddin'?" Spurr said, glancing over his shoulder at Fire Eyes, tugging speculatively at his chin whiskers. "This purty little gal is gonna . . . make me happy tonight?"

"Si," said Fire Eyes, jerking her head. "Go."

Spurr accepted Chokecherry's extended hand, and then the girl, quirking a bemused smile on her down-curved, thin lipped mouth, turned and began leading Spurr away from the camp.

Cuno watched them go, then turned to Fire Eyes. He was feeling a little left out, and the liquor had loosened his tongue. "If ole Spurr gets Chokecherry," he said, glancing around, "who do I get?"

Fire Eyes rose and walked lightly around the fire on her long, supple legs. The firelight danced in her eyes and glistened off the wedge of bare skin at her midriff. She knelt down before Cuno and shook her hair back from her shoulders. Her eyes were like warm coals caressing him.

"You get me."

A hard wooden knot grew in Cuno's throat.

She started to lean toward him, and he felt himself pull back slightly, instinctively. But then she wrapped her arms around his neck and, no fire suddenly blazing in her eyes and not reaching for a sharp knife with which to gut him, touched her lips very gently to his.

"I'll be damned," he said. "You mean it."

"I do not give myself freely to any man. Only those who earn me. This morning, you earned me."

She slid the deerskin jacket off her shoulders, then opened her vest, peeled it off her shoulders, and tossed it aside. The knot in Cuno's throat grew. His pulse throbbed in his temples. He extended his hands very slowly and slid his fingers along the sides of her fine, proud breasts. She closed her hands over his, pressed them more firmly to her bosom, and tossed her head back with a heavy sigh.

Finally, she rose, spread out his blanket roll, and lay her deerskin jacket down on top of it. Cuno kicked out of his boots and shirt and jeans and longhandles, all the while watching her shed her deerskin breeches in the firelight, her skin shining like a million copper pennies.

She lay down on the jacket and blankets, and now her eyes and hair shone as she faced the fire. Cuno stood naked before her. Her eyes drifted across him, the lids lowering a notch, her mouth corners rising in an alluring half smile.

"You are fine," she whispered.

Cuno dropped to his knees, and she spread her legs for him and reached for him, gently stroking, her eyes acquiring an almost startling dreamy cast. As he lowered his head to hers, pressing the length of his hard body against hers, the kiss with which she returned his was surprisingly gentle and warm and silky. There was none of the expected savagery in it.

Just as there was none of the wild zeal in what came

later—only slow, gentle, eminently erotic and boundlessly satisfying lovemaking with a tender, uninhibited woman.

They punctuated their coupling by taking a swim, then drying each other off slowly, kissing and nuzzling, and making love by the built-up fire once more. Cuno's anxieties over being trapped in the canyon with a whole herd of savage Yaqui burned off like Arizona ground fog.

He thought he'd died and gone to heaven, or as close to it as he was ever going to get.

24

GENERAL ARTURO CUESTA woke with a start. He jerked his head up as the echoes of the rifle shot, sounding like the detonation of a near cannon, echoed off the ridges around him.

"Mama mia," the general said, making the sign of the cross on his chest over his long silk underwear shirt revealed by his unbuttoned blue uniform tunic. "Those men are going to be the death of me yet. *Mierda!"*

Of course, it was better that the occasional shots echoing around the near ridges were made by his own men hunting the area around the train than by another batch of rampaging Yaqui. Still, Cuesta's nerves were shot, and with a groan he sleeved sweat from his brow.

The general was sprawled atop a red velvet settee that he'd ordered his men to set on the roof of his own private railcar. His car and the rest of his twelve-car military train sat at the end of the new railroad line, nearly at the foot of formidable Montana del Loco Oso. The general and his small army—around fifty federal soldiers—were stalled there until they could get more rails hauled up from Mexico City, and until they received the dynamite and badly needed, newer-model Gatling guns and ammunition that the general was having shipped down from Arizona. Mexico, it seemed, was low on both iron and black powder.

The general had ordered the expensive, ornately carved settee hauled up to the roof and a cream burlap canopy erected over it, because, after two months of being stalled here in this godforsaken sierra in north-cenral Sonora, four hundred miles from his home, the car's close confines were beginning to drive him as loco as the mountain he was assaulting, causing him to wake at night, heart fluttering, gasping for air, believing he was being buried alive.

And the intermittent rifle shots of the crew either hunting or target shooting wasn't doing his nerves any good, either. At least the lack of dynamite had halted the blasting of the tunnel through the mountain, though that would resume as soon as the dynamite arrived with Cuesta's business associate from Arizona, or with—Cuesta gave an evil, cunning grin—the notorious bandito, Carlos Riata, he'd sent to intercept the caravan and who would spare Cuesta about half the gold bullion the general had agreed to pay the *Americanos*. Of course, Cuesta wasn't certain Riata was up to the task, as the bandito's own ranks had been cut down in his own war with the Yaqui. But Cuesta had thought it worth the risk, as there wasn't much the *Americanos* could do about the double cross except to get angry about it.

In the end, they'd hand over the guns and ammunition, and be paid . . .

Cuesta looked around and yawned, his boredom a palpable thing, a weighing depression. Once the rail line, which his superiors including the president had ordered Cuesta to oversee personally, had made it this far from Mexico City, his crew had encountered one delay after another. And there was also the problem of the Yaqui who had, until recently, been making night raids on the work camps that had been set up on the far side of the creek from where Cuesta's private car now sat, waiting for supplies.

The pesky little Indians, viscious as wolverines, seemed to think the mountain was sacred, harboring the heart of their warrior god, the loco grizzly, and were intent on keeping Cuesta's crew from blasting a hole through it. So far, Cuesta's men had been able to hold off the swarthy hordes on their wild mustangs because most of the Yaqui were armed with only bows and arrows. But Cuesta's men were running dangerously low on ammunition, which was also hard to come by in Mexico City. Fortunately, since the blasting had ceased and the work crews released, the night raids had tapered off, but the general remained uneasy.

He spent many idle hours nervously wondering why he was uneasy.

"Where have you gone, my beautiful Fuega?" he said now aloud, dropping his stockinged feet to the car's slatted wooden roof, near his polished black boots, and sweeping the area around the train with his gaze.

There was only sagebrush and pinyons and low, flat-topped escarpments in three directions, under a dry, cobalt sky. Straight ahead of the train, a half mile away across a dry creekbed, Montana del Loco Oso rose like a massive, variegated, sandstone lizard's head lifted in stoic defiance of Cuesta's rails. At least, it looked like a lizard's head from Cuesta's vantage, though from a distance he had to agree it looked like a grizzly standing on its hind legs, jaws wide, on the verge of a deadly attack.

The mine was just on the other side, a half a lousy mile through the mountain—so close and yet so far. Probably a year's worth of tedious, hard, dangerous labor while Cuesta's soldiers held off the Yaqui led by the lovely, savage queen known even to her own people as *Ojos del Fuega*.

Again, raw desire chewed at Cuesta's gut. The girl had ravaged his nerves and harassed his men, killing several dozen in her early morning or late night raids. And yet, the image of her dusky, comely figure sitting that cream stallion just out of rifle range, armed with a Winchester as well as a bow and arrow, haunted his waking reveries . . .

"Incoming riders, General!"

Cuesta glanced at one of the lookouts standing atop the railcar to his right and followed the man's pointing arm to the east. Three riders, little more than moving smudges from this distance, were jouncing down from a low, dun ridge. Cuesta reached for his field glasses on the small table beside the settee and lifted the glasses to his eyes.

Three riders, two holding rifles straight up from their right thighs. White flags tied around the ends of the barrels blew in the dry wind. The rider in the middle sat his mount oddly, slouched forward slightly, both hands held close to the cream's saddle horn, as though tied to it.

Cuesta lowered the glasses slowly and frowned at the three riders as he watched with his naked eyes, his heart quickening faintly.

A cream?

No, it couldn't be.

Again, he lifted the glasses until the riders were bouncing around in both spheres of magnified vision. He gripped the glasses with both hands to steady them and swore under his breath as he made out the long hair, slender shoulders, and the deerskin vest that the beautiful Yaqui queen wore so beguilingly, showing just enough of herself to make a lonely man howl like a gut-shot coyote.

Could it really be her, or was the jouncing, black-haired image in his field glasses merely the lusty conjuring of his earlier reverie, the product of an overheated imagination?

Cuesta held the glasses firmly, staring, his heart beating faster, his lips parting as he drew more air. Now he could hear the rataplan of the horses as the three riders galloped to within sixty yards, dropped down into a wash, disappearing for a few seconds before reappearing again, galloping up and over the near bank.

"General?" The guard on the opposite car inquired testily. There was a guard on most of the rail cars, most holding rifles, some armed with Gatling guns, a few with cigarettes dangling from their lips, and they all had their heads turned toward Cuesta, awaiting his order.

The general lowered the field glasses in his left hand, raising his right to the guard. "Hold your fire, Sergeant. We will see what they want."

"Are my eyes paying tricks on me, General, or is that . . . ?" The sergeant crouching over the Gatling gun that was mounted like a giant mosquito on the opposite car, turned his mustached, sunburned face toward the approaching riders and drew two fingers over his eyes as if to clear them.

"I don't know," the general muttered, an unseen fist squeezing his heart.

As the three riders slowed their horses and swung their heads around warily at the guards holding rifles on them and at the sergeant crouched over his Gatling gun, Cuesta became conscious of his state of half dress. He set the glasses on the table and dropped down onto the settee, quickly stuffing his feet into his boots, then standing and fumbling nervously with his gold tunic buttons until he had the tunic properly closed. He brushed away tortilla crumbs, then reached for his leather-billed hat, inspecting it quickly before running a hand through his close-cropped, salt-and-pepper hair, setting it carefully on his head and tugging the bill down slightly over his eyes, giving him what he hoped was a slightly mysterious, commanding look.

Half consciously, he kept muttering silently, "Fuega, Fuega . . . ?"

He jerked his tunic down at the bottom, smoothing it over his flat belly—flatter than the bellies of most men in their fifties, he proudly noted—and watched the three riders approach a car near the rear of the train. Cuesta walked to the end of the roof, descended the metal rungs to the platform, and was turning just as the three riders rode up along the cinder bed, their horses' hooves clomping and crunching gravel.

Cuesta pursed his lips and clasped his hands behind his back, composing himself despite seeing that the girl riding with the old gringo and the young gringo was indeed Fire Eyes. Cuesta's mind hadn't been playing tricks on him. His breath caught in his chest, and his heart skipped a couple of beats as the Yaqui's dark eyes—he could imagine how they blazed when she was riled—met his, regarding him coolly, almost disdainfully. Her wrists were cuffed together and the chain between the two cuffs was tied to the woman's saddle horn.

The older man canted his head to one side, narrowing one eye at the sergeant crouched over the Gatling gun atop the railroad car to Cuesta's right, only about six feet away. He slid his gaze to the general. "General Cuesta?"

"*Sí*, I am Cuesta. Who are you, and how . . . did you manage to trap this wildcat?" The general slid his eyes around the trio, but he wanted nothing more than to feast the eyes on the savage, beautiful Yaqui before him, sitting the cream barb that was almost as legendary as the girl herself. From the very first time that he'd seen her, over a year ago and during a raid on the train on which he'd been traveling just west of here, she'd captured his imagination as well as every fiber of his male desire.

How he feared her and loved her!

He was a married man—he would even say a *happily* married man—but he wanted nothing more than to touch this Yaqui girl before him, to sniff her. To possess her body as well as her soul! He'd fantasized often of keeping her, as so many of his cohorts kept their own mistresses, in the apartment he kept in Monterrey. It would be like taking a mountain lion to the opera, of course, but where this Yaqui queen was concerned, Cuesta knew he was out of his mind.

"I'm Spurr Morgan," the older man said. "The younker's Cuno Massey. Yeah, we're gringos, but we understand you're offering a bounty worth two thousand of our American dollars for dear little Miss Fire Eyes here. Well, here she is. Alive, just like you wanted."

"Where . . . how did you come to capture this beastly creature?"

"We're bounty hunters," said the younger man, sitting his saddle casually, both gloved hands draped over his saddle horn. "And right good at it. Never mind the where and the how, General. If you fork over that two thousand dollars, we'll turn the Yaqui maiden over to you—to do with as you please."

The young man shaped a knowing grin, slitting his blue eyes.

Cuesta indulged in a close study of the Yaqui queen, who did not return his gaze but kept her eyes on the platform steps beneath his polished boots. She almost appeared to be in a trance—not defeated but merely subdued for the moment. The breeze tossed her hair lightly.

How smooth her cherry skin—how desirable even with its coating of desert dust! The gamey smell of the Yaqui queen drew his pants taut across his crotch.

Suddenly self-conscious, somehow feeling his thoughts might be plain on his features or elsewhere, Cuesta felt an angry burn and said crisply, "You will be paid when I am able to pay you, young gringo. You are the interlopers here. The gold will need to be weighed, and the officer in charge of gold payments is occupied with other work."

Despite his tone and demeanor, Cuesta was overjoyed, and he felt genuinely grateful to the bounty hunters for bringing Fire Eyes to him alive. He'd doubted that that could ever happen, even with the high price he'd placed on her head, but here she was . . .

"If you think we're just gonna turn this golden goose loose without so much as an IOU," said the hunter called Spurr, "you got another think coming, General."

"Does he?" said the sergeant crouched over the Gatling gun, one hand on the contraption's wooden handle. The deadly maw was aimed at the old man's face. The sergeant grinned, showed his large, tobacco-stained teeth beneath his black handlebar mustache.

"Well, now that you mention it," the old bounty hunter said, "I guess you done got us beat in firepower." He chuckled self-effacingly, and Cuesta was pleased. He hated the arrogance of all gringos, even those in Mexico, and he'd never known one who had not displayed such bad manners. Spurr reached into his vest pocket and produced a small pocketknife. As he reached over toward Fire Eyes, he said, "I reckon we'll turn her over to you, General, and rely on your honor to see that we're paid."

"You will be paid," Cuesta said, meaning it. However much he hated gringos, he felt truly grateful to these two, and it could never get out that he did not pay his bounties. He studied Fire Eyes as the man sawed through the rope binding her cuffs to her saddle horn and hoped the fervent beating of his heart did not show on his face.

Several other men had come up along the train from their quarters in the other cars, studying the Yaqui queen in utter disbelief, muttering amongst themselves. Cuesta knew what they expected—that he'd turn the girl over to them with orders that the last one to take her must cut her throat.

It wouldn't be like that, he thought. No, it wouldn't be like that at all. This was a wildcat he had to try taming himself. If she turned out to be untameable, which might very well be the case, he'd have her shot. But there was something in him that would not allow her to be corrupted by his men. It had something to do with his fantasies. She belonged to him and only him. To throw her to his men would be to cuckold him.

"What do you say, *chiquita*?" Cuesta said, trying not to sound nervous as he addressed the legend herself. "Are you going to make me throw you in a cage like a wild puma, or are you going to try and act civil?"

Slowly, she shook her head, and he was surprised to see no fiery flash of anger in her eyes. "I am done. When I can be caught so easily by two gringo cowboys, it is time to put down my weapons. I am a disgrace to the Yaqui." She lifted her gaze to the general's and curled her rich upper lip. "I will cause you no trouble if you shoot me right away!"

Cuesta rubbed his goatee as he studied the proud, sullen creature before him. He'd be damned if she didn't sound like she meant what she'd said.

His heart skipped a couple more beats.

He looked at the two gringos sitting their tired horses on the other side of the queen and canted his head to indicate the rear of the train. "You may stable your horses in the stable car. As a supply train recently arrived, there is plenty of hay and oats. We have a cantina car well stocked with beer and tequila." He gave a derisive smile. "It is also supplied with two senoritas I'm sure the two of you will find to your liking. They're cheap enough. In the morning, I will see that you are paid, and you will be free to leave."

The old man and the young one shared a doleful glance. Then the old one sighed. "This is how it always plays out in Mexico, kid. Best get used to it." He reined his horse away, and he and the young man trotted their horses down toward the stable car positioned in front of the caboose.

Cuesta turned to the small crowd of low-ranking Federales standing around in awe of the trophy that had just been handed over to the general. "Corporal Martinez," he ordered, "I want this woman placed in leg irons and brought to me in my quarters on the double!"

"*Si, si*, General. I and Lopez will stand guard on her ourselves!"

"Are you telling me I'm incapable of safely debriefing a female captive in leg irons?"

Martinez gulped.

He told another man to fetch a copper tub and hot bathwater. They all stood staring at him again, shrewd smiles beginning to brighten their tired eyes.

"Pronto!" the general ordered, then turned and pushed through the door of his quarters.

25

"DAMN RISKY," SPURR said as he and Cuno led their horses up the ramp and through the open doors of one of the train's four stable cars. Hooves clomped woodenly, and beasts and men made the rotten ramp boards sag ominously. "Cuesta could just as easily have her hauled off to the creek and shot against the bank . . . and us along with her."

Cuno glanced up and down the train, making sure no Federales were near, before continuing on up the ramp and into the stock car. "A girl who looks like her?" He chuckled as he and Spurr led their mounts toward a gap amongst the tied horses at the rear of the car. "Ain't likely any man with red blood in his veins could do that. Besides, she's convinced he's gone for her."

"I'll admit, ole Cuesta looked like he was about to fall on his ass when he saw her, but how in the hell did she know?"

"I reckon the 'wanted alive' bounty tipped her off."

"He could've intended to torture the hell out of her." Spurr tied the roan to a metal hook in the stable car wall, then hitched his pants and gun belts up higher on his bony hips, and walked over to a water barrel standing beside the open door. He leaned forward and turned his head to stare up the train toward Cuesta's private car. "And maybe that's what he's doin'. Sure would be nice to have a look-see."

That didn't look possible, as from this vantage he could see two rifle-wielding Federales milling around Cuesta's car, positioned there to make sure Fire Eyes didn't escape. There was probably another guard on the car's platform, and then of course there was the sergeant so proudly hunkered over the Gatling gun on the next car back.

"You worry too much," Cuno said, slipping Renegade's bit from his mouth, so the horse could drink and feed.

They had no intention of unsaddling the horses. Earlier that morning, a Yaqui scout for Fire Eyes's brother, Red Water, had reported that the gunrunner's wagons were headed toward Cuesta's train, within ten miles and moving at a clip of about three miles an hour. Barring delays, that would bring them on up to the train within two hours. By then, Spurr and Cuno hoped to have Cuesta dead and his men distracted enough so that they, Fire Eyes, and the twenty-three Yaqui hunkered down just over a low rise to the north, awaiting Fire Eyes's signal, could take over the train.

If all went as planned, it would be the two gringos and the Yaqui, not Cuesta's men, who would meet Bennett Beers, Dave Sapp, and Flora Hammerlich when they came lifting dust from the east.

Spurr took a wooden bucket off a nail above the water barrel, dipped up some water, and carried it over to Cochise, who gratefully swished his tail then dipped his head to draw the water. "Worryin' is how I've made it this far, kid."

"What happened to that tumbleweed in a cyclone?"

Ignoring the question, Spurr grabbed a scrap of burlap and began vigorously rubbing Cochise's rear quarters. "What kind of signal you 'spect she'll give us?"

"I don't know. She just said we'll know it when we hear it." Cuno watered Renegade and fed him a bucket of parched corn, and then he walked to the car's open door, staring out.

There were a good dozen Federales milling distractedly about the train, some sitting on rocks along the railroad bed, smoking and playing cards. Some lounged in the scanty shade provided by near pinyons while others gathered in groups to obviously discuss the general's new conquest, for they spoke in hushed, snickering tones while casting meaningful glances toward Cuesta's private car.

"Come on, you old codger," Cuno said, "I'll buy you a beer in the saloon car."

"Can you afford a beer and a shot of tequila?"

"No."

"All right, then, you cheap bastard," Spurr said, looking around at the dark blue–uniformed Federales and then casting a quick, furtive glance toward the low ridge behind which Red Water's Yaqui were hunkered, waiting. "You buy the beer and I'll buy the tequila."

Cuno and Spurr walked up toward the front of the train, passing the three other stock cars. The saloon car sat ahead of the third stock car, and it looked like any coach car except its windows were covered with red velvet, gold-tassled curtains, lending a gaudy opulence to the otherwise sun-bleached railcar. The light tinkle of female laughter emanated from one of the windows. Three Federales stood around below the platform, slack-shouldered drunk, and all three sneered as Cuno and Spurr brushed past them and climbed the platform steps.

Cuno paused inside the door, squinting into the car's deep shadows, as Spurr walked up beside him. To his left there was a short bar comprised of wooden planks propped over two beer kegs. A young, plain-faced woman in a sleeveless blouse and long, pleated green skirt stood behind it, leaning forward on the planks, one bare foot propped atop the other. She'd been looking toward the man and the woman seated at one of the tables near the front door when Cuno and Spurr had walked in, but now she turned to the newcomers, and the jovial smile faded from her lips.

The other woman, also a *puta* judging by her scanty dress, had been the one laughing as she leaned forward against her table, her forehead nearly touching that of the man with lieutenant's bars on the shoulders of his tunic. The lieutenant was facing Cuno, and he turned his head now to follow the *puta*'s inquisitive stare, sort of grimaced distastefully, and turned back to the *puta*, muttering drunkenly.

There was one more man in the saloon car, sitting toward the far end. He sat down low in his chair, chin dipped toward his chest, arms crossed, snoring. He was bearded and dressed in greasy buckskins, and a felt sombrero was tipped low over the top half of his face. Probably a trader of some kind, or maybe a member of the civilian work crew blasting the tunnel through the mountain.

Cuno let Spurr do the ordering, since the old man's Spanish was better, and when the *puta* had set them up and they'd both tossed her some coins, they took their drinks and sat at a table about halfway between the *puta*, the lieutenant, and the man in buckskins at the far end of the car. Cuno pulled a chair out from the side of the table facing the man in buckskins, and Spurr, looking beyond Cuno, flushed slightly, then sagged down into his own chair.

Cuno sipped his warm, yeasty beer and looked at Spurr, keeping his voice low. "What?"

Spurr glanced over his shoulder to make sure the *puta* and the lieutenant were still involved in their subtle game of slap-and-tickle, then said, "The man behind you. He lifted his head. I know him. Knew him. Mex outlaw I once locked horns with in Wyoming. Horse thief."

Cuno kept his eyes on Spurr, feigning a casual expression for the *puta* at the bar. "How long ago?"

"Two years. Must have lit out for the border when he busted out of that little jail I threw him in."

Cuno scowled. "You sure?"

"It's my ticker that's weak—not my memory."

"He still turned this way?"

Spurr shook his head. "Dropped his chin again. Just lifted it to yawn."

Cuno cast a quick glance over his shoulder, then took another sip from his beer mug and hiked a shoulder. "You wanna switch chairs?"

Spurr shook his head. "Too suspicious." He canted his

head toward the *puta* at the bar. "Why don't you see if she has a deck of cards?"

Cuno went over to the bar and managed to convey to the bartending *puta* that he wanted a deck of cards. She found one in a drawer behind the bar and handed it over rather snootily. Cuno returned to the table, where Spurr was sitting with his profile to the sleeping hombre at the back of the car. Cuno was more concerned with Fire Eyes's signal, whatever that would be, and what he and Spurr intended to do afterward, which was to take over at least one of the Gatling guns and give the Yaqui time to storm the train.

He figured that in the ensuing commotion he and Spurr would manage to wreak a little havoc and keep Fire Eyes alive, but they had a big job ahead of them, and he didn't mind admitting to himself that it wasn't only Spurr whose nerves were on edge. The buckskin-wearing gent was only a small fly in the ointment.

Spurr glanced over Cuno's shoulder again and lowered his own head to the card deck he was shuffling in his arthritic, age-spotted hands. "You gamble, kid?"

"Whenever I've had money it's gone into a savings account or my freighting business. Money's never come easy enough to risk losing it to old cardsharps like you."

Spurr shuffled the cards again, and looked across at Cuno incredulously. "How in the hell did a lad like yourself, with such an upright sense of things, land in so much trouble?"

"I've often wondered that myself," Cuno said, picking up the cards as Spurr shuffled them.

Spurr had tossed the last card down on Cuno's side of the table when he flicked a quick look over Cuno's right shoulder and winced. He bit his lower lip as though biting back a curse.

"Hey," came a low voice behind Cuno, who felt himself wince then, too.

"Shit," Spurr muttered, keeping his head down while still trying to look casual. "I hate a horse thief with a good memory."

"Hey," came the voice of the buckskin-clad hombre

again, louder. There was the squawk of a chair slackening and the trill of a spur.

"Follow my lead on this one, kid," Spurr said, tossing a card onto the table.

"This fella's gonna bust our little game wide open, Spurr," Cuno said in a low, accusing singsong, tossing down a paste-board and plucking one off the top of the deck.

"I know you," said the grating, Spanish-accented voice behind Cuno as the man's boots thumped loudly on the rough wood floor, and his spurs trilled annoyingly. "Don't I know you, amigo?"

Cuno glanced over his left shoulder. The buckskin-clad man was strolling toward him and Spurr, his dark eyes on Spurr, one dirty finger pressing the cleft in his jutting chin. He had a big, square head, goatee, and about four days' worth of beard stubble. He also had two Colt double-action Lightning pistols sheathed on his hips, with two cartridge belts. A Green River knife in a bearded sheath hung from his neck by a leather thong.

Cuno watched Spurr, wondering how the old lawman was going to handle this fly in their ointment that was grow-ing to ominous proportions. The buckskin-clad gent was casting a bitter pall over Cuno and Spurr's entire day.

Cuno didn't have to wait long for Spurr's reaction. The old lawman, not one to mince words, hauled his Starr .44 up onto the table with surprising speed, not batting an eye but only arching a brow with dire portent as he said, "All I can tell you, asshole, is that if you don't go sit back down over there and keep your goddamn mouth shut, I'm gonna blow a hole through your brisket big enough to drive this train through."

Still he did not blink as he stared up at the man flanking Cuno.

"Spurr," the man said, as though uttering an especially bitter oath.

"That's right, Rincon Charlie Robles."

The lieutenant behind Spurr suddenly climbed to his feet, scowling toward Spurr and Cuno, who slid his own chair back quickly, rose, and palmed and cocked his .45, aiming it straight out from his shoulder at the lieutenant's head. "No, no—you sit back down, too," he ordered. "You fellas are mixin' in something you shouldn't be."

With his free hand he quickly disarmed Robles, who stood with his hands raised halfheartedly, and tossed both pistols and the knife against the car's far wall. Spurr stood and pushed Robles back away from his and Cuno's table, and turned so that he could cover both the lieutenant and Robles, and glanced at the whore backing away from the bar looking angry.

"You two ladies utter a peep," he warned, "you're wolf bait."

The one still sitting across from the lieutenant, who'd retaken his seat and was holding his hands above his shoulders, gasped and covered her mouth, staring at the drawn weapons as though she'd never seen one before.

"That's right," Spurr said, "choke it down, senorita, and you'll live to dance another day."

The car fell silent. The lieutenant, Robles, and the two whores stared at Spurr and Cuno.

"Well," Cuno said, worrying his .45's cocked hammer with his sweaty thumb as he glanced at his old partner. "This is a fine turn of events."

He'd barely finished the sentence before a shrill, agonized scream from outside rose like the squeal of a dying buzzard.

26

THE SCREAM CAME again, shriller this time, stitched with unbearable pain. It was a man's groaning, wailing expression of godawful misery as well as an urgent plea for help. It was abruptly clipped by two quick, muffled pistol shots.

Cuno glanced at Spurr. At the same time, Robles made a grab for Spurr's .44. Spurr pulled the pistol back, then smacked it across Robles's head, and the big man in buckskins stumbled backward, groaning and clutching his head before he dropped to his knees.

The lieutenant's eyes jerked wide as he reached for one of the two Colt Navys on his hips, and Cuno's .45 roared, causing the whore sitting at the lieutenant's table to scream and the one standing behind the bar to curse sharply and clap her hands to her ears. The slug tore through the lieutenant's chest and punched him back against the car's front wall, and from there he dropped to the floor, knocking over a chair, quivering.

Spurr had his cocked Starr aimed at the saucy whore behind the bar, who raised her hands above her head and moved her lips as though uttering a quick prayer. Cuno shoved a curtain aside and looked out the nearest front window. Federales were running toward the front of the train, the direction from which the scream had come—the scream that Cuno did not doubt had come from the general and was, in fact, Fire Eyes's signal to unleash the dogs of war.

"I reckon it's time to dance," he told Spurr.

The old lawdog slid the Starr from the saucy whore to the one still seated and who looked half in shock as she slid her bright gaze from the still-shivering lieutenant to Spurr's cocked pistol. "You ladies sit tight and you won't get hurt. You poke your head or anything else outside, you're liable to get it shot off."

Cuno backed toward the front door, stepping over Robles. He stooped to pick up both the horse thief's pistols and tossed one to Spurr—they hadn't dared arm themselves with their rifles and risk drawing unwanted attention.

"Thanks, kid."

"Don't mention it," Cuno said, rushing out the front door and onto the platform. A few more yelling Federales were running along the train toward the front. Muffled pistol fire sounded, and Cuno could hear Fire Eyes shouting something in Spanish.

Cuno grabbed the ladder running up the rear of the car ahead of him while Spurr grabbed the ladder running up the saloon car, and they both climbed. With his head just above the lip of his car's roof, Cuno stopped and surveyed the situation before him—a corporal crouched tensely over the Gatling gun that he had aimed toward the front of the train and the sound of all the sudden commotion. His back was facing Cuno.

Cuno glanced behind him. Spurr was on the opposite car's ladder, and now as the Federale atop that car swung his Gatling gun toward the lawman, Spurr extended his .44 and blew the man back away from the cannon and off the car to land atop the cinder bed with a thud. He shot the Gatling gunner off the car behind the saloon car, then glanced, nodding, toward Cuno as he hauled his old, weary body up over the roof. His face was flushed and sweating, and he seemed to be gasping for air.

Cuno shot the Federale off the Gatling gun on his own car's roof, and ran up to man the gun himself. There were three more men with rifles on the three cars ahead of him, but Fire Eyes had done a good job of confounding the three enough that none had gotten their rifles leveled on Cuno before Cuno started turning his Gatling gun's crank.

Bam-bam-bam-bam-bam-bam-bam-bam-bam-bam-bam!

He'd never fired such a weapon before, and he blew up wood slivers from the three roofs before nudging the barrel up slightly and hammering his lead storm through the three rifle-wielding Federales. He watched all three through his puffing powder smoke lurch to their feet as the bullets shredded their tunics and caused blood to fly out their backs before, screaming, they twisted around and flew over the sides of their respective cars.

At the same time, Cuno heard the wicked belching of Spurr's Gatling gun behind him. He glanced around to see several more Federales going down in the same fashion as Cuno's had. A weird howling sounded, growing quickly louder. Cuno glanced to the east where a line of Yaqui riders, their faces streaked with ochre and their horses all painted for war, as well, galloped wildly toward the train, triggering carbines and flinging arrows.

Hoping the Yaqui weren't wild with their shots, Cuno bounded away from the Gatling gun, and, grabbing his .45 and the Colt Lightning he'd taken off Robles, ran forward along the roof of the car. To his right he could see several Federales lying prone against the side of the railroad bed, triggering rifles or pistols toward the general's private car. Smoke puffed from a rear corner window of the car as, presumably, the Yaqui queen returned fire.

Cuno leapt the eight-foot gap to the roof of the next car and began triggering lead toward the Federales. He pinked one in the thigh, thumped another slug through another man's shoulder before several rose to their knees and began firing at Cuno.

He kept running, bullets curling the air around his head,

and returned fire hastily as he leapt two more platforms. As he jumped down to the platform of the general's car, a bullet seared the top of his shoulder, and he winced as he rammed the opposite shoulder against the car door, triggering his last two bullets toward the Federales.

Suddenly, the door was gone, and he fell inside the general's car—not a hard fall due to the soft, wine-red carpet. Fire Eyes was down on one knee, looking tough but harried and holding two smoking, silver-chased, pearl-gripped pistols in her fists. As bullets hammered the car, flinging wood slivers and breaking the glass out of the windows, Cuno blinked at her.

She was also naked, water beading on every inch of her tan skin.

"Don't gringo mothers teach their boys it's not nice to stare?" she said through gritted teeth as she ran, crouching, to another rear window, and triggered each of her guns in turn at the Mexicans forted up against the railroad bed.

Cuno closed the door, and two bullets blew the glass out of its top panel. He pulled back against the wall beside the door and saw a long copper bathtub sitting in the middle of the well-appointed car. The general sat in the tub, head thrown back, face turned toward Cuno, his open eyes sightlessly staring. His arms hung down from the sides of the tub. The water around the general was red. A bloody, gold-handled Spanish sword lay on the floor near his sagging left hand.

"I decided he needed a bath more than I did," Fire Eyes said, casting a quick glance toward Cuno as she triggered another shot out the window before jerking her head to one side as a bullet slammed into the frame, spraying splinters at her. "If you wouldn't mind, I could use some help!"

Cuno quickly reloaded his Colt from his shell belt and glanced out the door's broken window. The Yaqui were swarming like ants on a beehive, and the Federales were dropping like flies, screaming, some bristling with arrows. A couple threw down their weapons and ran toward the train, intending to leap across the platform. Two wildly howling Yaqui drilled them from horseback before they reached the steps, and they both flew forward to sprawl on the cinder bed just outside the general's car.

Cuno stared out the window. Now, the only Federales he could see from his vantage were dead ones cloaked in sifting dust. He and Fire Eyes were attracting no more gunfire though Cuno could hear a veritable battle being waged on down the line, where the surviving Federales were trying to hold back the tide of swarming Yaqui raiders.

Fire Eyes stood and without a bit of modesty walked over to where her clothes were strewn near the tub in which the general lolled in the bloody water. She picked up her short doeskin skirt and stepped into it, her proud breasts jostling, and spat at the dead Cuesta. "Pig!"

Cuno stood. "How in the hell did you manage that?"

"To stab him with his own sword?" Fire Eyes laughed as she picked up her deerskin vest and shook it out in front of her. "The fool had it hanging on the wall. When I had him so aroused he couldn't think about anything other than what I was doing to him, I climbed out of the tub, took it off the wall, and gutted him like a javelina." She laughed again, and her dagger eyes flashed. "I took my time, as you might have heard."

Spurr's voice from the car's front platform said, "We heard, all right." He was crouched with his face just beyond the door's broken window. He was staring at Cuesta, then swallowed as he watched Fire Eyes pull her vest on.

Cuno said, "I figured you'd kicked off."

"Nah. When Fire Eyes's folks came, I hightailed it off the train and went back to pull those two *putas* out of the saloon car, squirrled 'em away where I figured they'd be safe in one of the stable cars."

Spurr cocked an ear to listen for a moment, as did Cuno. The gunfire had waned to only a few sporadic shots. The Yaqui had all but stopped howling.

To Fire Eyes, Spurr said, "Your people clean up right well."

"Of course," she said, grabbing one of the general's

fancy pistols off the table she'd set it on. A drawer had been pulled out of the table, and from it Fire Eyes plucked shells from an open cartridge box and thumbed them through the Colt's loading gate.

Cuno opened the door and stepped out onto the platform beside Spurr, who was reloading one of his pistols. "I reckon we'd better jump to the next step in our little fandago, eh?"

"Yeah, we'd best drag the dead Federales off and get as many of us into their uniforms as we can," Spurr said. "I can't wait to shake hands with them gunrunners." He stepped past Cuno and into the general's car, where he picked up the general's wool uniform trousers, and held them down in front of him. "You think they'll believe I'm Cuesta?"

"Best work on your accent," Cuno said.

An hour later, dressed in a Federale uniform he'd taken off a dead sergeant, hoping the blood wasn't too obvious, Cuno sat on the roof of the railcar flanking General Cuesta's private quarters.

He was dribbling some of Spurr's chopped tobacco onto the wheat paper he held between the first two fingers of his right hand. He could see Spurr below on his left, sitting on the platform steps of the general's car, elbows on his knees, smoking. Like Cuno and the Yaqui who had all donned the dead Federales' uniforms—all except Fire Eyes, that was, who was crouched out of sight in the general's car—he was waiting for the gunrunners to show. A uniformed Yaqui sat on each of the cars behind Cuno's, ready to man their respective Gatling guns, while several more, including Red Water, milled like bored Federales along the raised track bed. The others were waiting out of sight inside the saloon car, ready to bolt out at Spurr's signal, rifles blasting.

When Cuno had sprinkled enough tobacco on the paper, he pulled on the rawhide thong of the tobacco sack, closing it.

"How's it comin', kid?" Spurr asked raspily below him, not looking up but staring straight off across the desert, where the gunrunners were due to appear any minute.

When Fire Eyes had sent one of the braves out a half hour

ago to scout their position, they were only about a mile away. The old lawman was dressed in General Cuesta's spotless uniform, and while the pants were a little too long and loose in the waist, they fit him well enough for the few minutes he was going to need them. The general's leather-billed, gold-embroidered hat hung from his right knee.

Cuno started closing the paper, sticking his tongue out slightly with concentration. He'd never been much of a smoker much less a cigarette builder—his father had told him when he'd been bare-knuckle fighting back in Nebraska on Saturday nights that tobacco turned a fighter's lungs to raisins—but he wanted one now to help kill the time and ease his nerves. "I'm gettin' it."

"Don't waste none of my tobacco. That has to get me to the next town or tradin' post."

"I'm not gonna waste any of your damn tobacco."

Spurr chuckled. "Hell, I knew how to roll cigarettes before I was twelve."

"Smoking's bad for you, Spurr. My old man told me that early on. Ma never would have allowed it even if he hadn't."

"Your folks still alive?"

He felt as though he were wearing thick gloves, but Cuno managed to connect the two ends of the wheat paper. Now, to tighten and seal it without losing any of Spurr's precious tobacco. "Nope."

"Sorry to hear that." Spurr let the breeze shred an exhaled plume of cigarette smoke and leaned back on his elbows. "You got anyone else?"

"I got Renegade."

"A good hoss'll do you better than most people, by god."

"Not better than my people, but they're gone."

Cuno had gotten the paper nearly closed around the tobacco, making a nice, tight cylinder, when a Yaqui from around the middle of the train yelled something in his guttural tongue.

Out of sight inside the general's car but obviously watching for the gunrunners from one of the front windows, Fire Eyes translated. "They come."

27

CUNO'S FINGERS SLIPPED and the paper rolled away from the tobacco. The breeze caught the tobacco and blew it down toward Spurr, who scowled up at Cuno and said, "Damnit, kid!"

"Sorry." Cuno heaved himself to his feet beside the Gatling gun, brushing the remaining tobacco off his wool trousers and casting his gaze toward the northeast. "I bet Bennett has some tobacco he'll spare you, if you ask nice."

"Yeah, I'll ask *real* nice," Spurr said, rising and stepping up onto the top of the platform, donning his hat and throwing his shoulders back, Cuno supposed, to make himself look like a general.

As Cuno stared, two riders came around a distant camelback bluff, trotting their horses. One by one behind them, seven wagons jounced into view, one behind the other, spaced about forty yards apart. Five or so outriders trotted amongst the wagons, two ahead, one to each side, and another rider riding drag. The freight train was following an old Indian trail running along a shallow dry wash from the east. One of the lead riders raised his hand, and the men driving the wagons drew back on their reins, their bellowed "whoas!" reaching Cuno's ears on the breeze.

As the tan dust drifted over the wagons, the two lead riders heeled their mounts and galloped toward the train, keeping about twenty feet between them. Cuno's shoulders tensed, and he lowered the bill of his forage cap, hiding his eyes and the entire upper half of his face. He hoped that he, Spurr, and the Yaqui looked enough like Federales for the next few minutes to pull off the intended ruse, and he prayed that the Yaqui, as eager as broomtail mustang stallions to lift some dust, could restrain themselves until all seven wagons had pulled up to the train.

The riders dropped into the coulee and rode up the other side, Cuno now beginning to hear their hoof thuds. Bennett Beers was on the left, Sapp on the right. Both men would recognize him right off if they inspected him carefully, so he kept his head down and his blue eyes shaded. It wasn't likely they'd see past his uniform, however, and they'd never suspect he'd be here on the Federale train, waiting to take them down.

Beers and Sapp, unshaven and coated in dust, slowed their horses about forty yards away as they eyed the train suspiciously. Cuno felt his hands sweating in his gloves. Maybe he should have stayed out of sight with the Yaqui. Too late now. Besides, there was also a chance that Dave Sapp would recognize Spurr from the Gatling gun mounted in the bell tower, but they'd had no one else amongst them who had even the slightest chance of impersonating General Cuesta.

Cuno felt the taut muscles between his shoulders loosen slightly as Beers and Sapp gigged their horses up to Fire Eyes's brother, who, according to plan, walked out to meet them, one of the Federales' Springfield rifles held up high across his chest.

Red Water knew little English, so in response to Beers's query, he merely stretched his left arm out to indicate Spurr.

Beers and Sapp put their mounts into spanking trots, and they ran their gazes across the train fleetingly before they reined up in front of the old lawman. Cuno gritted his teeth tensely. Sapp needed to not recognize Spurr, and Spurr needed to get the accent right. If the wagoneers were alerted to trouble and had time to get out their own Gatling guns, they'd have a hell of a fight on their hands.

"Greetings, amigos!" Spurr intoned, throwing his arms out in what he must have thought was a hearty Mexican greeting. "Senor Beers, I assume?"

"That's right," Beers said, pulling his horse's head up as the mount jerked sideways. "Been a helluva pull. We lost a few wagons, but the bulk of the guns and ammo are here." The head gunrunner smiled at Spurr, and there was an inexplicable chill to it. "As long as you got the gold, that is."

"*Si, si*, senor," Spurr said, getting the accent almost right. "All the gold we discussed . . . as well as plenty of food and drink and even the company of two lovely ladies."

All right, don't overplay it, Cuno thought.

He hoped like hell they didn't want to see the gold before they brought the wagons on. He let out a little sigh between his pursed lips as Beers said, "All right, then—let's dance." He reined his horse around and rose in his stirrups to call back to the waiting wagons, "Come on, boys! Bring 'em in!"

Beers swung his steeldust around to face the train, as did Sapp, and Cuno felt his heart beat in his throat as he watched the wagons move toward him with maddening slowness. Beers and Sapp didn't say anything. They just sat their horses looking oddly self-satisfied. A few times they flicked their eyes toward Cuno, but they were fleeting looks, and obviously they hadn't recognized him. They were casting the same glances toward the other "Federales" perched atop the train cars over the Gatling guns.

When the first of the wagons was within twenty yards, Beers rubbed his stubbled jaw and turned to Spurr with that insolent grin. "Yes, sir, we lost a few wagons, we did. But not to banditos . . . though we were hit by banditos, that's for sure."

Spurr said, "Sadly, Mexico is dusted from one end to the other by banditos, senor. Banditos and Yaqui. I get so frustrated sometimes. But your guns and powder will be much appreciated, amigos. Of that, I assure you."

He'd be damned if the old goat wasn't enjoying the charade, Cuno thought, grinding his teeth.

"Well, you no longer have to worry about that rabid wolf, Carlos Riata," Beers said. "He hit us about three days up the trail." He pursed his lips until his cheeks dimpled. "Wasn't much of a fight, really."

"A very bad bandito, indeed," Spurr said, nodding. "I congratulate and thank you for sending him back to the hell he came from."

The first mule team was turned to Beers's left, swinging the wagon around so that the rear was facing the train. The next wagon in line made the same move, until it sat about fifteen feet from the first, the tailgate and rear pucker facing the train. As the other wagons followed suit, Cuno glanced at Spurr.

Now was the time to give the order, Cuno thought. Now was the time to turn loose the Yaqui. This was Mexico, after all, and Spurr was under no obligation to give these killers a chance to give themselves up.

Spurr started to raise his hand but stopped, turning and lifting his head to glance puzzledly up at Cuno. Just then Cuno heard what the old man's ears must have picked up first—the thud of horse hooves rising from the other side of the train.

A rifle cracked.

Cuno jumped as the Yaqui standing over the Gatling gun on the second car to his left gave a yowl and flew forward off his car to hit the rail bed with a crunching thud. Cuno swung around as a second rifle barked, and a second Yaqui was thrown off the roof of his railcar. He could see two shooters standing on a knoll about forty yards from the train, beyond a low screen of cedars. Mostly, he could see the smoke and flames spitting from their rifle barrels as, each down on one knee, they triggered lead toward the train, wildly levering rounds into their chambers.

Bullets sang around Cuno, one slicing across the side of his left thigh. He threw himself onto the car's roof and began returning fire, hearing the Yaqui suddenly start yowl-ing like demented lobos and seeing another brave blown off a car roof down the line to Cuno's left.

Behind him, he heard Beers yell, "Here's what you bought, *you greasy, Mescin, double-dealing bastard*!"

Cuno tossed a horrified look over his left shoulder to see the rear puckers on all five freight wagons open suddenly to reveal five Gatling guns set up on tripods, and five grinning men crouched over them. He also saw the Yaqui—some clad in uniforms, some in their own breechclouts, moccasins, and war paint—bounding toward the wagons while howling and triggering their rifles. Spurr made a mad, diving dash through the door of the general's car.

At the same time, the Gatlings exploded, fire jutting like red knives from their revolving canisters. The bullets tore into the rear of the general's car and through the charging Yaqui almost instantly, five or six going down in just the three seconds that Cuno watched—the bullets blowing out their backs in great gouts of spewing blood.

As the Gatlings kept up their bone-pounding cacophony, Cuno whipped his head forward to see the two riflemen— one a rifle*woman*, as he recognized the one on the left as the blond Flora—lower their Winchesters, then pick up second rifles lying at their feet.

Cuno triggered two quick shots, both blowing up dust around Flora's and the other shooter's boots, then crabbed forward to the edge of the roof, twisted around, and threw his legs over the side. Clinging to the roof's edge with one hand, holding his rifle with the other, he glanced at the ground wavering beneath his jostling boots then opened his other hand.

The gravelly rail bed came toward him at a slant, and he hit on his toes and knees, instantly grinding his heels into the gravel and hurling himself forward down the rail bed. He scrambled behind a boulder and glanced around it at the shooters continuing to blast away at him, hammering the rock.

Cuno drew his head back. When the firing stopped, he snaked his rifle around the rock, aimed carefully, and fired three rounds, quickly jacking the lever.

Flora and the male shooter jerked backward, dropping their rifles as they disappeared down the far side of the bluff.

Behind Cuno, a loud screeching wail rose. It was followed by the rat-a-tat-tat reports of one of the Gatling guns. He jerked his head down, thinking one of Beers's men had taken over a Gatling gun on the Federales' train. As he glanced behind and up at the car he'd abandoned, relief washed over him. Fire Eyes was crouched over the gun, turning the crank wildly and swiveling the barrel left to right and back again, screeching.

Agonized screams rose from the other side.

Cuno ran up the rail bed, dashed atop the platform of the general's car, crouched, and looked around, pressing his Winchester against his shoulder. The Gatling guns in all five wagons were silenced, the men who'd been manning the guns lying dead around the guns in growing blood pools. Dead Yaqui were sprawled around or hanging over the sides of both wagons where they'd died. Dave Sapp was draped over a wagon wheel with a war hatchet embedded in his skull. Near him lay Red Water, his chest blown out.

Left of the wagons, two men were limping off toward the northwest, Spurr about thirty yards behind Beers.

Both men had lost their hats. Spurr was dragging his right leg, and blood shone on his back around his right shoulder blade. Beers was even bloodier, dragging both his legs.

Now as he reached a fork of the dry wash, he stumbled forward and dropped to his knees. He twisted around and gritted his teeth as he raised a long-barreled pistol about halfway before dropping his hand suddenly, as though it were weighed down with lead. He wailed and flopped onto his back, shielding his face with his arm.

Spurr kept limping toward him, his Starr .44 extended straight out from his shoulder. "You miserable bastard," Cuno heard the old lawman rake out of his pinched lungs. "I'd love nothin' better than to take you back to the territories and hang your sorry ass in front of a howling crowd. To be followed by a goddamn barn dance!"

The Starr lurched in his hand. The crack echoed hollowly. Smoke puffed. Dust blew up from Beers's silk shirt and black frock coat, and he jerked back flat against the ground. He lay still for a moment then flopped one arm and a leg before falling still once more.

Spurr lowered the pistol and started to turn around. His left knee buckled, and he dropped to the ground, sagged back on one hip, the other leg curled beneath him. His deep-seamed face was a mask of agony.

Cuno ran to him, dropped to a knee. Spurr stared up at him, his tan face flushing crimson as his belly and chest heaved. Spurr tapped his left shirt pocket, and Cuno reached into the pocket quickly, pulled out a small hide sack, and poked his fingers into it. He pulled out a little gold tablet and, ignoring Spurr's outstretched hand, shoved the nitro pill directly between the old man's lips and into his mouth.

Spurr tossed his head back. His Adam's apple bobbed, and he drew a raspy breath. "Hope you washed your hands, kid."

"Shut up and lay still for a minute." Cuno took off his bandanna, looked at the wound in the old lawman's shoulder and the one in his thigh, and decided the thigh needed tending first, and wrapped the bandanna tightly around it.

"I reckon we got crossways in a cross fire," Spurr rasped.

"Between two double-crossing bastards."

"If I die, bury me deep."

"Sorry to disappoint you, old man, but you're too mean to die."

"Meaner jakes than me have kicked off, kid." Spurr, his color returning, glanced toward where Beers lay in a bloody pile. "Look at him."

"Became a whimpering dog at the end," Cuno said, removing Spurr's own neckerchief and pressing it onto the bloody crease across the top of the lawman's shoulder.

Spurr winced.

"The meanest ones do." Footsteps sounded from the direction of the wagons, and Cuno turned to see Fire Eyes walking toward them, a Winchester rifle resting on her shoulder. One of the wounded gunrunners groaned. Cuno recognized Lyle Carney, one of the outriders. Carney shoved a fist against his bloody chest, making a face and grinding his heels in the dirt. Fire Eyes swung toward him, casually lowered the Winchester, and drilled a bullet through his forehead.

He dropped to a shoulder.

Spurr chuckled.

"What happened?" Fire Eyes asked, jerking her head at Spurr.

"Ticker," Spurr said. "Hell—all your warriors dead, girl?"

"Si," she said tonelessly.

"Good lord—so many of your people gone." Spurr made a face and shook his head. "I do apologize for my part in it."

"For a Yaqui to die fighting is the greatest honor." Fire Eyes glanced back at the wagons. "There are many scattered bands of us. I will gather others, and now we will have enough weapons to protect the mountain from future attack . . . and to run off the miners from the other side."

Cuno placed Spurr's hand on the neckerchief he'd been holding on the old lawman's shoulder. "Hold that there. If you're not dead when I get back, I'll cauterize them wounds."

"Where you goin'?"

Cuno straightened. "Gonna see about Flora."

Spurr nodded, gritted his teeth. "If she ain't dead, try to take her alive. I'd like to hang at least one of these sons o' bitches at Fort Bryce."

Cuno glanced at Fire Eyes, then turned and walked back to the train. He crossed the platform of the general's car, jumped to the ground on the other side. He took one step and threw himself to his left as a pistol popped. The slug hammered a heavy iron train wheel, sparking.

Cuno rose to his elbows, aiming his Winchester. Flora tumbled toward him from the screen of cedars fronting the knoll that she and the man had been shooting from. She was dragging her boot toes, sobbing, holding her left arm across her belly. She tried to swing the pistol up again with one hand, but triggered it into the ground in front of her, spraying gravel. With a shrill curse, she dropped to her knees. She hung her head sobbing, and Cuno stood and walked toward her. When she lifted her chin, her blue eyes were sharp knives stabbing him.

"You son of a bitch!"

Cuno kicked the gun out of her hand.

Flora kept her hard gaze on him, tears streaking her cheeks. He'd drilled her arm and her lower right side, and she was shaking as though deeply chilled. "I was . . . I was gonna bring you into it. I was gonna bring you into it against Beers and Sapp!"

"And who were you going to bring into it against me?"

She gritted her teeth. "My father . . . deserved all this . . . !"

Cuno dropped to a knee in front of her, ran his sleeve across a streak of blood on his chin. "Did he really, Flora? Or was that just the story you told yourself and anyone else who'd listen? Maybe you felt so damn trapped at that fort, you were just desperate enough to kill the old man in cold blood."

She glared at him. Gradually, a faint flush rose in her paling cheeks. She belted out a chuffing laugh, then, almost too faintly to hear, she said, "You'll never know."

She fell forward. Cuno caught her and gentled her onto the ground, then rolled her onto her back, her ankles crossing. Her death-glazed eyes stared up at him now without acrimony.

Cuno rose, set his rifle on his shoulder, and walked back to the train. Fire Eyes stood in front of it, staring toward him and the dead blonde behind him. As he approached, she turned and walked off toward the back of the train. Cuno watched her for a time, before she leapt onto a platform between two cars and disappeared.

He went back to find Spurr sitting against a withered willow, rolling a cigarette.

"Kid," he said, "if you can get me back to Diamondback, New Mexico Territory, I'll be eternally grateful."

"Forget grateful. How 'bout getting me an amnesty from the governor or whoever's giving 'em out these days?"

"Can't promise it, but I'll give it a shot."

Cuno thought about it, looking off across the northern hills and mountains. He looked at Spurr. "Who's in Diamondback?"

"A sawbones who can breathe new life into me."

"What's her name?"

"June Dickinson."

"Good-lookin'?"

Spurr licked the quirley closed and narrowed an eye at Cuno. "What do you think?"

Cuno grunted. "I reckon I'd best build us a fire, tend those wounds of yours, then get started on a travois."

"I reckon you'd better."

Cuno grunted and turned to stride off toward the creek. Hoof thuds sounded behind him, and he spun around, lowering his Winchester. Fire Eyes galloped her cream out away from one of the stock cars and the gunrunners' bloody wagons, casting a long glance toward Cuno before reining the stallion around sharply and galloping east.

Her hoof thuds dwindled behind her.

Cuno looked at Spurr. "Where the hell you s'pose she's goin'?"

"Wouldn't know. But you can bet she'll be back for the guns." Spurr blew a puff of cigarette smoke and adjusted his wounded leg on the ground with a grunt. "Forget her, kid. I've said it before but I've never meant it half as much as I mean it now—the girl's dangerous."

"Yeah." Cuno scratched the back of his head. "She sure is."

He continued striding off toward the creek bed, glancing once more, longingly, at the Yaqui queen galloping away from him.